The Iron Man

The Iron Man
and Other Visionary Fantasies

by
Louis-Sébastien Mercier

Translated, annotated and introduced by
Brian Stableford

A Black Coat Press Book

ISBN 978-1-61227-759-2. First Printing. July 2018. Published by Black Coat Press, an imprint of Hollywood Comics.com, LLC, P.O. Box 17270, Encino, CA 91416. All rights reserved. Except for review purposes, no part of this book may be reproduced or transmitted in any form or by any means, electronic or mechanical, including photocopying, recording, or by any information storage and retrieval system, without permission in writing from the publisher. The stories and characters depicted in this novel are entirely fictional. Printed in the United States of America.

TABLE OF CONTENTS

Introduction

Louis-Sébastien Mercier (1740-1814) was best known in his own day as a dramatist, and in that capacity he became a rebel against convention and a voice calling for reform, attacking the tradition of verse tragedy whose principal figurehead was Racine, calling for a new kind of drama that would do away with poetic artifice and escape the hidebound rules of tragedy and comedy imposed in imitation of Greek models. He was a prolific writer, however, and a relentless propagandist for his own ideas, in various direct and indirect forms, including the idiosyncratic genre of visionary fantasy, of which the present volume is a sampler. He was not the only writer of his era to employ that genre, but he was the one who did so most prolifically, most inventively and—eventually—most successfully. That reflects his isolation within the general current of French eighteenth-century thought and art; he was not entirely a man alone, but he was certainly a man apart from what seems in retrospect to have been the main current of contemporary French philosophical ideas.

Although some contemporary *philosophes* sympathized with Mercier on his principal home ground—the Parisian theater—he was opposed to them in other arenas. In particular, he dissented fervently from their general allegiance to freethought; although by no means a doctrinaire Catholic, he was extremely devout. Although he was skeptical in many other regards, he regarded the existence and goodness of God as indubitable, and the entitlement of God to humble worship as unchallengeable. Although he often devoted himself to scathing satire of aspects of popular prejudice and conduct of which he disapproved, he let religion alone and directed his intellectual sarcasm at such targets as economic oppression, orthodox medicine, and scientific theory in general. Being humbly born—his father made a living repairing and polishing arms and armor—he was a fierce critic of the luxury of the rich and the corruptions of the aristocracy, but that did not incline him toward egalitarianism; he felt that the appropriate solution to society's ills lay in the rich and powerful—especially the king—becoming conscientiously benevolent and charitable, and employing their government to organize universal wellbeing. He was definitely not a political revolutionary, nor was he at all sympathetic to the philosophy of progress as popularized by such writers as the Marquis de Condorcet and Jacques Turgot.

That last point needs to be made emphatically because Mercier's image was distorted even in his own day, and was biased to a much greater extent in the twentieth century, by the legacy of the most successful of all his books, which turned out to be the best-selling illicit publication of his era. It was illicit because, prior to 1789, books required a royal license to be printed legally in France, and such licenses were hard to come by, never being granted to any text that the king's censors considered to be critical either of the monarchy or of the Catholic church. In spite of that prohibition, however, France in general, and Paris in particular, were awash with illicit publications, so vast in their quantity that only a minority could be pursued by active persecution and attempted suppression. Although printers, booksellers and authors alike were at risk of imprisonment, large fines or even exile, if they were proven responsible for unlicensed publications, that did not stop them, to the extent that defiance of the law became a point of principle and a source of pride to everyone who imagined himself or herself to be on the side of progress and freedom against vicious tyranny.

The great majority of the books that are nowadays thought to have made a major contribution to French thought prior to 1789 were initially published illicitly, and although there was certainly money to be made out of illicit publications, at least by booksellers and printers, it was a dangerous kind of commercial enterprise. Because of the involvement of the *philosophes* in that sector of the market, illicit books became generally known as "philosophical books," that label becoming a convenient shelter for a vast amount of what Jean-Jacques Rousseau categorized as "books to be read with one hand" (the term pornography was only belatedly invented, and had to be perverted from its initial meaning in order to reach its modern implication), which was also printed on the sly.

It is, of course, difficult to be sure, in the virtual absence of records, but it does seem highly likely that of all the illicit books produced in Paris before 1789 (all of which had false title pages, usually claiming to have been published in Brussels, Amsterdam, Geneva or London), the one that was by far the most widely read at the time was Mercier's *L'An deux mille quatre cent quarante, rêve s'il en fut jamais*, [The Year 2440, a Dream if Ever There Was One] (tr. as *Memoirs of the Year Two Thousand Five Hundred*), first published anonymously in 1771 and subsequently revised and augmented several times. Its accumulated sales have been vastly overtaken since 1789 by many other contemporary works, and it was probably very little read after that date, but at the time, it was sensational, and it remains notorious today, albeit mostly among people who have never attempted to read it.

The reason why *L'An deux mille quatre cent quarante* became retrospectively famous in the twentieth century is because it was identifiable by then as the first significant narrative set in the future, and thus the implicit ancestor of all futuristic fantasy, including the modern genre of "science fiction." Because science fiction accumulated a considerable cult following in the latter half of the twentieth century, and that cult following generated an enormous amount of bibliographical and quasi-academic historicizing. Mercier's visionary fantasy achieved a kind of totemic status, in spite of the fact that there is almost nothing "futuristic" about its imagery—inevitably, given his lack of belief in either the idea of social progress or the idea of technological progress that were linked together by Condorcet and Turgot and whose entanglement still provides much of the philosophical impetus for futuristic fantasy. It is

9

the least "proto-sciencefictional" of all the texts commonly identified as such with the aid of hindsight.

It was, however, undoubtedly the narrative device of setting a description of Paris purged of many of its contemporary evils in a hypothetical future that enabled and encouraged the text to become a best-seller. In all probability, Mercier did not think that he was doing anything particularly extraordinary. The idea that dreams could be prophetic was very old and had been used frequently in the literary deployment and exploration of oracles, which was prolific and commonplace. Applying the thesis to a city rather than an individual was not new in itself, but applying it to the city of Paris, and specifically to the amelioration of the manifold ills by which that city was presently plagued, was certainly sufficiently striking in 1771 to attract attention, and to hold that attention so well that by 1789 Mercier—who had owned up to having written it and begun signing new editions in 1784—had come to seem an important precursor of the Revolution. Partly as a result, he was elected to the Convention in order to help plan the future of the nation, but he voted against the execution of Louis XVIII—inevitably—and thus bought himself a ticket to the guillotine in 1793, avoiding it narrowly because Robespierre jumped the queue and enabled his release (the Marquis de Condorcet was not so lucky, having died in prison).

Before 1789, of course, very few of the book's readers could have had any idea that it was, in fact, an element in a long series of visionary fantasies by the same author, and when the text became famous again as a forerunner of futuristic fantasy, very few of its readers could have known that, or would have cared if they had. Indeed, it was not until the twenty-first century, when copies of Mercier's earlier visionary fantasies became available in electronic form on the Bibliothèque Nationale's *gallica* website and the International Archive Digital Library at *archive.org* that it became practicable for anyone to place *L'An deux mille quatre cent quarante* in its true context, within Mercier's pioneering development of philosophical visionary fantasy—a genre whose subsequent development has been stuttering, to say the least, inhibited by the commonplace notion that any story that ends "And then I woke up" should be awarded an automatic F in the qualifying examination for literary respectability.

Perhaps ironically, it is partly for that reason that much of Mercier's visionary fantasy still seems fresh and original, its exploratory zest not having been weighed down by an enormous burden of subsequent sophistication. In Mercier's work we can see the full effect of the liberation that the device of dreaming gave to his literary imagination, how it enabled him casually to toss aside conventional notions of narrative structure and conventional notions of narrative propriety, in order to become a genuine precursor of surrealism and to develop a number of what were to become conventional tropes of supernatural fiction in original ways. For instance the triply layered dream-portmanteau in *Songes d'un hermite* (tr. as "Dreams of a Hermit") featuring the Isle of Blood, is a very early and, in retrospect, very interesting, contribution to the development of the literary vampire.

Mercier's first collection of visionary fantasies, *Songes philosophiques* [Philosophical Dreams] (1768), was signed, although the title-page claimed publication in London, but *Songes d'un hermite* was not, and it gave its place of publication on the title page as "L'Héritage de St. Amour," so there was no manifest connection between the two books, or between either of them and *L'An deux mille quatre cent quarante*, but now that we know that the three volumes were by the same author and produced within a narrow timespan we can easily see not only the connections linking them but also an interesting pattern of development within them—a pattern that continued, in an equally interesting fashion, in a number of belated additions to the sequence. Several of the dreams from the earlier volumes were reprinted, in slightly revised form, in the 2-volume collection *Mon Bonnet de nuit* (1784; signed "M. Mercier" and ostensibly published in Neufchâtel in Switzerland) along with other stories and essays, and were then reprinted again, with other visionary fantasies, in volume

32 of Charles Garnier's collection of *Voyages imaginaires, songes, visions et romans cabalistiques*, ostensibly published in Amsterdam in 1788. The longest item added thereto, "L'Homme de fer" (tr. as "The Iron Man") was then reprinted as an appendix to *L'An deux mille quatre cent quarante* in the edition of 1899.

The present collection only includes five of the items from the 1768 *Songes philosophiques*, the first four and the sixth items in the section separated in that volume as Part I, the items in part II making less use of the imaginative scope of the visionary element in philosophical essays on various themes. Similarly, only a selection of the new items added to the volume in Garnier's series are included, but I have translated the entirety of *Songes d'un hermite*, which seems to me to be the most interesting of the three volumes in terms of its innovation, its eccentricity and its tentative pioneering explorations of "dream logic." It is certainly the wittiest of the three as well as the quirkiest, and hence the most entertaining from the viewpoint of today. Although all of the new materials added to the Garnier volume represent a partial reversion to the more ponderous allegorizing of the 1786 collection, they show very clearly the legacy of the 1770 volume in terms of their narrative strategy and whimsical wit.

The first item in the 1768 collection "L'Optimisme" (tr. as "Optimism") stakes out the principal philosophical territory of that collection, its title establishing it as a kind of ideological reply to Voltaire's most famous *conte philosophique, Candide, ou l'Optimisme* (1759), which mocks Gottfried Leibniz's theodicy. Faced with the dilemma posed by the existence and apparent prevalence of evil in the human world, which seems to require compromising either God's omnipotence or his omnibenevolence, Leibniz had plumped for the former option, proposing that God had done his best with the limited materials available to him—a hypothesis parodied by Voltaire in the philosopher Pangloss's continual assertion that humans live in "the best of all possible worlds."

Voltaire, of course, provided no solution of his own to the problem of evil, considering the question of whether the God in which he did not believe was less than omnipotent or less than omnibenevolent irrelevant, but Mercier could hardy settle for that, and he sets out robustly to wriggle out of the dilemma by proposing that what appear to be the evils and injustices of human existence are only apparent, and that the optimism that tries hard to find some good therein is not as stupid and misguided as Voltaire thinks. The sequel, "L'Âme" (tr. as "The Soul"), takes the argument a step forward, arguing—among other things—that human endeavor is capable of remedying all the world's ills, and that there is scope for optimism in that. Many of his subsequent fantasies, including *L'An deux mille quatre cent quarante* attempt to map out how that might be done, with the aid of a change of heart on the part of those largely responsible for causing them (Mercier would have loved Charles Dickens' *A Christmas Carol*, which is very firmly located in the tradition he helped to remold and carry forward.)

The most original and adventurous of the fantasies in the first volume—and consequently the most confused and problematic—is the fourth, "Les Lunettes" (tr. as "The Lunettes"), which provides a further argument in favor of optimism, on the basis of psychological necessity, and comes perilously close to arguing for the psychological necessity of illusion, although Mercier would presumably have been hostile to any suggestion that his own faith-based optimism was nothing but an illusion. (Voltaire, who was still alive, but very old, might have made that suggestion to him had the two of them been on speaking terms.) It is the bold imagination of "Les Lunettes" that is reproduced in many of the most interesting thought-experiments conducted in *Songes d'un hermite*, which includes a brief account of another pair of revealing philosophical spectacles. It is not surprising, however, that within his first story-sequence he chose to go in a different direction, producing in "D'un monde heureux" (tr. as "A Fortunate World) an image of a world that really does seem to be "the best of all possible worlds," and then undermining it ingeniously with the earnest argument that a comparison of that world with our own does not work entirely to the advantage of the former, and suggests that ours is the one that has the greater capacity for virtue precisely because of its faults.

The interplanetary voyage of "D'un monde heureux" is also recapitulated in *Songes d'un Hermite*, but in a much more flippant, almost absurdist manner, which reduces its significance somewhat within the history of interplanetary fantasy, although it is worth noting in passing in 1768 and 1770 Mercier appears to have had no doubt that the Earth is spherical and that planets orbit suns, although he seems to have become skeptical about both those assertions late in life, when he wrote *Satyres contre les astronomes* [Satires against the Astronomers] (1803) and *De l'impossibilité du système astronomique de Copernic et de Newton* [On the Impossibility of the Astronomical Theory of Copernicus and Newton] (1806). Those late essays are, however, not entirely disconnected from the satirical spirit of *Songes d'un hermite*, which has no qualms about venturing into the realms of pure farce in pursuit of skeptical notions, in a quasi-anarchic spirit.

There are traces of that imaginative quirkiness in the early pages of *L'An deux mille quatre cent quarante*, in the formulation of its key narrative device, but it changes its tune completely in its sustained and angry assault on the avoidable evils afflicting life in contemporary Paris and the attempt to map out practicable solutions to the corollary problems. That was to become the focus of the two journalistic texts that were to become the foundation of Mercier's posthumous reputation throughout the nineteenth century, *Tableau de Paris* [A Depiction of Paris] (1781; revised and expanded 1788) and *Le Nouveau Paris* [The New Paris] (1798), the detailed observations of which make them important historical documents. The three works are emphatically not "dreams of a hermit" but the very opposite: the practical propaganda of a deeply concerned and actively involved city-dweller.

"L'Homme de fer" is clearly related to the Parisian works, but it is equally evidently related to *Songes d'un hermite*, and represents an interesting hybrid of two contrasted elements of Mercier's productivity and personality; it certainly does not seem completely out of place in the 1786 collection, where it rubs shoulders with vignettes that recapitulate the spirit of the eremitic dreams in a more direct manner. Its reputation has not been yet redeemed in recent times by fans of superhero fiction hailing it as an important precursor, but there might still be time for that to happen.

The most interesting of the other new pieces contained in the Garnier version of the *Songes et visions* is "Nouvelles de la lune" (tr. as "New from the Moon") which provides a brief vision of the afterlife somewhat reminiscent of a schema of cosmic palingenesis mapped out by the Chevalier de Béthune in *Relation du monde de Mercure* (1750, posthumously; tr. as *The World of Mercury*).[1] It is also reminiscent of the schema that Mercier's friend Nicolas-Edmé Restif de la Bretonne began to map out in the late 1780s in a manuscript that was belatedly completed and published as *Les Posthumes*, (1802; tr. as *Posthumous Correspondence*)[2] and it might well have emerged from the same discussions in Fanny de Beauharnais' salon, to which Mercier had introduced Restif. Restif's work clearly shows some influence from Mercier's visionary fantasies—one of the few contemporary authors that does—but the influence surely worked both ways, and "Nouvelles de la lune" is not the only item in the 1786 collection that might have taken a little inspiration from Restif, "Je suis mort" (tr. as "I Am Dead") probably being another.

It is perhaps odd that neither *Mon Bonnet de nuit* nor the 1786 *Songes et visions* reprinted any of the dreams from *Songes d'un hermite*, although Mercier had published that volume anonymously and it was not generally known at the

---

[1] Black Coat Press, ISBN 978-1-61227-410-2.
[2] Black Coat Press, 3 vols. ISBNs 978-1-61227-513-0, -514-7 & -515-4.

time to be his work (but there can be no doubt about the attribution). The material in that collection is certainly not inferior to the material in the other volumes, and it is equally important, if not more so, as an innovative and experimental text. Perhaps Mercier felt that the dreams in *Songes d'un hermite* gained something from their presentation as a set, and that its elements might not have shown to their best advantage if extracted. If that is an arguable case, however, it is equally arguable that the items in the present sampler gain something from being presented as a set, which allows the evolution of the author's thinking and methodology to be more easily perceived and better appreciated. That is, at least, my hope and conviction. At the very least it provides a fascinating cross-section of the work of a unique writer, whose originality and enterprise has never yet been given the full credit that it deserves.

The translation of the stories from *Songes philosophiques* were made from the version of the 1768 text reproduced on *gallica*; the translations from the 1786 *Songes et visions* were also made from the copy reproduced on *gallica*. The translation of *Songes d'un hermite* were made from the scan of the 1770 edition reproduced on *archive.org*.

Brian Stableford

OPTIMISM

I had been reflecting for an entire day on the happiness that is the share of the wicked and the misfortune that pursues the virtuous man; but who can sleep in a feather-bed while the unfortunate suffer and their plaintive groans criticize our repose, while they awaken an invincible sentiment of pity in our hearts? There is no philosopher—or, to but it better, qualifier—who is not a friend of humankind; his sensitive soul is too firmly linked to the fate of his peers for him to isolate himself, as the wicked do. The soul of a virtuous man does not want to be happy unless everyone else is too.

My enfeebled senses had ceded to the poppies of slumber, but my free and potent thought followed the course of its meditations nevertheless. I did not lose sight of the destiny of the unfortunate man; my heart was awake and interested on his behalf. I was still irritated—albeit in a dream—by the spectacle that the wretched earth offers me, in which indolent vice triumphs, and where timid virtue is stigmatized and persecuted. I experienced those torments, from which a man who does not seal his being within the situation of his own existence cannot defend himself.

Saddened, I traversed at a slow pace the beautiful country of Azora, but the tranquility that reigned over the cheerful face of Nature did not penetrate my heart. All the scenes of injustice, crime and tyranny offered themselves more vividly to my thought. On one side I head the cries of famished indigence that were lost in the atmosphere; on the other, the foolish and noisy joy of insensible and barbaric men replete with superfluities.

All the misfortunes that overwhelm the human race and all the chagrins that ruin and devour it were retraced in a host in my memory. I sighted, and bittersweet thorn of pity wounded my heart delectably. Hot tears streamed over my cheeks; I exhaled my laments and I forgot wisdom to the extent of murmuring against the powerful hand that arranges the events of the world.

"O God," I cried, "let my ear no longer hear the sighs of misery and the howls of despair; let my eyes no longer fall of men murdering their fellows; let me no longer witness the glittering sword of despotism and the shameful chains of slavery, or give me another heart in order that I no longer suffer with a world of unfortunates! Alas, you have given life to so many innocent creatures who did not ask you for it! Was it only to see them be born, suffer and die? Dolor passes through this sad world like an impetuous hurricane, while pleasure is as rare and light as the inconstant wing of the zephyr."

I was about to continue my laments where I felt myself lifted up in the air by an unknown force. The earth trembled, the sky lit up with flashes of lightning, and my eyes measured fearfully the immense space uncovered beneath my feet.

I recognized that I had sinned. I cried: "Mercy, O my God, mercy for a feeble creature who adores you, but whose heart is too sensible to the woes of humankind."

Suddenly I felt my feet set firmly on an unknown soil; I found myself in a profound obscurity. I remained plunged therein for some time, but then a radiance more rapid and more piercing than lightning came to dissipate the darkness that enveloped me. A Spirit dressed with six bright wings appeared before me; by the celestial flame that shone over his head and the characteristics of divinity imprinted on his luminous face, I recognized him for one of the Eternal's angels.

"Listen," he said to me, in a tone that rendered me courage, "listen, and do not censure Providence any longer for want of knowing better; follow me."

I followed him to the foot of a mountain, the summit of which cleaved the heavens. I rose up, or rather, I climbed. Picture for yourself enormous rocks suspended one above another, which, at every instant, threatened to fall and crush the plains. In the midst of those fearsome viewpoints, the eye sought in vain for a tree or a plant that might remind it of animate Nature; it only discovered a chain of rocks half-charred by thunderbolts.

I followed my guide tremulously, and the roars of tigers and lions, rendered more frightful by the echoes, terrified my ears; at every step I needed the arm of the obliging angel to sustain me, and I saw by my sides—a terrible spectacle!—unfortunate companions who, wanting to scale those high rocks, were holding on, suspended from the spurs, but who soon wearied of the effort, tottered, shouted in vain for help, slipped and fell, were crushed, and became the prey of tigers, which found over their palpitating limbs in the valleys.

I was thinking that a similar fate awaited me, when the angel said to me: "Thus Providence punishes the reckless audacity of mortals. Why do humans want to penetrate that which is impenetrable? Their first duty is to recognize their weakness; everything is propelled invisibly by the hand of a God; that God wants to pardon you; he wants more, he wants to enlighten you."

With those words, he touched me with his hand and I found myself at the summit of the mountain. What a pleasant surprise! The opposite slope, which we descended, was a garden, simultaneously agreeable and magnificent, where verdure, birdsong and the perfume of flowers enchanted all the senses; a superior charm impassionate the most indifferent being there. My divine conductor showed me, in the distance, a temple of astonishing structure; the road that led to it was so mysterious that it was impossible to reach it without a guide.

As we approached, the doors of the temple opened; we went in, and they closed again suddenly with a sound of thunder under an invisible hand.

"No one can open them, and no one can close them, except for the powerful voice of God," said my august protector.

Gripped by respect, I read these words written in letters of gold: *God is just; his way is hidden; who would dare to want to fathom his decrees?*

I darted a glance at the magnificent height of the temple; the whole of that magnificent edifice rested on three columns of white marble; in the middle stood and altar; from the place of the image of the Divinity an odorous smoke rose up, whose sweet vapor filled the temple. To the right of the altar a black marble tablet was suspended, and facing it was a mirror composed of the purest crystal.

The angel said to me: "It's here you will learn that, if Providence sometimes renders a good man unhappy, it is in order to lead him more surely to happiness."

Having said that, he disappeared.

It was no longer cold terror that froze my senses; it was a pure, sweet, ineffable joy that filled my soul. I shad tears of tenderness; my knees buckled, my arms were raised toward the sky, and I was only able to adore supreme Goodness in silence. A majestic voice, which had nothing terrible about it, said to me: "Get up, look and read."

I raised my eyes to the mirror, and I saw my friend Sadak therein: Sadak, whose constant and courageous virtue had often astonished me, and who was able to brave indigence and even make it respected. I saw him in a chamber whose walls were bare; he was leaning his weary head on the last item of furniture that remained to him, his heart consumed by hunger and by a despair that was even crueler. A single tear escaped his eyelid—a tear of blood! Wretched, he dared not weep.

Four children were crying for their father and asking for bread; the youngest, weak and languishing, lying on a litter of straw, no longer had the strength to moan; he was exhaling the last sighs of an innocent life. The wife of the unfortunate man, emaciated by misfortune, forgot her natural tenderness and mildness in order to reproach him for the excess of their misery. Those cruel plaints tore his heart and added to his torment.

Sadak gets up, turns away from the sight of his children, and, ill as he is, drags himself away in order to seek help.

He encounters a man to whom he had once rendered great services; the man owed to him the honest employment that he enjoyed. Sadak explains to him the deplorable state in

20

which he finds himself; he describes his children, ready to expire in his arms for want of a little nourishment….

The other blushes at being forced to recognize him, and looks around anxiously to see whether anyone can see him talking to a man wearing the livery of indigence; he brushes off the poor supplicant with vague promises and cold politeness, and suddenly draws away at a rapid pace. It is at least the tenth time that he has treated inhumanely the man to whom he owes everything.

Desperate, Sadak is directing his steps at random when one of his creditors stops him, heaps him with insults, gathers people around the unfortunate, threatens him publicly, and is ready to strike him, more out of scorn than anger.

Finally, I see him wandering from door to door, extending and imploring hand, sometimes rejected, sometimes receiving the alms that one gives to importunity. He buys a loaf of bread, carries it home, shares it with his children, weeps with joy in appearing their hunger and thanks Providence on his knees for the rich blessings that it has just lavished upon him.

I uttered a cry of dolor, astonishment and fright. My eyes, charged with tears, turned toward the tablet of black marble, and an invisible hand traced these words thereon:

Finish contemplating Sadak, and condemn, if you dare, the Providence that regulates everything.

I redirected my sight at the mirror, and I saw my friend Sadak again, but how changed he was! How different the scene was! It is no longer the indigent Sadak: poor, it is true, but tender, virtuous, sympathetic, full of honor and humanity. It is Sadak in abundance, having become opulent by virtue of an unexpected inheritance; it is Sadak who, in the corrupting bosom of wealth, has forgotten the virtues that were dear to him. Torpid in luxury, he is harsh, he commands sharply and, no longer suffering, he does not remember that there are unfortunates, and that he has been one of them.

I immediately read, with a respectful admiration, what the mysterious tablet informed me:

Virtue often suffers, because it would cease to be virtue of it did not fight. When August Providence causes misery to descend upon the head of a mortal, its sister, patience, accompanies it, courage sustains it, and it is by that gift that virtue is sufficient to itself and becomes happy even when misfortune seems to overwhelm it.

My avid eye did not delay in returning to the mirror. What object could there be more interesting for my heart? It was my homeland that I perceived, my dear homeland, the happy city where I was born—but O Heaven, what am I seeing? Suddenly, a formidable army has inundated its fields, surrounded its strong walls, and has prepared, for its ruination, the infernal machines of destruction. The iron is ready, vengeance and rage light their torches. O superb city, you are trembling in spite of your proud defenders! Your treasures are inflaming the thirst for pillage in the heart of the enemy.

You want to oppose a courageous resistance to him— vain efforts! He climbs, he scales your vainglorious towers; blood flows, death flies, flame ravages; you are no longer anything but a sad heap of stones covered by thick smoke. My unfortunate fellow citizens who have escaped the conflagration are wandering in the woods, but horrible famine awaits them in those deserts; it devours them slowly and prolongs their torture and their death.

"Just God," I cried, "a million people will fall victim to one ambitious man. Children will be killed on their mother's bosom; the white hair of old men will be dragged in the blood and the dust; innocent beauty will become the victim of a murderous crowd, an entire city will disappear because the cupidity of a monster will have coveted its wealth!"

A land full of prevaricators, responded the tablet, *merits the punishment of a Divinity too long scorned. Those who were not culpable are extracted from the danger of becoming so, and if the hand of Providence has struck them, it was to preserve them from a more horrible shipwreck than the torment of a temporary death; their refuge is in the bosom of the clemency of an eternal God.*

The palace of the Minister Aliacin, the gilded pyramids of which pierce the clouds, rose up with too much magnificence for it not to strike my gaze. How many times indignation had seized my heart at the sight of that happy monster, who, with a venal soul, a barbaric heart, depraved morals and a despotic spirit had, it seemed, enchained fortune to has chariot.

His elevation was the fruit of his base actions, his treasures the price of his treason. He had sold his fatherland for gold, and vices struck with opprobrium had had decorated the rare dignities. An entire province groaned under his harsh oppression. Sometimes he laughed at the faint murmur of a people reduced to slavery; sometimes he dealt with their stifled groans and cries of revolt. Every day he committed a new crime, and every day success crowned his audacity.

Meanwhile, the interior of his palace only offered features of generosity and examples of virtues, as many on silk as on canvas. The busts of the great men of antiquity ornamented the house of the most cowardly scoundrel, and those mute marbles, far from speaking to his heart, did not even make him shudder when he looked at them.

I considered that wicked man, dressed with power, surrounded by flatterers, feared by his enemies, publicly covered with incense, and only cursed in whispers. A thousand precious rarities decorated his cabinet, and each of them had only cost him an injustice. The purple with which he was covered was at the expense of those who went naked, and the wine that was poured into his cup ornamented with gems could be considered as an extract of the tears that he caused to be shed.

He emerges from a sumptuous table and goes to put himself at the feet of a concubine, the patrimony of an orphan. He stands with her at the window, and from there he sees, tranquilly, a sensitive and courageous citizen put to death, who had dared to represent to him the abuse of his power. The good man is strangled, and a courier comes an hour later to announce to the Minister that the Sultan, in recognition of his signal services, is making him a present of considerable lands.

The monster smiles, and, in becoming more powerful, he dreams of rendering himself more terrible.

My hatred against that odious tyrant became so strong that I turned my gaze toward the tablet, impatiently, several times, as if to hasten the verdict that it was about to be pronounced, but nothing appeared there yet. My sight returned sadly to the marvelous crystal.

I perceived the monster entering a secret cabinet. What a satisfaction for my heart! Nature, the unfortunate and the earth are avenged! That powerful man, who seemed the most fortunate of men, reads a letter, goes pale, trembles, cries out in a low voice, and strikes his forehead with the same hand with which he murdered the innocent. Agitated by a despair that he cannot vanquish, he goes back and forth, wandering in fury, racked by dread more than by remorse. He tears away all the marks of his dignity, tramples them underfoot, and in his range, he weeps like a child.

I was trying to divine the subject of his fury when one of his favorites, viler than his master, came into his cabinet and I learned the cause of his despair. One of his confidants, a spy at the court, had just written to tell him that a new storm was brewing, that he was going to lose his rank and his credit if he did not have sufficient skill to ward off the blow. Immediately, that shameful favorite gave his master advice, in a firm voice, which no one else would have been able to hear without punishing him with his own hand.

That frightful advice pleased the barbarian. He ordered that his daughter be brought into his presence. Nouremi appeared. She was beautiful, and she had virtues. Gods! With what horror she learned that her father wanted to deliver her to the Sultan, like a victim immolated to his insatiable ambition.

She almost falls unconscious at her father's feet, she makes the tears of her beauty, nature and innocence speak.... A severe gaze commands her to obey; she obeys, and dies.

Has Aliacin become any happier? I see him in his refuge of repose; lying on the soft bed, or plunged in a delightful bath, one would think that he were lying on thorns. He fears for his life; he gets us, he wanders around his Palace with tremulous steps; he finds his slaves asleep, and envies their peaceful slumber. Day dawns; still anxious, still suspicious, he shivers when he eats and goes pale when he drinks, uncertain whether he is pouring nourishment or death into his bosom. He even fears the caress of the women he tyrannizes and whose slave he is. If someone stands up, a thousand serpents gnaw at his bosom; it might be the man who will one day overthrow him, the redoubtable man who will one day sit down in his place.

Full of a respectful expectation, I consulted the tablet of the august judgments of the Eternal, and I read:

The truth is terrible for the wicked man; it is incessantly present to his eyes; it is what constitutes his torture; he only sees that redoubtable mirror, in which he reads his injustice and the deformity of his soul.

Suddenly, a muffled sound, like that of distant thunder, became audible. I turned my sight toward Aliacin's palace. His gardens, his pyramids, his statues, even himself—everything had disappeared! In place of that abode, where all sensual pleasures were assembled, nothing could any longer be seen but a nest of impure snakes crawling in a miry marsh. Such is the foundation of palaces that crime has built. These words engraved on the black marble told me what had become of Aliacin.

He has been swept from the surface of the earth like vile dust, and future races will doubt that he existed.

That frightful tablet will never leave my memory, and since that time, I groan when I see a powerful man; other people contemplate his wealth, but I see him exposed to the arm of divine justice.

My eyes, more attentive, flew back to the mirror and I perceived Mirza and Fatima, tender, generous lovers, at the age at which one knows the enthusiasm of virtue. That very day had just united them, and their mutual tenderness promised them a long sequence of similarly fortunate days. The sweet intoxication of happiness shone in their gaze, their hands were interlaced and their sighs were confounded with a touching tenderness. Fatima had the beauty of a virgin, its modesty, its grace and the soft incarnadine whose splendor is so fleeting. The most beautiful bosom enclosed the noblest heart. Mute with amour, his soul plunged in an inexpressible delight, Mirza kissed Fatima, halting words were the only and feeble interpreters of the emotions of his heart. Fatima recompensed her lover's tenderness with an amiable smile; she blushed, and that adorable blush was the work of the purest amour. How their silence expressed what their tongues could not! My heart shivered with joy at the seductive picture of Virtue crowned by the hands of Amour. How could a friend of humankind see those fortunate hearts without being moved by pleasure and without applauding their happiness?

The two lovers were glad to be united, because they would be able to do good together. They were rich, and satisfied thereby because they would be able to relive the host of the unfortunate. On the day of their wedding they wished that hearts as sensible as their own might savor the same felicity. They would marry young women to their young lovers when misfortune was the only obstacle that opposed their union. Mirza wanted all hearts to be in unison with his; his sublime soul would have lived to blow a universal, unalterable sensual pleasure over Nature entire.

"Dear Fatima," he said, "in the bosom of happiness, we will be able to say: We are not the only ones to be happy. We are in joy, and at this moment we are being blessed; we have caused Hymen to descend into sad cottages. Innocent hearts are opened to joy; consoling Amour has effaced the image of their misery, and we shall see their children smile at our approach. Fatima, their caresses will be our sweetest recompense!"

Those tender and virtuous souls formed the plan of a useful and beneficial life; their children would be raised in the sound maxims of wisdom; they would be taught above all, to be simple and good, because simplicity and goodness are the principles of all the virtues; in their flexible and tender souls, impressions of humanity and sympathy would be nourished, because it is necessary to be sensitive in order to be humane. That charming and respectable couple were inflamed by the transports of their hearts, already seeing their posterity heir to the generous blood that ran in their veins. In the delight that Amour, Virtue and Good Fortune inspire they fell it their knees before the Supreme Being.

"Great God," they cried, "give us children worthy of you, in order that they will be humane, that they will walk in the paths of your justice; or if they will stray from the sound laws that we cherish, rather strike us with sterility, and let them not receive an existence that would debase them in our eyes as in yours."

Their suppliant arms are interlaced when the ceiling of the room creaks and shakes. Fatima faints in terror; Mirza could still save himself, but how can he abandon his dear Fatima? He tries to lift her in his arms; the wall totters and falls, crushing and burying the two lovers. The world loses its most worthy ornament and the human species the example of the rarest virtues.

I hide my face in order to weep freely. I wanted to be crushed under those sad ruins with Mirza and Fatima; motionless for a long time, I dared not risk my gaze upon the tablet.

Finally, I lifted a trembling eye and I read:

The blind human eye only sees the present; Providence alone knows the future; the most sudden death has been the recompense of the virtues of Mirza and Fatima; it has enabled them to pass into a state of delight of which this world has no idea, at the same time as it has saved them from bringing into the world descendants unworthy of them.

I concluded that I ought not to decide anything henceforth, being a feeble atom whose limited sight could not embrace my own existence. On looking again into the incomprehensible mirror, I had a further subject of astonishment; I perceived Agenor, an unfortunate young man given to every form of excess, and the most decided libertine in a dissolute city.

He was pale, distressed, and violently agitated; he was striding back and forth in his room, putting his hand to his forehead furiously and pronouncing imprecations in a low voice. He paused momentarily, as if irresolute; soon, all his rage burst forth; he ran to a secret cupboard, took out a piece of paper, and poured some kind of powder into a cup....

"Yes," he said, with his eyes ablaze, "this poison is the only resource that I can embrace; it will save me from the opprobrium that awaits me. The infidel Roxane has sacrificed me for the unworthy Dabour; my father no longer wants to pay for my pleasures; my creditors are threatening me with prison every day. Let us avenge ourselves simultaneously on Roxane, my father and my creditors."

He raised the cup to his mouth, and I was scarcely afflicted to see the world lose a furious debauchee, when he suddenly stopped.

"What!" he cried, in a dull and stifled tone. "I'm going to die, and without being avenged! Perfidious rival! Oh, I want to redden the earth with your blood! You'll fall under my hand and your death will satisfy my fury!"

Having said that, he put down his cup, picked up his scimitar, and went out.

Scarcely was he in the street than his father, a venerable old man, went up to his son's room. Alas, he would have been happy but for his son. Legible in his face was the sharp dolor that distresses a parental soul. He was coming to represent to that ingrate son the laws of honor, probity and duty. He hoped to touch his heart, to bring him back to virtue. His wrinkles, his noble wrinkles, his white hair and the tears that bathed his face all inspired respect and pity. On seeing him, the hardest heart would have been moved.

That unfortunate old man, fatigued by the efforts that he had made, was thirsty. He perceived that fatal cup; he drank, fell to the floor and rendered his soul in the most horrible convulsions.

I dared to confide my surprise to Supreme Justice, and it raced the following words on the redoubtable tablet with its invisible finger:

Agenor's father had rendered himself, by his culpable negligence, the cause of his son's doom; it was just that Agenor become in his turn, the instrument of his torture. Fathers, know the full extent of your duties, and shiver! To tolerate vice is to commit it.

Scarcely had those words been traced than they disappeared, and these took their place:

Consider the whole, in order not to go astray.

Immediately, I perceived in the mirror a great island, separated into two by a river. The right hand part formed a lush plain covered with sumptuous palaces and magnificent gardens; it was populated by richly clad people. The left hand side, on the contrary, presented an arid desert in which a few wretched cabins, partly open, allowed the indigenes to be seen, who led an obscure and difficult life there.

That island might have been considered as an image of the earthy globe. The land to the right was called the land of the fortunate: songs, dances, feasts and spectacles seemed to be their only occupation. Sensual pleasure smiled in the eyes of the tender beauties who accompanied them; they allowed themselves to be drawn meekly toward solitary shade. However, I remarked that the majority of them only considered themselves to be fortunate while they perceived the people who lived on the opposite bank.

In the most splendid feasts they appeared to be extremely joyful, but I, who was able to see their hearts laid bare, could see that they were devoured by gnawing worms. They seemed to be drinking nectar at the table of the Gods, but the inferno was within their breast. Although in the bosom of abundance, their desires were far from being satisfied; they only had one mouth with which to savor aliments but their active and insensate imagination depopulated the land and the sea in order to furnish new dishes to a palate worn out be sensations too frequently repeated.

Among those supposedly fortunate individuals there were some who suddenly quit their pleasures in order to run after a certain will-o'-the-wisp, to the sound of drums and cannons. They came back covered in blood, sometimes mutilated, and then they were called "heroes."

Others made the greatest efforts to reach the top of a flight of steps, which was occupied, whereas they could have found a more comfortable spot a little lower down. They tormented themselves in a strange manner. Sometimes they were mocked, and often they were thrown down to the bottom of the stairs. Nothing put them off; they climbed again, and of they succeeded, either by skill or by importunity, they did not even have the time to sit down, sufficiently embarrassed and occupied in repelling the ambitious who, in their turn, wanted to usurp their place.

Further away, I perceived scatterbrains who were running back and forth, without occupation and without affairs, sowing gold coins without pleasure and ending up setting fire to their palaces in order to rejoice the eyes of a concubine momentarily. Afterwards they were forced to return to the desert country known as the land of the unfortunate.

In that miserable abode nothing could be heard but laments and cries; every inhabitant went about bowed down beneath a fleshy tumor that oppressed the back of his neck. It was with a sad and envious gaze that they contemplated the land of felicity; and what did they obtain by those vain desires? The hump they bore became much heavier; if they approached those fortunate men they heard the piquant mockeries launched at them by the others, against the bearers of the fleshy tumors.

It was not easy, but not absolutely forbidden, for the inhabitants of the unfortunate country to swim across the river and establish themselves in the land of the rich; but after they had tried the air of the region for a while, almost all of them came back voluntarily, preferring to wear a heavy hump than always to be at war with their own conscience.. If someone complained because his tumor was much heavier than his fellow's, he had the power to exchange it, but he usually repented of the bargain and resumed his original burden.

Those masses of flesh did not appear to me to be as insupportable as their bearers affirmed; in general, it seemed to me that in the land of felicity, people exaggerated by appearance the sentiment of pleasure, and in the land of misery, people exaggerate by weakness the sentiment of pain, for there is an ancient mania, still subsisting, of wanting to be pitied. I noticed that the lack of skill of the latter rendered the burden much more difficult than it was. Those who were able to bear it lightly appeared content and healthy, habit having rendered the burden scarcely sensible, whereas those who were unable to maintain a precise equilibrium lurched at every step and rendered walking very difficult.

Another advantage of the land of misery was that its inhabitants confided themselves with assurance to the irritated waves. Their hump always sustained them on the surface of the water; they could be tossed about but the rudest shocks of the tempest did not bring any damage to their situation. On the contrary, the citizens of the land of felicity, often seeing the unified plains of their beautiful countryside, were suddenly overturned by the slightest moment of the liquid empire. Carried away by the currents, they were unable to swim, and the gold that covered their garments made to small contribution their being engulfed.

I also observed that in the fortunate country, people were much less skillful, much less industrious, much less humane, and much less charitable than in the land of the unfortunate.

My avid eyes were searching for some other object of comparison when the sky of the island was covered by somber clouds; thunder was heard, furious lightning split the clouds sand a frightful hail fell upon the land.

All hearts were consternated, but now the abysms of the sea rose up; impetuous waves climbed all the way to the heavens, laying siege to the double isle and soon swallowing it along with all its inhabitants. I could no longer see anything in the mirror but a lugubrious and pale obscurity that covered an immense mass of waters, pierced by a few confused moans.

At that very moment a supernatural light filled the temple, the odorous cloud of smoke above the altar was transformed into a column of flame, and the vault of the edifice was suddenly removed, offering me the spectacle of a luminous throne, which descended slowly, to the majestic sound of thunder. I fell down fearfully before the Divinity of ht redoubtable place.

A divine arm deigned to lift me up again, and I saw beside me the angel who had deigned to serve as my guide. His voice rendered me courage; I read these words written in streaks of fire on the mysterious marble:

Death renders humans equal. It is eternity that assigns each human being his veritable share; justice is slow but it is immutable. The just man, the god man, finds himself in his place, and the wicked man in his. Mortals, the balance of an eternal God swings in the abysms of eternity.

Then the mirror became perfectly clear and I saw a tall and beautiful woman clad in a celestial majesty standing on a demi-column. She was holding a balance in one hand and a faming sword in the other. Millions of people of all nations and all ages were assembled around her; she was weighing virtues and vices, and pardoning faults that were the children of weakness. Patience and resignation were recompensed, and indiscreet murmurs were punished.

I saw with an inexpressible joy that the tears of the unfortunate dried up under the benevolent hand; those unfortunates blessed their past woes, the source of their present happiness; the more they had suffered, the greater was their recompense; they entered into the eternal dwellings where the God of bounty took pleasure in exercising clemency, the first, the greatest, the finest and the most adorable of all his attributes. All those that the Eternal had deigned to animate with his divine breath were born to be happy. The stains that the vile mud of the body imprinted on the soul disappeared in the radiance of the true Sun; his splendor absorbed those temporary shadows.

The Creator of this vast universe was a tender father who was collecting his children after a long and sad pilgrimage, and who did not arm his hand against their pat faults. Those who had opened their hearts to justice, to tender pity, who had helped the innocent and relived the poor, received a double degree of glory. An immortal canticle of praise, repeated by the entire human race, announced the reparation of things.

The time of dolor, dread and despair was elapsed forever; the beautiful days of eternity opened, the face of this world had vanished; no groan was to trouble the celestial harmony of that universal felicity. The good God, whose magnificent hand is imprinted on all of Nature, which has even embellished the place of our exile, embraces all his creatures in his bosom; the father and the children were no longer any but the same family.

Then a thunderous voice made itself heard.

"Go, feeble mortal, audacious and limited mind, go and learn to adore Providence, even when it appears to you to be unjust. God has pronounced one and the same decree, he is eternal, he is irrevocable, he has seen everything before bearing it away. Finite beings, your theories, your prayers and your thoughts enter into his plan; submit, hope, and do not criticize his work."

Then the temple collapsed on my head. I woke up, uncertain as to whether I had seen an apparition or a reality.

Ought I, then, to be indignant at the prosperity of the wicked? Ought I to murmur at the misfortune of the just man, or ought I rather to wait for the great curtain extended over the universe to be drawn over our eyes by the hand of death; that is what must enable us to live, by uncovering the immutable, eternal truth that orders he course of events for the greater glory and for the greater felicity of human beings.

THE SOUL

I found myself on a high mountain at sunrise. My gaze turned toward the orient, surveyed the magnificence of varied and renascent Nature. After having embraced that immense horizon, returning to what surrounded me. I perceived under a young cedar the same Spirit that I had seen the previous night. Penetrated by respect and gratitude, I bowed down in order to embrace his knees. He lifted me up with a majestic generosity and spoke to me in a voice whose softness inspired confidence and joy.

"Friend, I want to enlighten you further, since you have such a keen desire to be enlightened. I shall unveil to you what it is permitted for you to understand regarding the spirit hidden within you, which animates and orders both your thoughts and your action. Before the body that you drag under the will of God has returned to the dust of which it is formed, I shall try to make the celestial things that are within our grasp descend."

I tried to embrace his knees for a second time,"

"Leave these genuflections to the vulgar children of men," he said. "My eye can read your heart. Look to the west."

I obeyed, and I saw an agreeable plain surmounted by a hill that was crowned with lemon trees embalmed by clumps of roses. I thought at first that it was uninhabited but I soon perceived a beautiful woman with a luminous body of majestic and superhuman stature, who was coming down the hill; she was surrounded by young children, with a light step and gracious smiles. They announced joy and gaiety; thus Fable depicts for us the Amours, Laughs and Games accompanying the Goddess of Beauty.

"That majestic Nymph," my conductor said to me, "is named the Soul; she obtains her origin from the Heavens, from which she is exiled; but the cause of that exile is in the range of things that are hidden. Some say that it is because she drank too much of the nectar of Olympus, and others because she conceived an unreasonable sentiment of pride in herself. Whatever the reason, cast on to this unfortunate globe, she became partly terrestrial."

While the Spirit was speaking, the Soul came closer, and I was able to consider her and her retinue more carefully. Her face still seemed to be astonished by her new estate; her uncertain physiognomy was mingled with two almost opposed sentiments; she appeared to be debating with herself as to whether or not she ought to be proud of the objects that surrounded her, especially the children who were accompanying her, who were called Desires. Their physiognomy was simple and credulous, announcing inexperience rather than depravity; they all had an agreeable and very seductive form. However, I thought I could perceive a certain fickleness in their brilliant vivacity

The Soul often turned her gaze toward the heavens, and by her contemplative smile and the sighs that escaped her, it was easy to deduce that she had not lost the memory of the divine abode in which she had lived.

Not far from that place was an eminence covered with flowers, which formed an embalmed bed. A woman was lying thereon whose facial features were fine and delicate; however, her effeminate forehead bore a certain imprint of boldness. Down here she is named terrestrial Felicity, but the inhabitants of Olympus do not hesitate to called her Folly. She was surrounded by a multitude of sylphs and sylphides of all forms and colors, all as light as the air. In the same way, one sees differently colored butterflies wandering amid odorous flowerbeds with inconstant wings, sometimes alighting on the tufted stems of flowers and sometimes in their open calices. They bear the name of fleeting Pleasures; they are children of Folly; she has raised and nourished them in secret embraces.

That swarm of Pleasures resembled the colored flies that flutter and buzz in the last rays of the sun on the evening of a beautiful day. They formed a certain flattering noise, which awoke the Soul from her demi-lethargy. The Desires ran to the Pleasures as soon as they perceived them; they were attracted to one another by a strong and secret sympathy. They embraced with the keenest ardor, and each couple resembled a young shepherd united with his nymph. The Soul, indecisive by nature, did not know which way to turn. She listened with a secret complaisance to the attractive sounds of Felicity; she wanted to go toward her, but something unknown to me drew her in another direction, and when I tried to understand that mystery, I perceived a little angel with golden wings hovering over her head. He fluttered his wings joyfully when he saw her drawing away from the deceptive path of Pleasures; on the contrary, he trembled with fear when he saw her set foot on it again, and his dolor went as far as shedding tears.

I begged my divine conductor to explain what he had just revealed to me.

"As often as you see the Soul approach impatiently the direction in which Felicity invites her by means of her siren voice, a shadow of sentiment takes possession of her; you see her drawing away sadly in spite of the keen Desires. That is an effect of the memory of her previous estate, which that charitable angel renews for her with his ever-vigilant tenderness.

"Once she lived under the celestial roof as a sister and companion of pure Intelligences. She was accustomed to a daylight compared with which this is merely darkness. Her ears heard a harmony of which no one here has the slightest idea. On the day of her banishment she was forced to drink from the river of Forgetfulness, but the impression of her past happiness was so profound that a confused memory of it remains in her.

"As soon as she looks at the sky, her sublime order is stirred; she recognizes her former domicile, and the majesty imprinted on the face of the stars elevates her, transports her and causes her to sigh. But when the attractions of the deceptive goddess whom mortals call Felicity masters her, to the point that she is ready to succumb, that angel of heaven, who has always loved her, a sympathetic protector, insinuates a supernatural strength into her with his divine wings; she abandons the dangerous routes, and the beautiful angel that heaven has charged with the care of her guidance brings her back, with transports of joy, to the narrow path that alone can return to her past grandeur.

"You can see, however, that he is often too weak to set aside the powerful lure of a present sensual pleasure; you can see how she is gradually drawing closer and closer to the dangerous hill You can see how the hand of the Desires is leading her gently. She is in peril, alas, she is going to yield to their power. The angel is beating his wings in vain; his sighs, his tears and his efforts are impotent. The Pleasures blindfold the eyes with garlands of flowers; those garlands are enchanted; they all surround her, they are all gently violent, smiling at a futile resistance, and draw her into the arms of Folly."

While I was considering that scene, a great change suddenly overtook the troop of Desires and the troop of Pleasures. Those children, once so attractive and so mild, who were embracing one another with the moist ardent transports, were suddenly transformed into serpents of various kinds and horrible specters. The prettiest became the most hideous. The Desires separated, quivering, from the Amours. I saw the Soul herself extract herself with disgust from those embraces, which became odious to her, but she had scarcely taken a step back than all those little enchanters resumed their first and seductive form.

Weakly, she allowed herself to be drawn away again, abused as she was by their new and deceptive grace. At the same time, secretive Felicity played the prude; she seemed to want to flee the Desires, in order to be pursued by them with more ardor. When the Desires, sometime repelled, turned back grumbling, the ingenious magicienne ran after them. Alas, in their naïve credulity, they always came back to rejoin the indefinable goddess. She fled again, in order better to draw them into her traps. Nothing could be seen but a multicolored whirlwind in continual and rapid movement, which made a confused sound. The plaints of deceived Desires, the impetuous impatience of the Pleasures, their regrets, their reproaches, and the cries of furious Jealousy, sometimes plaintive and sometimes loud, gave rise to a perpetual murmur.

And what was the Soul doing? The Soul was asleep beside Folly on a bed of roses; her hand nonchalantly let go of the reins of the Desires; she awoke at the tumultuous sound of so my discordant voices and saw that she was enchained; she tried to recall all the vagabond Desires, in order to put them in irons and imprison them in her bosom. Vain attempts! Folly, the stronger, held her feeble will captive, submissive to an imperious instinct; she could not command obedience.

Then a heavy woman with a dull face, named Habitude, came, and with an invincible arm, bound her with further knots to the bed of the false Felicity; and the Desires, whirling around her with a continuous rapidity, wearied her so much that she became drowsy, or, rather, torpid, in a profound lethargy.

In the midst of that deadly calm and in the bosom of that death-like sleep, the Soul heard a few distant, but sweet and piercing sounds, which woke her up by degrees and mastered her in such a powerful manner that she made the greatest efforts to get up again and rip the garlands that retained her. I perceived then that the angel with the golden wings, whom I had not seen for a long time, was wandering around her urgently, stimulating her with his gestures and his voice, weeping with joy while she increased her strength and courage.

She struggled for a long time before ridding herself of her bonds. She went to wake up the host of sleeping Desires, who were lying here and there; her voice engaged them to direct their steps toward the heroic and sublime symphony, which seemed to draw away, and the last sounds of which, still delightful, had just expired in her ears. But I believe that she would never have been able to tear herself away from the altar of Folly, in spite of that celestial music, and in spite of the beautiful angel with golden wings, if she had not found, at the right moment, a beautiful woman with a noble face, which seemed serious at first and even slightly austere but whose charms one discovered on considering it more closely.

My conductor told me that her name was Reflection. In one hand she was holding a mysterious glass lens; she gave it to the Soul and ordered her to look through it at Folly and her daughters. What a surprise! Those nymphs who had seemed so charming dropped the mask that covered their deformity. What a contrast! It was the hideous ugliness of crime and remorse.

The Soul examined terrestrial Felicity through the same crystal; her smile was false and cruel; her eyes, which had seemed so soft, were scintillating with the fires of hatred and vengeance; artfully-interlaced serpents formed her hair; it was legible in her gaze that she thought of nothing but deceiving humans, of hollowing out beneath their feet the abysms of woe and shame. The Soul was obliged to blink her eyes in order to sustain the sight of her.

The sage Reflection ordered her for a second time to look with her into the distance, and she discovered a beautiful Spirit on a sheer mountain, whose brightness surpassed everything that the human imagination can create. After having considered it for a long time, the Soul thought she remembered having seen something similar in the abode where she was happy. She flew as if she had wings on her feet to the place from which the divine melody that filled the air seemed to be coming. The Soul ran, accompanied by the beautiful angel with the golden wings, which preceded her steps, smiling with delight and indicating the route to her. The Desires flew after her, full of impatience, and appeared to divine by means of a secret presentiment that the void they experienced in their hearts would soon be filled.

They arrived at the foot of the mountain and stopped there; at first it appeared to them to be difficult to go to, but now three women, similar to goddesses, not in the richness of their attire but by the majestic simplicity of their stride and the nobility and mildness of her features, came down toward them. They were Temperance, Moderation and Patience. They offered to transport the Soul in their arms to the summit of the mountain; as for the Desires, irritated by the obstacle, they thought them too active and too hasty not to attain their goal without help and guidance.

Then it seemed to me that, by a prompt and imperceptible movement, I was carried to the face of the mountain myself, and I considered at close range the august and brilliant scene that met my gaze.

I saw an esplanade surrounded on one side by tall cedars and on the other by odorous bushes. The slope was sown with salutary plants. One respired in those locales the pure air of life and immortality. One found more serenity of mind there, and something celestial in the heart; but the Divinity of that abode struck my sight, in the body that she had wanted to put on. She advanced under the cedars. Her face was as brilliant as the sun ornamented with all its radiance; it was the same Divinity that the Soul had perceived in the distance through Reflection's admirable lens. When one has been fortunate enough to behold her, one cannot desire anything more beautiful, but it is impossible to draw a portrait of her for the eye that has not seen her. She wears a golden band over her forehead, on which her name is written in sacred characters; it only belongs to celestial intelligences to be able to read it; profane morals must lower a respectful gaze in her presence. Down here we call her Virtue.

To her left was a goddess similar to a ravishing daughter, but of a beauty so noble and so touching that, on seeing her, one feels moved by an inalterable pleasure. My divine conductor told me that she was Harmony, that the golden lyre she carried on her alabaster shoulders was the one that regulates the movement of worlds and suns, at the same time as it accompanies the eternal hymns of the angels consecrated to the praises of the Creator. Although she was not touching the lyre at the moment, a harmonious quiver was flowing from it that delighted me with ecstasy, as when the sun sets behind the mountains it still extends golden lances through the layers of the atmosphere, which announce the magnificence with which it crowns its head when it pursues its course in the burning summit of the skies.

As soon as the Soul perceived Virtue, who was coming toward her with an expression of tenderness and goodness, she hastened to throw herself at her feet and to embrace her knees; it was then that she felt, for the first time since she had abandoned the celestial roof, something similar to the divine felicity that she had enjoyed in the assembly of the angels. She even thought that she discovered in the face of Virtue, as in the garments in which she was clad, a few features of the eternal beauty that she had once adored without veils.

Virtue embraced her tenderly as she lifted her up and led her to the side of her sister Harmony, on a smooth lawn, on which they sat down. I discovered a radiant contentment on the face of the Soul; it seemed appropriate to the order of her excellent nature. She appeared to me to be in her veritable state next to those august goddesses. I judged them to be made and created to live together, and that they ought never to be separated. How beautiful the Soul was then! Everything that she said caused me an intimate satisfaction; I no longer doubted her celestial origin; something divine struck me.

In the meantime, the host of languid, astonished Desires, lying on the ground, were like children devoid of strength and light; their eyes were unable to support the radiant majesty of Virtue, their ears could not hear her virile and sublime language; but as soon as Harmony picked up the lyre that commanded the universe and they saw all of Nature obeying that sweet and powerful music, suddenly metamorphosed, they emerged from that state of weakness and indolence, raised their arms to the heavens, clapped their hands in cadence, joined in the ensemble and formed a majestic dance while surrounding the august Virtue.

Their dance imitated the course of the heavenly bodies, suns and planets that, in various orbits, rotate at the behest of the laws of a constant harmony; for the beautiful order of a physical system is doubtless only the feeble image of the moral order that reigns in the eternal world. The Desires had never been so happy or so satisfied. They were no longer light, fickle, inconstant and capricious; they sensed the peaceful equilibrium that is the fruit of true contentment; their hearts were full, and in that moderate agitation there was a mild enjoyment that did not produce lassitude or disgust. But what was most admirable for my enchanted eye was that each Desire that obeyed Harmony is dancing around Virtue immediately received her amiable and vivid imprint; you would have seen something like as many mirrors all reflecting faithfully one and the same object. One might have taken her for a mother surrounded by a laughing troop of children, each bearing a few of their mother's features, although the resemblance as not entirely perfect.

A delightful voice struck my ear; it was that of Harmony. That voice gave a new brightness to the heavens and the earth. The beverage of the immortals is not as sweet as those words.

"Children of the Creator, behold the order that reigns above your heads, fix your eyes on that high viewpoint; let it be your light; neither wealth, not glory, nor sensual pleasure can content your desires; you will be tormented and miserable in the arms of those deceptive phantoms; a frightful void will always remain in your heart.

"And by what can that void be filled, O mortals? Only by Virtue. In the whole extent of creation, is there anything as beautiful, anything more perfect? How sweet it is to possess her! Fortunate is the man who says to himself: *I have only a moment to live in this mortal prison, but I can perfect my soul, I can ennoble the faculties with which it is ornamented as long as it is in me, I can render it worthy of the gaze of the God who created it!*

"You, who live under its amiable empire, mortal, your hours will be sweet and peaceful; moderation and simplicity will preside over the wishes of your heart. It is moderation that creates sentiment, the sentiment that smiles upon the wise. Then, whether you traverse enameled plains or lush pastures, Pleasure will perfume the air for you; it is you whom the spirit will embrace in its meditations, and the globes of fire that I cause to roll, and the worm that I lodge and nourish in a grain of dust.

"Remember, remember, above all, that the God whose daughter I am, is the most lovable of all beings. Oh, it is not given to me to be able to depict him, but we are marching toward him. Everything passes, all these changing scenes will fall into the gulf of annihilation; soar in advance in the regions where I have my throne near his, see everything flee, and Virtue alone will survive, pompous and unshakable, the immortal human soul, the faithful guide to happiness, the treasure and recompense of hearts that revere and adore him.

CUPIDITY AND VIRTUE

I was in a dark wood, not knowing in which direction to turn my footsteps. The moon's rays, broken by the vault of a dense foliage, cast a pale light that rendered the darkness of the night even more frightening. I had the weakness of a child abandoned in a desert. Everything frightened me, every shadow appeared to me to be a phantom; the slightest noise made my hair stand on end and I stumbled over every tree-root. Aerial beings that I could neither see nor feel made themselves my guides without my consent. They told me a thousand ridiculous tales to which I added faith; they led me among brambles and thorns; then, insulting my ignorance, they laughed at their malice and my credulity. Not content, they caused perfidious glints to pass before my eyes to stun me or drive me to despair.

I always wanted to advance toward a faint but pure light that I could distinguish at the end of a long pathway. I hastened my steps, but at the end of that long avenue, where I expected to emerge from the wood, I only found a little empty space, which offered me the impenetrable barrier of an even darker wood. How many tears I shed during that long night! Hope and courage reanimated my heart, however, and patience, and, above all, time, finally caused the dawn light of my deliverance to shine over my head. I emerged from the somber forest, where everything had frightened me, but only to enter another abode whether everything astonished me.

I perceived vast plains enriched by the gifts of fecund Nature; never had such a radiant aspect struck my eyes. I was weary, I was hungry, the trees were laden with the most beautiful fruits, and vines rose up by the favor of their branches, from which gilded clusters were attached in festoons. Transported by joy, I was running to slake my thirst, thanking from the bottom of my heart the God who was the creator of all those good things, when a singularly dressed man opposed an arm of iron to my passage.

"Innocent," he said to me, "I can see that you have just emerged from infancy and do not know the usages of his world; read on this stone portico, its laws are engraved there, and it is necessary to submit to them or die."

Sad and cruel human destiny! I read with a chagrined astonishment that the whole of that beautiful country was rented or sold, that it was not permitted to me to drink there, to eat there, to walk there, or even to lay my head down there without the express permission of the master. He was the exclusive possessor of all the fruits that my hungry stomach coveted in vain, and in the entire extent of that globe, I did not have a single point for a refuge, or a single apple for property; everything had been invaded before my arrival. I was going to die of starvation for want of certain small pellets of silver, very easy to lose, which that harsh man demanded of me to exchange against the nourishing fruits that the earth produced.

I said to myself: *This man has no more rights over this terrain than me; he is assuredly a tyrant, but I am the weaker, and it is necessary to submit.*

I saw that in order to have some of those fugitive little pellets it was necessary to put a thick chain round the body, at the end of which hung another lead ball, a hundred times heavier than all the little pellets that one could ever receive.

In fact, I noticed that the man who had stopped me was following an order; he saw the embarrassment that I was in, and told me in a charitably imperious tone: "If you want to eat, look, I'm good; come closer and put around your neck a link of this big chain, until you get a taste for it."

I was dying of hunger and I did not prevaricate. In giving me something to eat he accompanied the gift with a hard flick on the end of my nose; I murmured a good deal, but I ate anyway. I was still muttering between my teeth when I saw another man, even more heavily laden with chains than the first giving the latter a sharp slap, which he received humbly, kissing the hand that had struck him.. It is true that at the same

45

time he received a lot of the little silver pellets, which he seemed to idolize.

Forgetting my resentment I could not help saying to the man to whom I was attached: "Why do you put up with such an affront? Why does that man have the insolence to insult you?"

He looked at me, sniggering, and said: "You seem to be brand new, my friend. Learn that it's the fashion of the land: every man who gives something always satisfies his pride or his harshness at the same time, at the expense of the recipient. But is it as they say, a loan repaid. Although I'm enraged by the slap I've just received, I don't let anything show, for the reason that the man who gave it to me has received many others, and I hope one day to be able to distribute them at my leisure. Unfortunate as I am, though, I've only been able thus far to give a few miserable flicks here and there. What! That language renders you stupefied? Poor young man! It isn't time to be astonished yet. You'll see many other things. Come on, follow me."

I followed him.

"Do you see those sheer mountains in the distance?" He said. "One of their summits is almost in the clouds. Well, the eternal object of the desires of all men resides there. Between the rocks, an abundant spring gushes forth of this subtle silver, of which I, alas, only have a few drops. Come with me, let's overcome the obstacles; let's fight. Support half the chains with which I'm going to load myself; they'll be much heavier, but we'll succeed. Oh, if I can ever draw from that fortunate well as I please, I swear that I'll give you a share."

Curiosity, a passion that never abandons me, even more than the fatal necessity I as in, drew me in his footsteps. God, what a railway! What a crowd! What insults and pains! I hid the redness of my face under the weight of my chains. My conductor affected a cheerful attitude, but I sometimes glimpsed him biting his lips until they bled and despairing in a low voice, while crying loudly to me: "Courage, friend, it's going well."

Avidity gave him supernatural strength, and, as my chain was linked to his, he dragged me along with him.

We arrived at the foot of the mountain; there was another tumult altogether. The valleys were covered by a multitude of men, who were agitating with their irons, and who were extracting with all possible politeness a few drops of the quicksilver that was flowing from the fountain.

It scarcely seemed possible to me to get through that impenetrable crowd, when my conductor, with a reckless audacity, set about violating people's rights. He struck to the right and the left with all the violence of cupidity; he trampled those he knocked down underfoot, inhumanely. Shuddering I felt that I was marching over the palpitating entrails of those unfortunates. I wanted to recoil, but there was no longer time. I was dragged away involuntarily.

We were covered in blood; the horror of their plaintive cries and maledictions chilled me with fear.

In that horrible manner we reached a little hill. He looked at me complacently. "We're doing well," he said. "The first step is taken; the rest ought not to frighten us. You see how we've made them fall on top of one another. Here, it's a different matter; we're at the court, in a terrain full of gorges; it's necessary not to go so forcefully; it's necessary to be able, with a skillful, studied finesse, to give an appropriate dig of the elbow, always without quarter. One puts one's man down just the same, but what it's necessary to avoid with the greatest care is scandal."

My heart was too constricted for me say a single word in reply; such a man did not seem to me to be made by to listen to virtue or humanity. I was chagrined to be attached to him; I feared constantly that he might try to prove to me that he was right to act thus. In any case, he had many examples that seemed favorable to him. What a horrible and disgusting spectacle! What variously frightful scenes! All the passions were giving rose to all kinds of crimes. No one had any virtues except to sell them, and without that traffic they were considered ridiculous.

One monster had put on the mask of Justice and was filing his sacred balance with mercenary weight. Men still covered with the mud from which they had emerged were honored, and insulted public misery. Others were rubbing their bodies with those pellets of quicksilver and marching with their heads held high, pride in their eyes and debauchery in their hearts. They deemed themselves superior to other men, and were scornful of anyone who was not whitened like them. Although they did not always slap those they encountered, their gestures were offensive, their smile an outrage.

Often, however, the quicksilver wore away, and those same men, so proud and so harsh, became humble, submissive and crawling again. The disdain of which they had made a show was then returned to them with interest. Rage transported them secretly, and they did not spare iniquities in order to climb back to their former estate.

It is also necessary to admit that the deadly quicksilver had gone to their heads, with the consequence that they had lost their reason. I saw one who had come down from the summit, oppressed beneath the weight that was choking him. Motionless, as if in ecstasy, he contemplated his silvered body, and did not want either to drink or eat. I tried to help him to get up; he thought that I had come to rob him, and he opposed me with a closed fist in order to defend his quicksilver; and at the same time he held out a suppliant hand with a pitiful expression, begging me to assist him with a little pellet, that he might die content.

A little higher up, forty strong and wiry men were carrying a prodigious quantity of the metal in barrels. They had not been to draw it from the spring; it had been snatched from the weak hands of women, children, old man, cultivators and the poor; it was stained with their blood and sprinkled with their tears. Those exactors had an army in their pay, which exercised detailed brigandage and pillaged the hearths of indigence. The people crushed by those two terrible levers did not know which tyrant they ought to heap with maledictions; all the treasures of the earth passed into those avid hands. I observed that those who possessed the substance in abundance were never sated by it; the more they had, the harsher and more intractable they became.

However, my conductor only saw in those objects models for emulation.

"Come on, come on," he said to me. "You're dreaming, I think, with your fixed and observing eyes; let's go. Can you see through those rocks? What a ravishing object! Can you see that dazzling spring flowing in great waves, precipitating in cascades? Oh, let's run, I fear it might dry up! How everyone is fighting over it! But let's be careful, we're not there yet; the last steps will be the most dangerous. How many, for want of prudence, have fallen from the summit into the abyss! By knocking over the others, we'll preserve ourselves from a horrible fall; it's necessary to profit cleverly from the misfortunes of others. Come on, I've discovered a path that will take us more reliably to the desired terminus."

As he said that, he led me into a little path that few people dared to follow; it was a kind of tortuous staircase, narrow, pierced in the rock and covered by a vault.

We advanced for some time, but the path was soon blocked by three figures of the finest white marble. It was only their dazzling whiteness that could deflect the mind from the idea of flesh, so truthfully, nobly and gracefully was it expressed. The three figures were linking arms, united as if to close the passage to imprudent mortals. They represented Religion, Humanity and Probity. At the bottom was written:

These figures are the masterpiece of the human mind; the originals are in the heavens. Respect these images, O mortals; let them be sacred for you, may they be made to stop you in the perfidious path that leads to the abyss. Woe betide the person who is not touched by them, and accursed forever be the sacrilegious individual who dares to damage them.

At that sight I felt a respectful emotion mingled with love. I looked at my conductor; it appeared to me that he was momentarily troubled and indecisive, but having heard cries regarding a new eruption of the spring, his face went a dark red color and he seized a stone, which he detached from the rock. I tried in vain to stop him; he broke the sacred monument with an impious fury and stepped over the debris.

My redoubled efforts, contrary to his finally broke the odious chain attaching me to that monster.

"Go," I said to him, in my indignation, "go, insatiable, frenzied man, run to satisfy your appetite for crime; the lightning of divine justice is ready...."

Already he could no longer hear me; I followed him with my eyes. The wretch, led astray by his crime, and wanting to draw too avidly from the deadly spring, hurled himself into it blindly. Carried away by the torrent that he had made his god, he was broken by the spurs of rock, and his blood reddened the dazing whiteness momentarily.

As for me, I remained in shock, trembling, contemplating the adorable debris scattered around me, fearing to tread on the fragments, not daring to take a step. Tears of affliction ran from my eyes. I was looking at the sky, my hands together and my heart sick with dolor, when a divine power suddenly reassembled them, as beautiful, as majestic and as touching as before. I prostrated myself, and I adored the God who had not permitted the hand of the miscreant, or that of the tyrant, ever to destroy those sacred effigies: immortal, unbreakable, they will be throughout time the refuge of the unfortunate and the consolation of the human race.

Promptly, I retraced my steps. I encountered an active multitude scaling the rock by various paths; I was the only one descending voluntarily. Some were carrying the chain of an individual who rose above the others momentarily on some eminence, but if his foot slipped, there were loud bursts of laughter, and the fall often ended up being more frightful. Others were lamenting like children; they had acquired a good deal of quicksilver, but it had evaporated so subtly that they could not find the slightest vestige of it. All those scenes, and others even more pitiful, made me scornful of the spring and the unfortunates who besieged it.

I was irresolute as to the path I ought to take when I encountered a man whose physiognomy was noble and had even more mildness than nobility. He was descending in a free and easy manner and carrying his chain with dignity; it appeared to be imposed on him not by the hands of servitude by those of duty. He possessed a meager portion of little pellets, and he was distributing them liberally in the bosom of the poor. He was holding an ancient book, and smiling with joy at every page; he was exhorting everyone to be content with what they had and not to risks themselves foolishly on the heights. In order to avenge themselves for his advice, people called him "philosopher" and thought they were insulting him lavishly.

I saw him refusing the most gilded chains that were offered to him, in spite of all the pompous hopes that companied them. I felt drawn toward that sage by a sympathetic impulse.

"Deign to conduct me," I said to him, "you who seem to be marching over these steep rocks with such surety. I don't know where I'm going or where I ought to go; serves as my guide, help me to get out of this frightful labyrinth in which I find myself engaged by the hand of fatality."

The age stopped, and after having stared at me for a few moments, he said: "Young man, you've interested me too much at the outset for me not to help you. It's not at your age that one ordinarily finds oneself in this frightful abode. What sacrilegious man has corrupted your youth? You merit being taken out of this inferno, but before then, it's necessary that you observe with me the scene revealed to our eyes. Let's stop; we can see enough to discuss it usefully.

"See with what prodigal magnificence the hand of Nature has sown riches over the surface of the earth. But that earth has only responded to stubborn human toil; it is imprinted on these fields, which indefatigable arms have rendered fertile. Brambles and thistles once filled these fields but they have been organized to produce crops. The laborious cultivator undoubtedly has rights over the terrain that he has mastered; it is necessary that he be compensated for having supported the heat of the day and the vicissitudes of the seasons;

so distributive justice reigns, nothing is overturned, every heritage is shared; they flourish enviably, and everything is arranged by a social contract perhaps as astonishing as Nature herself.

"Well, the peaceful harmony that reigns in those fields is founded on the disorder of this mountain. The point at which the thunderbolt is formed in the atmosphere is fiery, but when it bursts, it carries afar the fecund and refreshing rain; similarly, the active principle of the moral world excites tempests at its source but it spreads life and activity throughout the orders of the State. The shiny substance that sparkle and leaps at hazard comes and goes, is eclipsed and is divided, one part becoming a thousand others of proportionate value, is recombined and re-divided, is the pledge of all wealth and all labor, and gives and active soul to this great body, all of whose movements would be slow and uncertain without that useful ferment.

"It is an admirable marvel, that ever-present sign, ever fecund in its relations, and the misfortune that results from it is only in the prodigious abuse that people have made of it. Reason and humanity can correct it, if people listen to their touching voice. The fruits of those trees are made to extinguish the imperious sentiment of hunger; if a man uses them soberly, he enjoys his rights and health will recompense him for his temperance; but if a glutton devours the share of three of his neighbors he will give himself a cruel indigestion, and cause the others to die of starvation.

"If people, therefore, instead of being insatiable, instead of consuming themselves wretchedly beside that spring, were able to limit themselves, they would have the wherewithal to be happy and would also be able to share their happiness with hundreds of their fellows. It is cupidity that comes to break the fortunate equilibrium that balances people gently; once broken, it arms them against one another in fury.

"Yes, the rich and ambitious man is a devouring wolf unworthy of the name of human, since he has become a scourge. He will be unhappy and he will be held in horror;

always avid and discontented, he will harden his heart against the cries of need that he would be able to appease; he will put all his art into denaturing his soul, and he will succeed in that. It is him, and those who resemble him, who cause all the calamities of the earth; they are the rue authors of blasphemy, and an inhumane rich man cannot possess his wealth without shuddering at the sight of the man who has nothing.

"Friend, contemplate all the paths that lead to that height. How few of them are straight! Some are soiled by pride and the abuse of power, others by the baseness of slavery. One sees many people who pass through the most shameful crimes, and do not blush."

"But if there are culpable hearts in that crowd," I said to the sage who was taking to me, "they are not all wicked; we arrive involuntarily in society and we receive at the outset the irons that have been prepared in advance for each of its members; how can we get rid of the immense chain that binds us forcefully to one another and forces us to march toward the common goal whether we like it or not? How can one do without that indispensable metal, since without it, one cannot satisfy any of the numerous necessities of life? And since it is so prompt to vanish, is it not prudent to amass a certain quantity of it?"

"It is because it flows away easily that it is wise not to be too attached to it. I don't say that it's necessary to scorn that conventional sign, but it is better to put a brake on our desires than content them in that regard.

"Look at that insensate, who, after having consumed the best years of his life accumulating a mass of that false wealth, has collapsed under the burden; no one deigns to pick him up; his treasures are dispersed before his eyes; his fall leaves him nothing but the remorse of having acquired them badly and the more frightful regret of not having been able to retain them.

"What a contrast is presented down there by that good man going to dig the soil! After having searched hard all day he finds one of the small pellets toward nightfall, thrown at hazard by the flow of the spring; he returns home content to take it to his wife and his children; he lets them admire its gleam for a while, and he goes to present it in order that he might be granted a few ears of the grain that he has caused to grow. The bread he eats, however, is more delicious than that served at the table of the rich, for he shares it with the offspring that Nature has given him, whom his heart cherishes and by whom he is loved, while the latter only nourishes parasites whom he despises and who detest him.

"It is sometimes good to have a great deal of that substance, but that is when one relieves the unfortunate with it, when one waters some desiccated tern in order to render it fertile and splendid; then, the usage that one makes of it proves that one has climbed by way of straight paths. But those paths are rare. I have searched for them, and I have succeeded. I watch myself continually, in order not to engage in any of the tortuous paths that are easier and broader.

"I often have the pleasure of extending a hand to a few imprudent individuals ready to go astray; having got up they block the passage by way of gratitude, but I have done good and I have no regrets. I have given myself a reason to descend with the same contentment with which I climbed. No, it is not there that I find my pleasures.

"Young man, if you feel that you have a soul great enough to follow me, I will show you another abode, where people savor a happiness as pure as it is immutable. The inhabitants of this country consider it to be a chimerical realm; all these opulent, heavy and malevolent men would like to have it regarded as such, not being able to conquer it by means of their vile riches. But it is not a matter, in this case, of violence or metal amassed in coffers; in order to enter it, what is necessary is a great soul, and above all, a head that quicksilver has never intoxicated."

"O my father," I said to him, clasping his hands, "have pity on me, on my youth delivered to inexperience and full of sensibility; magnify my soul, purify the vile stains that I might have contracted in this poisonous atmosphere; be my guide; I sense, yes, I sense where you want to take me; my heart is inflamed with joy. Oh, go on, my father, go on to the end. I love this holy virtue, my soul was born for it. How ingrate Nature would be if the heart that honors her the most were not made to be happy!"

"I like that enthusiasm," he replied. "Come, you are worthy to follow me."

He took me by the hand and made me descend a few paces. Everyone laughed in our faces, shrugged their shoulders and asked where we were trying to go.

"Let them pass," said the greater number. "So much the better; don't you see that they're making room for others?"

"Don't be embarrassed by their vain clamors," said the sage. "Follow your project with firmness; leave them to amass those frivolous pellets; a richer treasure awaits us; but I won't hide it from you that we have several obstacles to overcome. In fact, it's necessary for us to go by way of rude paths, called the paths of patience, and the paths of temperance."

I took so much courage from my noble model, however, that I marched cheerfully, without experiencing any lassitude.

At a certain bend I had a horrible fright; a fleshless woman who was gnawing the rocks over which we were walking threw long snakes at us. The insensate was trying to hollow out precipices under our feet with her teeth and fingernails; foam covered her lips and a somber rage inflamed her gaze.

I recoiled, but my courageous guide looked at me, smiling.

"What!" he said. "Masks scare you! Come on, be firm; so much the worse for her if she's so ugly and so wicked. See how a tranquil and proud gaze causes all these snakes to die; they only devour those who are afraid of them; just be careful not to place your foot on their traps; but they're perceptible from a distance and they're crudely set. We have more dangerous moments to overcome. It's here that it's necessary to fight, young man; now is the time for courage."

I perceived a large lake that it was absolutely necessary to traverse; its pure waters presented a mirror in which the charming landscape that decorated its banks was reflected. The amiable breath of zephyrs rippled the polished surface, and a cool and voluptuous air brought a thrill of pleasure all the way to the heart; everything announced its presence.

"If you were a celestial spirit," my guide said to me, "I would say to you: 'Extend your wings, rise into the air and soar above this dangerous and seductive passage;' but you're a man; instead of wings, you only have arms and tardy legs. Come on, my son, it's necessary to submit to the laws of Nature; it's necessary to swim here, and with all your might; the condition is harsh, but it's inevitable."

Stimulated by those words, I launched myself into the river, and I set about traversing it. Gods, what moments! A subtle languor spread through my veins; I was in an ocean of sensual pleasures. Naiads emerge from the depths in order to stop me; amour was smiling in their eyes, sometimes sharp and sometimes languid; their dazzling breasts, and the contours of their adorable charms, showed through the moving crystal of the water which multiplied their attractions. They extended their alabaster arms and sought me for the object of their caresses.

I needed all my courage not to sink to the bottom. With one hand I was clinging firmly to my guide's cloak, but I could not help abandoning the other to an engaging and gentle hand that invited me to follow it. I was ready to succumb; my resistance was involuntary, and in the trouble of my intoxication I was obliged to repose momentarily on the breast of one of the young naiads; I savored sweetness there that robbed me of the strength to follow my route. I was about to deliver myself entirely to that enchanting power, which triumphs over all the faculties of the soul, when my conductor spoke into my ear:

"Young man, before reposing, it's necessary to cast a glance at the trajectory that remains to be traveled; see how short it is; too long a repose numbs the limbs; look at the unfortunates who have not used their courage."

Then he pointed with his finger at several drowned cadavers that were floating. I understood that language. I kissed my young naiad rapidly; I promised her a tender gratitude; I closed my eyes and I continued my route, swimming. It was not without combat that I tore myself away from that seductive beauty; I regretted that keen pleasure, which, having only inebriated me for an instant, had left in all my senses a deceptive taste for its attractions. The hope of passing over that lake again in order to slake the thirst of my desires there was the idea that consoled me.

As he gave me his hand to help me go ashore, my guide said to me: "Oh, my son, you had a narrow escape from the nets of death; these redoubtable waters burn all the way to the spiritual substance; one more instant, and you would have been consumed.

"Oh!" I replied. "Why does sensual pleasure have such sweet allures?"

"Feeble mortals even succumb to less sweet pleasures," replied the sage. "There is a sensuality more sublime for the reasonable man, which is to submit them to one's will. But before going any further, my son, it's necessary to complete here the mastery of all these desires. You are going to see men the sight of whom will destroy you, if you present yourself before them in your present state. It's already a great deal to have come this far, for how many have remained in the darkness of the forest and how many have perished next to that accursed spring? How many great men, foolishly wishing to avenge themselves on that horrible fleshless woman, have allowed themselves to be devoured by her snakes? And a greater number, as you have seen, have perished in the enchanted lake in the arms of those deceptive naiads. It's impossible that you can be absolutely stainless, after having passed through such rude ordeals. Take this polished tablet and read the words written around it."

I read: *The art of knowing oneself.*

In fact, I saw myself within, all transparent. I perceived my heart. It was spotted with vain and ridiculous little passions; I removed that miserable dust, which was disfiguring it, but it was very tenacious. I even tore away the portrait of my naiad, but not without a sigh, for it was so prettily painted!

All that having been done, I found myself lighter than a bird that cleaves through the air; I inclined naturally toward the vault of heaven. What a delight for my heart!

I soon discovered the same three figures of white marble, which were opposed to my passage; they were elevated with a rare magnificence at the entrance to a profound pathway that was crowned with superb laurels. My gaze plunged into that route, which extended as far as the eye could see; its nobility and its majestic simplicity imprinted a delectable sensation in my soul that made me cherish my own existence.

"Let's stop here," said my conductor. "Let's renew our oaths at the foot of these sacred effigies. O august Religion! O touching Humanity! O holy Probity! You who reveal to us God, Nature and our duties, fill with your pure radiance hearts that, without you, would only belong to vile matter, in order that they might live, and be inflamed by your celestial fire, in order that, marked with your divine imprint, they might merit the gaze of the Eternal Being; it is through you alone that a feeble creature can elevate himself as far as his throne. You are his cherished daughters; adopt the hearts that adore him in honoring you."

We entered into that majestic pathway; a mild and re-splendent sun was shining; characters of pure and sparkling fire traced in mid-air the legend: *Abode of Virtue*. Several altars were established between the odorous laurels. Each of them was erected in honor of some virtue. There, good kings and faithful ministers surrounded the altars of strength and equity. There, Louis XII and the conqueror of the Ligue and the Spaniards embraced d'Amboise, Sully, Turenne and Colbert. Their recompense was in their hearts, in the full knowledge of having done good; that thought, which ennobled their being, made their happiness.

Further on, magistrates, men of letters and painters whose brush had been consecrated to heroism—in sum, all those whose genius had been turned as much to the glory as to the utility of the human race—were enjoying the esteem of humans and the sweet sentiment of living honorably in their memory. Surrounded by the celestial air that they were breathing, they only knew amity, the sacred knot that links souls and augments their value and their price; the pleasure of finding themselves gathered far from the wicked, far from frivolous hearts, inspired them with a mild and lively joy.

They communicated to one other the treasures of thought; they formed great projects together and united for the happiness of humankind; they all worked together on the execution of vast and sagely organized plans—a pleasure unknown to those leaden beings who, having never had a taste for great things, drag around obscurely a body that oppresses them, masters them, and which they have never been able to command.

There, they encountered none of the basely avid souls that have only ever turned her gaze on themselves, but rather the heroic hearts that a stainless and unpainted virtue has consecrated to immortality and the respect of their nephews. Worthy spouses, docile and respectful sons, citizens who died for the fatherland, virtues friends, lived there together.

There, Decius was seen, still bearing the scars of the arrows by which he had been pierced; with Codrus, who saved Athens and had the glory of being the last of its kings; and Regulus, the victim of faith; and the generous Roman who ordered Nature to interrupt her laws for his most fortunate triumph; and the modern hero who bore the chains of a convict in his father's stead, which ennobled him, rendered him respectable, and almost made him envied. All of them looked at one another complaisantly, and formed a corps that reconciles the gaze of Heaven with the earth.

In that divine abode, I was rapturous, as if in ecstasy. Oh, if I were only able to report all that my heart experienced! But souls born to understand me will go beyond my feeble discourse, and those who will not understand me will regard my words as vain, insensate and chimerical.

I would have liked to remain eternally in the company of those living models of wisdom and virtue; I could not have wished for a greater happiness; but the venerable mortal who had introduced me informed me that only the appearance of those beautiful places was permitted to me. I was too scantly worthy to remain there. As I retraced my steps I turned my head, sighing, toward the divine simulacra, radiant with a beauty that was ever new.

The sage began speaking and said to me: "Well, friend, is it necessary to ask you whether you will go again to besiege that culpable mountain or bathe in that dangerous lake? Cease to afflict yourself; your place is here, if you love virtue constantly."

"Oh, my benefactor," I said to him, "When one has seen this abode, how can one not desire uniquely to inhabit it?"

"Doubtless," he said to me, "When one has seen it with unfascinated eyes; but how many feeble humans, after having glimpsed celestial things, have lost the memory of them, and have resumed once again the shameful chains that an instant of courage had allowed them to break; how many others have gone astray in a vainglorious confidence or an infantile frivolity! They have quit these beautiful pathways of a majestic symmetry in order to walk beneath profane myrtles; in the midst of dances and games, crowned with sterile heather, they imagine that they are scenting the odor of these divine laurels!

"It is not sufficient to desire to inhabit these august retreats, it requires a noble perseverance, proof against anything. Whoever wants to enter these immortal pathways will go astray if he had not first passed under this holy portico where Religion, Humanity and Probity ought to receive his homage and his oaths; then, let him enter, let him seek his model here; let him contemplate his thoughts and his actions, in order to act in conformity with his virtues; let him attach himself to following that heroic and living example.

"That, young man, is what remains for you to do; it is then that you will be able pluck a branch of the tree of immortality that rises into the clouds; you will plant it with respect a few paces from his, and one day, its shade will be the delight of your last years. Here is mine, which seems to be flowering already. Oh, my son, it is going to bear the fruits for which I am waiting; a sweet joy is intoxicating me, a supernatural force is taking possession of my senses; I'm dying—or, rather, beginning to live forever."

In fact, his eyes turned toward he havens, gradually extinguished, he uttered slight sigh and his soul flew away. I launched myself forward to embrace him, and the effort I made was so great that I woke up.

THE LUNETTES

I had seen one of those traveling charlatans who boast of being able to predict the future. While he was lying impudently and imposing on souls delivered to curiosity and terror the singular ascendancy that the vilest of men are able to obtain over the weakness of others, I said to myself: *This rogue is an impostor, but if his science were not vain, would it not be useful to divine something of future events? Is prudence not already a manner of perceiving what might happen? Are there not secret presentiments that more attention might be able to improve? How many times people sin more out of error than malice! Why is the future an impenetrable wall, while all times past culminate in a single point, overwhelming and saddening our imagination in vain? The past is no longer in our power, but we could, up to a certain point, modify the future.*

I went to sleep in the midst of those ideas, and I found myself in a vast library. I wanted to open a few books, but all of them were sealed. I only perceived one that was open, on a table. I looked at it, and I read the following tale, which I transcribed as soon as I awoke.

One day, from the height of his aerial palace, Xuixoto, the God of India and the Earth, cast his eyes upon the human race, which appeared at his feet like an ant-hill, moving and buzzing. He deigned to listen, and was surprised by the continual plaints that struck his ears. Everything that he had done was not done well; he never sat on his throne without a thousand insulting voices immediately censuring his justice and insulting his omnipotence.

The little people, in spite of their pious mummeries, were not those proffering the fewest blasphemies. Mutinous and seditious in their ignorance, they said a great many prayers but uttered even more murmurs. As for those who took the pompous name of philosophers, they mingled their reasoning with the bitterest mockery, and saw nothing but imperfection in the most admirable works of Nature.

Always chagrined and discontented, they only seemed sensible to the pleasure of criticism; everything was frightful as soon as they had a toothache, and when there was thunder, their pride was wounded in hearing such a majestic voice rumbling above their heads. If Xuixoto had deigned to take their advice the world would be much better organized; but all the reasoners, stupid or vainglorious, fantastical or impious, united their clamors to form one single complaint:

"Why is the future closed to our eyes? That is surely a gratuitous cruelty. If we could read future times, we could avoid false steps, the source of our misfortunes; we would have more courage in adversity, we would prevent a thousand accidents that our own prudence often only precipitates upon us; finally, we would be able to make preparations in accordance with the absolute necessity of events. Instead of which, wandering in thick darkness, dread poisons our days; the future becomes redoubtable to us and we never live in the present moment."

"When will these insensates learn," said Xuixoto, in his paternal wrath, "that it isn't me but they alone who pursue and determine their woes."

Oradou, the prime minister of his will, immediately received an order to publish over the globe of the Earth that whoever had any complaint to make about his lot should come to the fore of the mountain of Valepuzi, and that Xuixoto would deign to respond to them in person.

The resolution of the God of India astonished the human race. Our declaimers were nonplussed by it. It Xuixoto was going to grant all their wishes, they would have no more occasion to exhale their satires and their quips, and what gift could compensate for that loss? In any case, everyone was very irresolute in trying to decide exactly which favor to ask.

A certain number were in accord with regard to asking for immortality; by means of that gift, every passion seemed to be satisfied. The hero would no longer see a term to his glory; the miser could hope that several centuries of parsimony would increase his treasure to the extent of his avidity; the lustful, at the renaissance of every dawn, could flatter his imagination with the varied image of a pleasure, fleeting to be sure, but so frequently renewed that it would appear durable; the scholar would be able to abandon his entire soul to his vast ambition, hollowing out the abyss of the sciences, tearing away all the veil of Nature, seeing everything, fathoming everything and no longer envying the privilege of inanimate beings who, in their inertia, brave the revolution of the centuries while the thinking being descends into his tomb when he had scarcely sketched out his work.

Everyone, therefore, presented a different request, but the conclusion of each one tended to beg Xuixoto to lift the blindfold that hid the future from them. The motive for that request was that by that means they would be able to foresee their misfortunes, and arm themselves in advance against dolor. They awaited the appointed day with impatience, in order to raise a unanimous cry.

The day arrived, and the environs of Mount Valepuzi were populated with an innumerable multitude; that was the assembly of the malcontents.

Needless to say, thunder preceded Xuixoto's descent. He was seated on a scintillating cloud, lightning flashes departed from his eyes, thunderbolts burst between his hands, and whenever he twitched an eyebrow, the earth and its inhabitants trembled. Even Zelon, the exceedingly audacious philosopher, pen in hand, was gripped by terror. The design of the good Xuixoto was not to exterminate the human race, but only to show them what he was like when her armed himself in wrath.

Suddenly, a radiant and pure light succeeded the inflamed thunderbolts; the unleashed rumbles only struck the mountains any longer with an expiring sound. Zelon, recovering his courage, regained his audacity; he had seen Xuixoto smile, and, trusting in his bounty, he had the temerity to address these words to him:

"You, who are God, and, as such, sit at your ease above all the miseries that torment the poor human race, who are impassive and happy while we suffer, if you want us to support our miserable existence, a fatal present of our almighty hand, take away the blindfold that only serves to lead us astray; our desires seduce us only to deceive us more thoroughly; enable us to see what is, and that which we can reasonably expect.

"It is not only the interest of our happiness that addresses this prayer to you, it is also the love of your greater glory. Blind as we are, curbed under the weight of our woes, having nothing to sustain us but an illusory hope, how can we adore you worthily, while, deaf to our cries, you remain silent and, only enveloped in your grandeur, you veil yourself from gazes that are only seeking you?

"Can we, sensitive and groaning beings, offend you in desiring to know what our generosity, goodness, wisdom and power reserve for us? Then, our charmed eye would doubtless embrace the plan of your admirable works, and we would await with respectful patience the dawn of the beautiful day that would determine our felicity. If we had to suffer before that time we would suffer with more firmness. Yes, the sage might be shaken by an unexpected accident that would strike him down instantaneously, but the dolor against which he could arm himself in advance would no longer bear him any but feeble afflictions.

"O powerful Xuixoto, your unveiled justice would become the object of our eternal homages; you would be greater in our eyes when we know you better. If this prayer ignites your anger, strike an unfortunate earthworm to whom you have given a heart that aspires for happiness; but what are we asking of you, except to know our intelligence, your love and our clemency?"

Zelon fell silent, and Xuixoto replied, with a proud and tender smile of compassion: "Feeble mortals, you want it and I shall grant your request. You shall know the future, but if you complain, in the regrets that will trouble your present felicity, complain of yourselves, and remember that it was not Xuixoto but your impudent curiosity that prepared your misfortune."

Then he gave orders to Oradou, his Minister, who set about distributing the lunettes that he was holding in his hands.[3] Those lunettes had a double virtue; in one of their lenses they showed the sum of happiness that one could enjoy, and in the other, one perceived the full extent of the misfortune that one had to dread.

After having made those gifts to mortals, the God slowly rose up into the heavens, in the midst of lightning flashes, and in the same apparatus in which he had come. A thousand cries of joy and applause accompanied him all the way to the luminous arches of his palace; humans caused those transports of delight to burst forth because he had granted their folly. If the great Xuixoto had sent down upon them a real but hidden ben-

---

[3] The French *lunette* is ambiguous; employed in the plural, as it is here, it usually refers to a pair of spectacles. In the singular, however, it usually refers to a telescope. Not only does the idea of a telescope have a certain propriety in connection with the idea of peering into the future, but descriptions of the way that the optical instrument featured in the story is used are more suggestive of a single device with an interchangeable ocular lens than a pair of modern spectacles—but in Mercier's day, a pair of spectacles would not necessarily have had arms in order to hook them on to the ears for permanent use, but would have been more likely to be akin to a pince-nez or a lorgnette. It might even be appropriate to think of these lunettes in terms of a pair of loose lenses, but the author seems to have refined his ideas in the course of the story, because he replaces the plural term with its singular in its later phases and mentions one of the instrument's users polishing its *cuivre* [usually copper, but in this instance, probably brass], implying that it is, indeed, something akin to a small refracting telescope, which provides different perspectives depending on which end is applied to the eye.

efit all the people would have murmured, so far does our ignorance extend even in regard to our true interests.

If it is necessary to believe the story, Oradou must have been made of celestial substance, for the crowd that pressed him in order to obtain the lunettes was so great that a mortal body would inevitably have succumbed thereto.

If I had a hundred tongues it would be impossible for me to recount the various effects that those marvelous spectacles produced. I can only choose a few examples here.

Aline, a young beauty fifteen years old, was the first who satisfied her curious desire. She was stuck to the Minister's breast and had snatched the lunettes from his hand with a kind of violence. Vivacious, fickle, dazzling, an enemy of everything known as chagrin, reflection and ennui, she avoided even the shadow of seriousness; she did not apply to her beautiful eye the lens that prophesied misfortune, but rather the fortunate lens that anticipated happiness.

Young Aline was ambitious; she was fed on a certain self-regard that one could call vanity, and, above all, she was amorous to a supreme degree. How her heart palpitated with joy when she perceived a felicity such as she had desired! She saw herself beautiful, and beautiful to extent of exciting the jealousy of goddesses. The king of the gods was ready to subject himself to a new metamorphosis in order to surprise her heart; the eyes of her rivals were ablaze with anger at the aspect of her charms; the princes of the earth and the heroes of the century fell at her knees.

Aline triumphant, Aline proud of her beauty, in the intoxication of her glory, thought that her soul was strong enough to support the opposed lens. She only darted a glance into it, and uttered a piercing scream. Alas, that flattering reign was only to last five years; the terrible malady that destroys beauty would one day hollow out those cheeks polished like ivory, swell that fine and sensual nose, and furrow that forehead so full of grace. She loses the most precious wealth that she possesses, the treasure that was her unique merit; she sees a long series of years dragging by in sadness and disgust; she no longer has lovers, and the rivals she once eclipsed now insult her ugliness.

The fortunate five years go by too rapidly; Aline has a thousand adorers, but she is devoured by a secret chagrin. She sighs at every new homage from her lovers when she remembers that she will soon become the object of their scorn.

If she consults her mirror, it is no longer those shining eyes, that florid complexion and that enchanting mouth that she sees; she only sees the sad wrinkles engraved forever by a desolating hand. Oh, if only she had remained in her fortunate ignorance, at least she would have had five years spun by the hand of pleasures, that tender but deceptive hand.

Milnar was honored as the most valiant captain in India. In the midst of the packed crowd, the admiration and the respect that his name inspired permitted him to approach freely. He was one of the first to obtain the dangerous present; he received it with a mocking expression and an ironic smile, as if indifferent and superior to his own destiny.

What Milnar discovered to begin with flattered his ambitious pride. He saw brilliant victory attached to the wheels of his chariot, and himself, lying on laurels, receiving the honors of the triumph in the midst of public acclamations. Entire people reposed in the shadow of his sword. Over the debris of every enemy city rose a column of glory that would transmit to the future the exploits of his genius and his courage. Poets deified him; every day increased his renown and gathered the host of pleasures around him.

Milnar would die satisfied with the sweet sound of the songs of his glory; but he wanted to know what that name would become in posterity; he turned to the other lens.

What a change! His name is held in horror; the voice of sages ranks him in the class of fanatical brigands who have taken a frightful pleasure in shedding human blood. History, with a serene forehead and a redoubtable eye, presents to future races the faithful mirror in which the truth—the inflexible truth—is reflected; she had been disguised during his lifetime by the host of his adulators; now alive and formidable, she causes the deceptive radiance to fade of a glory founded on murder, tears and the screams of innocent weakness.

Those columns and obelisks are reduced to dust; those names of *hero, conqueror* and *victor* have been changed to *furious, ambitious* and *unjust man*; he is only remembered like one of those earthquakes that are only recalled fearfully, or rather with the secret pleasure of not having felt their redoubtable effects. Milnar sees all the vile springs of his heart laid bare forever. Everything dies except his opprobrium and that of the poet unfortunate enough to have sung the praises of the enemy of the human race.

Milnar has remained immobile with astonishment; he is seen for the rest of his life insensible to the palms that shade his brow. At the brilliant fêtes instituted in his hoot, in the midst of the sweetest concerts, he hears the voice of posterity speaking in his ear: "Man of blood, you were once praised in public; today you are cursed; you have only sown misfortune, you are the scourge of the world, you will be forever odious to the spirit of humanity."

Young Elmire appeared, and on her face the sharpest dolor was painted; the entire city was interested in her fate. How unhappy she was, groaning under the tyranny of an aged husband, miserly and jealous; her father had sealed that cruel knot by force. In secret, she loved young Damon, and was loved in return. Could her breast, which was animated by youth, amour and sensuality, respire the air without exhaling dolorous sighs?

Separated from the only man for whom she could support the light of day, her life went by in chagrin and tears. She extended a tremulous hand to seize the prophetic lunettes, and remained indecisive momentarily. She dreaded reading therein an eternal misfortune; but Elmire was a woman and curiosity prevailed.

At the first glance her heart swam in joy; she cried: "What a good God Xuixoto is!"

In fact, she perceives the funeral procession of her aged husband, which is making its way slowly toward the Temple; his coffin is covered with a richly ornamented mortuary cloth; and three days later, not far from the tomb in which her tyrant is sealed by unbreakable marble, she receives the oaths of her lover at an altar sparkling with the sweetest nuptial candles

Her imagination savors in advance the fruits of that union; the desires so long constrained shine with a new vivacity; they will fade away in the bosom of that cherished lover from whom she expects all her happiness. She sometimes forgets herself in that enchanting dream, and, full of fervor, she embraces the septuagenarian with the same fervor that she will embrace young Damon.

The gout-stricken old man, is astonished by those enthusiastic caresses; he observes that her beautiful eyes are no longer inundated with tears but shining with a tender languor; he fears a hidden perfidy and punishes her tenderness by redoubling his inflexible vigilance. The old debauchee struggles for a few more months against the gout, asthma and a violent cough; finally, he dies.

Elmire is free; mistress of considerable wealth and mistress of her fate, she marries the handsome Damon.

But what a reversal! The image of her lover had been so powerful in her mind during her slavery that it could not fail to weaken. The reality of her happiness is well below its expectation; our passions have no other nourishment than difficulties. Elmire and Damon are united. What does their felicity lack? It lacks sweet surprise, the sole charm of amour. Their ardent imagination had expended all the wealth they were to enjoy, and their fires relented in achieving the desired goal. Elmire regrets the times when she made such a tender depiction of a sensuality that is no longer anything for her but an illusion; she groans like Psyche at having destroyed the charm of amour in wanting to know it.

Adiram had received from Nature a fortunate character, an honest heart and a sensitive soul. He was young, he could not resist the general example. Curiosity is a contagious folly. Honor was his idol, honor rendered him capable of any noble enterprise; but, it is necessary to admit, impetuous in his passions, they carried him too far. He was at the age when the human heart, while balanced in equilibrium, is equally open to the impressions of vice and virtue. A single grain can make it incline in the fatal direction.

Adiram would have followed the peaceful path of virtue if, content with the fate that the gods had made for him, he had not wanted indifferently to penetrate the future. Unfortunately, one of the lenses of the lunettes informed the young man that he was to play a considerable role in his fatherland. What heart, endowed with strong passions is not ambitious? And what more can a heart delivered to the thirst for grandeur desire? Adiram perceived the position of Prime Minister that awaited him, which was very little; the heart of his mistress, that superb and rebellious heart, would become his conquest.

Occupied with that delightful scene, which he scanned slowly and with delight, it was in vain that he applied the other lens to his eye. His inflamed imagination abused him, in only representing to him what he had just admired with so much complaisance. In his presumption he did not discover the deadly effects that his frivolity and the abuse of his talents were preparing for him. Plunged in his illusion, he returned to the fortunate lens and mistook the error of his desires for evidence of an unalloyed good fortune.

Proud of his destiny, his conduct became arrogant, haughty and insolent; he made those who had the misfortune to approach him sense the superiority of his talents, and the scorn that he had for other people. He abandoned himself to all his desires because he knew that success could not fail to crown them.

The proud Ismene is enchained under the yoke of marriage, but he seems to be honoring her by deigning to admit her to his bed. Her caresses are, so to speak, graces that he accords; she would like to make her own pride speak but she encounters a more terrible vanity that crushes her and reduces her to silence.

Adiram made as many enemies as he encountered men; he believed that he was humbling them in abasing them, but he really collected hatred, and universal indignation repaid his disdain. The God's verdict was accomplished by degrees. Adiram rose as far as the terminus from which one cannot rise and further. He believed himself to be triumphant over the crowd and his enemies because he was so elevated that clamors could longer reach him. He had experienced everything, except misfortune.

Misfortune came, falling upon him as lightning falls upon an oak neighboring the clouds. Like a voyager having scarcely reached the summit of a steep mountain, that ambitious man found a slippery slope, fell and rolled into a precipice. His fall was horrible; everyone applauded it and avenged themselves on his pride. Everyone humiliated him, including his wife, who did not bemoan the reverse of fortune that felled her husband. His immense wealth, with whom he had not contrived to attach, I do not say a friend, but a single grateful individual, became in an instant the prey of those who had meditated his ruination.

The pains that one takes to harm someone are rarely fruitless, and human pride could not have had a more agreeable victim to immolate. He was scorned as much as he had scorned his fellows; the disdain that he had lavished was returned to him with interest. The days of his debasement dragged on for a long time; the butt of public derision, he died in the horrors of despair.

What rendered that young man superb and unfortunate? It was the fatal knowledge of the brilliant future that awaited him; his success enabled his audacity, and impunity rendered him wicked. He had virtue when his fortune was still doubtful; he could have made friends and he might have achieved a happy and respected old age, but he was justly hated, and woe betide any human heart which—even without consulting any lens—knows its high destiny too soon.

On his heels, two individuals were seen to arrive who were filed with a profound scorn for one another. One was a poet name Neothete and the other a philosopher, the same one who had harangued Xuixoto. The poet took the optical instrument first and the philosopher set about observing him, for there was no sight as risible, in his eyes, as the vanity of a poet.

Our poet spent his time polishing the brass with all imaginable care; he made a prodigious expenditure of intellect to ornament all the knick-knacks of the century. What a spectacle! His pamphlets reposed on dressing-tables; he forbade his readers the fatigue of thinking; what author was more charming, more amiable, more delightful? He rotated the lens in order to consult the image of posterity a little. He perceived a slight renown of about fifteen years, as long as it could extend, after which he would descend, still alive, into the river to Forgetfulness, made to bury every fine intellect in the world.

I believe that Neothete might have been able to deceive himself, that he could have done so if there had been a few more years to diminish. The philosopher saw with pleasure the cloud that had just spread over his face, and was greatly amused by his astonishment.

The philosopher took the instrument in his turn and saw on the favorable side the Genius in person; he was a beautiful angel radiant with glory; two splendid wings sustained him in the air; a pure and sacred flame shone on his immortal head; in his hand, a flaming sword truck down the monsters of the universe, such as Fanaticism, Error and Intolerance. At his voice, the useful arts enriched the earth; humankind was ennobled before his eyes; a plan escaped from his hand traced the well-being of nations. He poured forth a durable light that illuminated the world, and Fraud, Calumny and Violence sought darkness in vain in order to bury their shame. His piercing darts showed posterity the names devoted to opprobrium, and immortalized the virtues.

Our philosopher did not fail to believe that it was his own Genius that was offered to his sight. He consulted the opposed lens airily.

What a change! That brilliant and luminous being is no longer there; it is a fury enveloped in fire and torrents of smoke; she proceeds in unequal leaps, a torch in one hand, and a dagger in the other. She sets ablaze in her blind and reckless audacity the altars where the gods are severed and the thrones where kings sit. She shakes the foundations of empires and soars over the debris of human opinions.

Sometimes leading the likes of Alexander, Caesar and Tamerlane, she orders the murder of several million men, who cut one another's throats artfully, she instructs despots in the profound art of enslaving human beings; she puts the name of humanity in their mouths and cruelty in their hearts. More ingenious in her barbarity, she inspires the Spinozas, dictating to them their monstrous and despairing systems, attacks the dogmas of the world, overturns the sacred supports of the human race, shakes the hope and consolation of the unfortunate, plunges the mind into frightful doubt or stupid derangement, breaks the effigy of touching morality, laughs at virtue, insults its candor and, in its place only breaths the impure fires of debauchery and the contagious poison of atheism.

Such appeared in Zelon's eyes that Genius, so different from his own when its powerful authority is abused. I do not know whether the philosopher—or the man who usurped the title—recognized himself therein, but he broke the veridical spectacles while praising himself for always seeking everywhere for the truth.

The blind Myope, in spite of the tiny share of understanding that Nature had lent her, possessed enough madness to want to know what she had to dread or hope for in the future. She took the instrument with the greatest vivacity, and saw nothing. Very angry, she turned it around and did not see any more. Furious, she heaped Oradou with reproaches and insults.

Claiming that she had been cheated, that Xuixoito's gifts were made for her as well as for everyone else and that she too must have a destiny marked in the decrees of Heaven: a very particular destiny in sum. The poor woman did not understand that the fault was only in her eyes.

"Oh, the foolish woman!" cried those around her, forgetting that their eyes were little better.

Myope continued to vegetate with her short sight, and while vegetating, to complain about Xuixoito and Oradou. She still retained in the depths of her heart a profound self-esteem, and preferred, for that reason, her own eyes—which she thought excellent—to the piercing eyes of eagles.

A virtuous young man, full of sensibility, still in the hands of Nature, also wanted to know the future. His pure soul launched itself toward all objects in order to know truth, confidence and happiness. He saw nothing in the world but generous hearts. He populated it with sincere friends, sympathetic human beings; he only knew calumny, lies, dissimulation and malevolence by name; he was as prodigal with his tenderness as with his gold, his ingenuous soul overflowing in sweet confidences of amour and amity. His open soul did not sound the somber labyrinth of hearts.

Touched by his virtues, when he reached out his hand to take the fateful gift, Oradou said to him: "Good young man, remain placidly in the obscurity that surrounds you; you would lose too much by being undeceived. Believe that Xuixoto acted wisely when he condemned you to a reciprocal ignorance; it serves to hide from you in the shadows perfidies that would make you despair if they were exposed to broad daylight."

That speech revolted the young man. "Give," he said. "Give, atrabilious destroyer of human nature; you do not see the mildest and the strongest bonds of the human heart, amity and esteem; I sense them delightedly. My heart, born for virtue, recognizes it in my fellows; give, that I might contemplate this friend, this beauty that I love, and the thread of the happy days that I will spend, by turns, in their arms."

Oradou handed him the double lunette, sighing.

At first, the young man saw his friend attached to his footsteps, sharing his pleasures, ready to shed his blood for his slightest quarrel. He saw his mistress clasping him to her beautiful bosom, with the appearance of benevolence and tender interest.

"Ah! he said. "I knew full well that humanity was thus made, and that happiness resides in the need to love one's fellows. It is necessary to extend the sphere of amity in order to extend that of pleasure."

He exchanges the lens. What arrows that exposed heart is going to receive, alas!

He sees a little black monster, always implacable, always envious, piercing the heart of his friend with a poisoned dart.

That little monster was self-regard. It looked at itself in a mirror and, deformed as it was, it compared himself incessantly to what surrounded it. It was unable to sacrifice any of its desires, or suffer any enjoyment that it did not have exclusively.

That faithful friend is poisoned by the infernal vapor. A secret enmity is engendered within his heart. Constraint renders the poison more active; he smiles while he is burning with rage; he caresses while he meditates vengeance. Finally, his fury, composed of a thousand compressed passions, suddenly bursts forth; his arm raises a blade over the same bosom that he has clasped to his heart so many times. He sees the woman he adored consummate her perfidy with the same friend, and blush, not at being discovered, but at having been unable to abuse him for longer.

The lunette falls from the hands of the unfortunate young man. He sees happiness precipitated from its brilliant throne, stripped of the radiance with which the creator embellished it. That amity of which he formed a living, active and courageous image, is no longer anything but a cold, motionless, inanimate statue, or, rather a fury armed for its own benefit. That divine amour was a base thirst for gold.

He flees. He goes to bury in deserts the regret of having been horribly deceived; he falls into a somber misanthropy; and for the rest of his life he pays with tears for his imprudent curiosity.

Poor Irus, an unfortunate whose legs had both been amputated, dragged the remains of his mutilated body toward Oradou. The poor fellow was scarcely two and a half feet tall. He was obliged to wait until Oradou had satisfied the avid crowd of the curious; he lamented in his impatience; he raised a halting and imploring voice, but, disfigured and covered in wounds, the least of men pushed him away brutally.

Irus was not even fortunate enough to lose his life in the crush. His hands were covered in bruises, several of his wounds opened and inundated him with blood. His days had been nothing but a long chain of calamities. Well, what could enable him to support the burden of existence except hope, the faithful companion of the unfortunate? It gave strength to his enfeebled organs; it softened his suffering gaze.

The wretched Irus never goes to sleep without a pleasant and deceptive dream immediately arriving to promise an amelioration of his woes. When dawn shines, Irus quits his meager bed; he hopes; but the following day aggravates his misfortune. Irus sighs and, resigned, raises his hands toward Heaven and says: "Oh, powerful Gods, it's tomorrow that you'll cast a compassionate eye on my misery! Yes, it's tomorrow." He goes to sleep in that idea; it is the only thing that diminishes the horror of his troubles.

"Oradou," he cried, in a piercing and plaintive voice, "see the inhumane crowd that is crushing me; don't let me groan any longer. The uncertainty of the future is a hundred times crueler to me than the present. Lower your eyes, see the remains of a human being, mutilate by the thunderbolts of the gods, of whom ravage has only spared to breath. I'm convinced that Xuixoto is a just God, and that he will not let me suffer eternally. Equitable Minister of his bounty, let me perceive the end of my woes! The measure is full, Heaven must be satisfied. If I can see that happy day, even if it is unique, I shall die content."

Oradou, who was as eloquent as the god Mercury, employed the best reasoning in order to dissuade him, but in vain. Irus uttered lamentable cries, and forced him with his ardent prayers to grant him that deadly gift. He seized it with an avid hand, and applied each lens in turn to the one eye that remained to him.

Pallor comes to blanch a visage that was already extenuated. He sees misfortune pursuing him indefatigably, rising with every dawn to overwhelm him relentlessly; not one consoling hour is to suspend the course of his woes. His fate is to be incessantly unhappy, until his last sigh.

He loses all hope; hope, the precious elixir that, mixed in the chalice of misfortune, gives us the strength to rink therefrom. If the unfortunate falls, exhausted by suffering, on to the hard stone, a more terrible tomorrow arrives to bear a frightful bitterness into his heart.

He recognized then, but too late, the wisdom of Xuixoto, which hid such a redoubtable future from him. He would have fallen into the arms of death while enjoying until the edge of the grave the sweet illusions of hope; now, nothing will weaken the sentiment of his distress; he sees nothing to console him but the specter of death; but he recoils at the aspect of that horrible consoler.

History reports that a crowned head, in his pride or his fear, also wanted to consult the decrees of destiny. In spite of the monarch's disguise, he was recognized by his military manner and the arrogance of his stride.

Oradou, who, in his quality of demigod, had no more respect for kings than for the likes of Irus, did not prostrate himself in his presence, but he presented him with a lunette with a kind of urgency, as an excellent lesson that she surely would not hear from the mouth of his poets.

He wanted to see everything, as he did in all things, and to know what posterity would think of his exploits, his government, his politics, his prose, and even his verses. I think that he might have learned the true judgment of posterity, but a clever courtesan, on adroit pretexts, always turned the lunette slyly to the favorably side, so that, man of genius as he was, he became at that moment similar to other kings.

Further examples would be superfluous. The insensate wishes all had consequences just as deadly, and humans were unjust enough to impute their new woes to Xuixoto.

"Was it necessary to torment us with the discovery of the misfortune that threatens us?" they cried, in concert. "That Xuixoto presented us with agreeable scenes of felicity was well done; but to offer us the evil that is suspended over our heads is to want, gratuitously, to fill our life with troubles. Xuixoto is nothing but a tyrant, and if he accords us some benefit, he poisons it."

Xuixoto smiled in pity on his throne, and was insensible to these new reproaches. He even deigned to grant them a mercy that they did not merit; and the signal his clemency, he took back from humans the fatal gift of being able to read their future destiny in those misfortunate lunettes.

A FORTUNATE WORLD

Lifted into the air by a chariot harnessed to two superb eagles, I thought that I was traversing the etheric plains with the rapidity of an arrow departing from a bow flexed by a supple and muscular arm. A thousand blazing worlds were spinning beneath my feet, but I was only able to cast a rapid glance over so many varied globes, all heaped with the benefits of the Creator.

Impelled by a powerful and invisible hand, I traveled the frightful depths of the universe, and every instant offered me a new and interesting spectacle: here, worlds from which songs of delight departed; there globes where I heard sighs and prayers; further away, a mixture of sadness and joy. O prodigious diversity! O astonishing fecundity!

I tried in vain to slow such a precipitate flight; it did not seem to be permitted to me to perceive those curious worlds in detail. I only observed the striking colors that diversified them infinitely.

Suddenly, I perceived a world so beautiful, so flourishing and so fecund that I felt a keen desire to descend there. Instantly, my wish was granted; I felt myself borne gently to its surface. I traversed its embalmed atmosphere and at the renaissance of the dawn I found myself sitting on a grassy bank.

I stood up, and I thought that I had been transported into the Garden of Eden. Everything in that abode of peace inspired a mild tranquility in the soul. Nature there was ravishing and incorruptible; a delicious freshness held me senses open to joy; a suave odor flowed into my blood with the air I breathed; my heart, which was quivering with an unaccustomed force, entered into a sea of delights; and pleasure, like an immortal and pure light, enlightened my soul in its utmost depths.

The inhabitants of that fortunate abode advanced to meet me; after having greeted me they took me by the hand; their noble physiognomy inspired respect; several of them had a head covered with hair of a dazzling whiteness. Innocence and happiness were painted in their gaze; virtue shone in their elevated speech; they were wise and good, in imitation of the Supreme Being. They often raised their eyes toward the sky, and at the sight of it, tears of love and tenderness inundated their eyelids.

I felt very emotional in conversing with those sublime beings; their hearts overflowed tenderly with the most sincere testimonies of amity; the voice of reason—a majestic, soothing voice—made itself heard in my charmed ears. I soon realized that such a dwelling was not made for vulgar mortals. A divine force made me fly into their arms and press myself upon the bosoms that contained such noble hearts; I had a foretaste of celestial amity, the amity that united their souls and composed the greater part of their felicity.

The angel of darkness, with all his cunning, had never discovered a way into that world; in spite of his vigilant and profound malice, he had been unable to steal that fortunate globe from the Creator. Anger, envy and pride were unknown there. Like a peaceful family, in which the happiness of one make the happiness of all, that people enjoyed the gifts of Heaven in peace, and only disputed the concerns of benignity; an ecstatic transport rose up incessantly in their souls at the sight of the prodigal and magnificent hand that assembled the most marvelous prodigies of creation above their heads.

Lovely morning, with its moist and gilded wings, was distilling pearls of dew on the bushes and flowers, and the rays of a nascent sun were multiplying the most vivid colors, when I discovered a wood filled with a soft clarity. On going into it I thought I was entering into a sea of perfumes.

I saw young people of both sexes there; they were not delivering themselves to terrestrial sensual pleasures, but, plunged in a mild and tranquil contemplation, with arms extended toward the firmament, they were filling themselves

81

with the grandeur and majesty of the God who moved almost visibly above their heads; for, in that innocent world, he deigned to manifest himself by mans of features of grandeur unknown to our feeble eyes. Everything announced his august presence: the serenity of the air, the colors of the flowers, brilliant insects; I know not what universal sensibility was distributed in all beings and vivified the substances that seemed least susceptible to it; everything showed signs of sentiment, and the tone of pleasure that resonated along streams and arbors seemed to spring from even the hardest rocks.

But what brush could depict the ravishing faces of young beauties whose breasts respire amour? Who could paint that amour, of which we have no idea, that amour which has no name down here, that amour shared by pure intelligence, a divine amour that they alone could conceive and define? Human language is found impotent and mute, and the mere memory of those beautiful places suspends all the faculties of my soul at this moment.

The sun rose; the brush falls from my hands; O Thompson,[4] you have not seen that sunlight! Let us one say that every particle of richly colored air became melodious under the song of birds; that the cedar agitated its superb crown therein, that the butterfly, in extending its multicolored wings, offered a scene in which harmony made itself felt even in the slightest particles. What a World, and what magnificent order!

I trod as if regretfully on the flowery plants, endowed, like our mimosas, with a keen and prompt sentiment; they lay flat to relieve my footfalls, more brilliant and more beautiful. Fruits detached themselves complaisantly from the branches; they scarcely moistened the palate before one sensed the delectable juice running through one's veins. The most piercing eye sparkled with a brighter gleam, the ear became more cheerful, and the heart that blossomed over all of Nature seemed to possess and enjoy her brilliant and fecund extent;

---

[4] Presumably the engraver and print-seller Richard Tompson (1659-1693).

the universal pleasure did not cause torment to anyone; union multiplied delights, and one esteemed oneself happy less by virtue of one's own happiness than that of others.

The sun did not resemble the paler and feeble light that illuminates our tenebrous prison; one could stare at it without lowering the eyelid; the eye plunged with a kind of sensual pleasure into the soft and pure light; it recreated sight an understanding simultaneously; it passed all the way to the soul; it was as if the bodies of those fortunate people became transparent; everyone could read in his brother's heart, then, the sentiments of mildness and tenderness by which he was affected himself; from all the leaves of the bushes that the star illuminated sprang sheaves of luminous matter, in which all the colors of the rainbow were painted; its face, which was never eclipsed, was crowned with sparkling radiance that the audacious prism of our Newton would never have been able to decompose.

When that star set, six brilliant moons of different sizes floated in the atmosphere; their progress, variously combined, formed a different spectacle every night. The multitude of stars that seem to us to be scattered randomly was discovered from its true point of view, and the splendid order of the universe showed itself in all of its pomp.

On that fortunate world, when a man abandoned himself to sleep, his body, which hardly participated at all in the terrestrial elements, did not oppose any barrier to the soul. His soul contemplated the throne of the Eternal, to which it would soon rise, in a dream that held to the truth of the luminous region. The man awoke from that light sleep untroubled, without anxiety. Enjoying the future by virtue of the intimate sentiment of immortality, he did not cast the somber gaze of remorse upon the past; often, he fell to his knees to thank God for the bounty of the present happiness that he savored, while intoxicating himself with the image of a future felicity with an even more enthusiastic transport.

Pain, the baleful result of the imperfect sensibility of our coarse bodies, was unknown to those innocent humans.

Warned of objects that might wound them by a slight sensation, Nature distanced them from peril as a tender mother removes her child from danger by drawing him gently by the hand.

I breathed more freely in that abode of concord and lightness. My existence became dear to me, and such was the charm that surrounded me that I thought for a moment that I had been transformed into one of those fortunate mortals.

"Alas," I said to those who surrounded me with benevolent smiles, "the world I inhabit once resembled yours but innocence, inalterable peace and pure pleasure soon vanished; death covered the earth with its funereal veil. Why was I not born among you? O fortunate globe, how I love your pure air and your Heaven! Connected to one another by virtue, you form and endless chain, each link of which is formed by two hearts united by amour. What a contrast! The Earth, which was my sad dwelling, resounded incessantly with cries and moans, while you float in abundance, tender equality presiding among you.

"There, a small number oppress the majority; the demon of property is infectious, and what it touches, it wants to possess. Gold is a god there, and on profane altars people make the sacrifice to it of love, humanity and the rarest and most cherished virtues. One might think it an ocean in which shipwreck is universal, and where the unfortunate only seek to save themselves at the expense of others. The greatest enemy of man is man himself, his leaders are tyrants; they inflict the cruelest wounds on humankind. Conquerors make blood flow there under the mask of glory.

"No mortal there can say: 'Tomorrow I shall repose in peace; tomorrow, the hand of despotism will not crush my head; tomorrow frightful pain will not grind my bones; tomorrow the howls of a futile despair will not emerge from my oppressed heart.' O my brothers, appreciate all the benefits that the Creator has deigned to spread over you!

"On the wretched world where I was born, the monster of war, vomiting flaming saltpeter, agitating a thousand hands armed with clubs, legitimates everything there is of the most frightful; its orders and consecrates murder, it emboldens in the name of the Creator the timid hand that recoils in horror or pity. O my brothers, weep, weep for us!

"The chains of oppression extend over our lamentable world from one pole to the other. Almost all men are slaves, but everything depend on the seasons, the elements, the vastest insects; Nature entire is rebellious to us, and if we tame her, she makes us pay for the benefits that labor extracts from her by force; the bread that we eat is washed with our sweat and our tears; avid tyrants come then and rob us a part of it in order to squander it on their idle supporters or their dogs. Weep with me, my brothers!

"Calumny, hatred and vengeance have never made you curse the air that you breathe and the sunlight that illuminates you. You only know the virtues that embellish and elevate the soul. How far we are from your felicity!"

While my heart was giving free rein to its plaints, equally delivered to the sweetest delights and the sharpest regrets, I saw resplendent Seraphim descending from Heaven, and exclamations of delight rose up from the entire race of those fortunate humans.

As I stood there, astonished, an old man said to me: "Adieu, my friend; this is the moment of my death approaching, or, rather, the instant of a new life. These ministers of the clement God have come to remove us from the surface of this earth."

"What, my brother!" I replied. "You do not know the agonies of death, the anguish, the disturbance, the horror that accompanies our last moments?"

"No, my son; every year, these Angels of the Lord come on an appointed day to take the heads of numerous families, whom you see assembled; that separation, instead of sadness, spreads a sage and universal joy. If a few uneducated children sometimes shed a few tears, our mouths inform them that today is a day of triumph; our mouths console them, and their hearts, soon enlightened by reason, only experience a moment of weakness."

I saw those fortunate people ready to take flight toward the throne of God. What luminous smiles shone on their lips! Their heads already seemed to be crowned by an immortal splendor.

Their children kissed their hands with a most profound respect; they said: "Father, remember us near the throne of the Eternal; take him our prayers, our canticles and our actions of grace. We congratulate you on reaching the end of your days, on the commencement of a bliss of which we only perceive the shadow down here. Alas, we still have a hundred years to spend in this garden of delights before being reunited with him. How slowly the time goes by! When will the moment come for our hair to turn white…?"

"My children," they replied, "We do not condemn the secret desires of your heart, but remember that you owe everything to what God wants; we leave you the memory of our life, the accomplishment of our duties engraved on all the hours that composed our days. Adieu, adieu; love the Eternal…."

Then I saw their faces radiant with a new brightness; the closer they approached God, the more his august image seemed to be reflected in their dazzling faces. Their children squeezed one of their sacred hands for the last time, while they abandoned the other to the Seraphim who were already extending their wings in order to lift them into the sky. They all took off at the same time, like a flock of bright swans taking flight, and rose in a majestic and rapid light above the summits of our palaces. The gazes of their children fooled them into the air. Those venerable patriarchs were lost in the silvery clouds. Then, all the inhabitants assembled, dancing and celebrating the fortunate day, and concluded with a hymn to the Creator…..

But I shall stop; it is not permitted to the weakness of an indigent tongue to render those sublime chords.

My imagination filled with those magnificent objects, I moved away from the crowd in order to walk under a solitary shade. A somber and gently melancholy took possession of my soul; as I respired the air of that divine abode, I could not help casting a sadder glance upon the world that had given birth to me; that contrast between felicity and misery caused my tears to flow, and I said in the bitterness of my heart:

"How fallen you are from your primitive beauty, once-blessed and fortunate earth; delivered today to the wrath of a vengeful God, you have lost all your attractions; arid and despoiled, you appear to have escaped from a conflagration, and your hardened flanks only open when they are torn by fire. But what am I saying? It is not those enameled plains that I regret, those plains where eternal spring sowed flowers perpetually under majestic human footfalls, that balm of the air, that ambrosia of the fruits. Oh, no; but that lost innocence, that universal amour of our unknown days, that flame of sentiment, a precious flame henceforth extinct, the harmony that once subsisted between sensible beings; yes, that is what my heart regrets; that is the loss my soul deplores, Be sad, my heart, be said; my brothers are torpid in thick darkness; plunged in forgetfulness of themselves, they deliver themselves to errors and passions; they consume the time of a temporary life, the time granted to them to reconcile themselves with Heaven, in frivolous hopes.

"Oh, from what heights human nature has descended! How it has obscured the intelligence that is the pure radiance of the Divinity. It could discover without difficulty truth, virtue and perfection. Alas, everything has vanished; the temple where the flame of divine love ought to burn without interruption is no more than an impure lair where insensate desires crawl and disorderly passions quiver.

"Scarcely a few feeble rays remain to us of the sunlight of verity that shone over our heads; they spread a dubious light through the darkness of our understanding, but they no longer warm our soul. The truth, when it is pure, goes straight to the heart, penetrates it, sets it ablaze and fecundates the seeds of virtue there. It is thus that it acts upon these innocent souls, but on miserable mortals like us....

"We have long the truth as well as happiness. What am I saying? We flee the dying light. Unfortunates that we are, if the truth appeared in its splendor, as it appears here, where would we flee, where would we hide? Shame and confusion would hold out tongues mute at the memory of the outrages that we have committed. Philosophers, masters of the earth, you who have so often offended it, all your pretended rights, all your frail theories would fall like old edifices that time has undermined with a hidden hand, and which a gust of wind suddenly brings down.

"A miserable, terrible collapse, which cannot be imagined by the very people who have fallen into that abyss of woes, in order that you could make us regret the day, the glorious dawn, when Heaven was united with the earth! Today, our soul is corrupted before it can think; is it delivered to the poison of crime before knowing evil. Everything that surrounds us flatters and nourishes our depravity; habitude comes and even steals remorse from us....

"O Heaven! How can you see such disorder in your empire? How can you suffer such a deformed world to rotate with the celestial spheres in the immensity of the skies? How can you permit that it bears the impious to imagine and say that it can only be an evil God that is the Creator of so many woes?"

Suddenly, one of those just men appeared before me; a divine wrath illuminated his eyes. He stared at me, as if he would have liked, in reading in my heart, to recognize wiser thoughts therein. I was too touched to retain my tears; they flowed abundantly; I confided to him my dolor regarding the fate of my wicked and unhappy fellows, a fate that seemed a hundred times more horrible by the ever-renascent comparison of this innocent and fortunate world.

The just man listened to me tranquilly; my heart was relieved in his presence, with all the vehemence that sentiment can bring to a soul.

He directed a gaze at me that mingled compassion and amour, and said to me: "I like the noble sensibility that makes you weep for the destiny of your brethren; how rare those tears are, shed in favor of the human race. On your planet they would be a subject of derision for the fools who have never reflected on anything, but that sadness of your soul pleases me.

"That glance cast upon the general disorder that give rise to so many individual woes, those sighs rendered bitterer by a longer contemplation, and that desire for the happiness of all, announce in you an honest heart, which you have nourished with useful emotions; but what you name dolor, suffering, debasement, misery, and even death with its horrible apparatus, all those woes, however sensible they might be, are nothing compared with other misfortunes; it is there that it is necessary to weep and tremble.

"There are men who have blinded their reason and hardened their hearts, men who do not love God, who see the sun rise without rending him any action of grace, who abandon their souls as the threshing-floor abandons straw to the wind; men who flee the truth in order to throw themselves into the arms of lies, who divine monstrous phantoms, and who render themselves the victim of their desires, simultaneously impetuous and fleeting; insensate men who brave the thunderbolts of Heaven and only tremble when the time of mercy is past. That is what saddens even the Angels, and when we learn that a culpable individual has returned to God, the entire world celebrates that day as if it were celebrating the birth of a new universe.

"But refrain, in contemplating that deplorable scene, from raising the faintest murmur against the Creator. See the august and sage Providence that embraces that culpable and unfortunate globe in its bosom; it has thrown a veil over this immense universe, which no created hand can lift. Groan because humans are not what they could be, but believe at the same time that this world, fallen as it appears to be, possesses what is necessary to it in order to fill the place assigned to it among the innumerable spheres that circulate in the presence of the supreme Architect.

"Yes, this world, the theater of crime and death, through the black vapors that surround, exhales the pure prayers and sighs of a few just people, worthy to join in the immortal canticle of praise due to the Creator. This world circles under his gaze, it enters into the constitution of the universe, and the virtuous individuals who inhabit it render it as precious in the eyes of God as some other innocent worlds brilliant with their original beauty.

"In order to be enlightened in these lofty speculations, remember that it is a consequence of the weakness of the necessarily limited human mind if it cannot perceive the order of the great whole, which it even divides into infinitely various particles. Humans only see the details and cannot perceive the ensemble, but it would be necessary to be born perverse to imagine that the world, divine as it appears to us, has nether a spirit nor an intelligence to rule it; it is only malevolence that depicts a hard and chagrined God, and only a corrupt heart that can engender such frightful and abominable thoughts about the Supreme Being.

"Can you believe that the supreme wisdom has abandoned anything to chance? Can you believe that its plan is traced in a tremulous and uncertain hand? Can you believe that it has done poor work, like a bed workman making trials? No, every idea has been shaped, executed and followed. Intelligence has discovered, conducted and sustains that vast harmony; its designs are fixed and immutable; its gaze falls complaisantly even on this globe, the aspect of which indisposes because you can only see the obscure part, whereas, placed in the rank it has to occupy, it contributes to the splendor of the whole.

"It is enough for humans to know that God directs everything that exists; moral beauty is an invisible beauty, which God alone enjoys. It will be permissible one day for humans to contemplate that intellectual beauty, and, astonished and seized with admiration, they will confess their past folly and the profound omniscient wisdom of the dispensation of the Eternal.

"Embrace that consoling hope; God has planted the seed of it in your bosom. Magnify your being with the sublime idea of an imminent elevation; let the grandeur of God always be present in your mind, and you will be able to conceive your weakness in a holy and respectful gladness. It is useful to you to believe, and to believe that all is well. It is useful to you to honor your Creator, to put your confidence in his supreme bounty; submit to the dictates of that divine hand, which lowers you in order better to lift you up,

"Do not say 'This world is evil.' In the eyes of the Creator, it might appear more resplendent than any other. There is a virtue that can only belong to humans who fight, a sublime virtue that only inhabits your unfortunate world. There is nothing more beautiful than the patience of a firm and sensitive soul, which humiliates itself voluntarily under the yoke of dolor because it regards it as imposed by the great mater. What is more glorious under the heavens than the combat delivered by virtue against vice—which is to say, terrestrial passions? Then the Eternal lowers his eyes upon the mortal who, in a body of mud, has recognized the dignity of his soul and has struggled stubbornly against misfortune.

"The more obstacles virtue has to overcome, the greater and more beautiful it is. Victory rendered terrible and difficult puts into a brighter light the strength and merit of the victor. The chastity of a Joseph prevails over the purity of Seraphim, because it had to combat attractions of which all men are idolaters; it was necessary for him to vanquish, simultaneously, beauty, pleasure, Zuleika and his heart.

"Our actions do not have that merit. We obtain everything from the clemency of the Creator, nothing from his justice. Unlike you, we do not have entitlements to pretend to happiness, we receive it as grace and not as recompense; but the spectacle that charms our gaze the most is when we see on your globe a soul surrounded by so many needs, difficulties and troubles seeking the truth with an indefatigable ardor, pursuing it, although it escapes continually, and, in spite of renascent storms, lighting the torch that ought to illuminate the universe.

"Socrates, that martyr of the Divinity, drinking the hemlock, makes us weep with admiration. Marcus Aurelius, virtuous at the age of twelve, and virtuous on a throne, wearing in the eyes of the world the mantle of a philosopher over the royal mantle, makes us envy even his diadem.

"When, in the most debased ranks, we discover a mortal marching with a firm and sure tread along the roads of wisdom, respecting his soul, monitoring his actions and thoughts, directing them all toward the glory of the Creator and the happiness of his fellows, trembling to commit the slightest fault, closing his eyes to the charms that surround him and might corrupt him, seeing death accompanied by all its horrors, and raising toward the heavens a submissive and dying eye, our eyes do not perceive anything more admirable, or anything more august in the vast extent of creation. The soul of that mortal, or, rather, our friend, our brother, contains the perfection of its essence; it reflects the universal beauty, and the moment when it abandons its terrestrial bonds is the one when it becomes one of the rarest ornaments of the heavens.

"Thus, virtue shines and reigns in a world where crime would like to establish its empire; thus, the Earth is the battleground where, under the eyes of the eternal, they deliver a combat that will be eternally glorious for triumphant virtue. Soldier of the living God, honor the temple in which he resides; that temple is your heart; it is there that he talks to you and judges you; apply yourself to doing everything with gravity, with tenderness, with liberty and with justice; life is short and is only given to you in order to merit it.

"It is God who made you; conceive all the profundity of that thought. You are a man, you are a citizen of the word, you are a son of God; think about what those names require of you. See the world as a glorious arena, in which there is an honor that must be defended. If death surprises you in a generous action, useful to humankind, you can then hold your head up superbly in the midst of Nature, while raising your pure hands toward the God who recompenses.

"O supreme intelligence, ocean of glory, power and happiness, our souls are feeble trickles escaped from your eternal and majestic flow, but they tend toward their source; it is our soul that senses you, you who enlighten it and penetrate it with the sentiment of love; it enables you to perceive your magnificent attributes; a sweet delight comes to swell the heart that is filled by you; it knows you then, it adores you, and delightful tears flow from the eyes fixed upon the celestial vault. Oh, what felicity the soul enjoys which conceives the good fortune of being your creature!

"Mortals, esteem yourselves fortunate under the omnipotent hand, advance in life at a firm pace; the decrees of the Almighty will be accomplished in time. If you direct your sight into the future, you will see enough light springing forth to guide you in the darkness. Convinced of the existence of a God, what more do you need? Do you not sense beyond it all the great verities that flow from that primitive truth? A limited being can be susceptible to anger, vengeance and jealousy, but the perfect and universal Being is far from human passion.

"Whoever does not know God to be a good being, infinitely surpassing all humans in goodness, has neither religion nor confidence; he has never raised his thought to what is morally excellent he has never had an idea of virtue, which is nothing other than supreme goodness. It would not be a duty for a human being to do good if he did not have to imitate the sovereignly good Being. We cannot admit any majestic and magnanimous character if we deprive ourselves of the one who possesses it par excellence, and if we mistrust his clemency, we would do better not to recognize him."

He had stopped speaking, but my delighted ear thought it could still hear him. Awakening dissipated my illusion, but it will always be dear to me, and I shall conserve it in the depths of my heart until death.

DREAMS OF A HERMIT

Dream I

A hermit does not always savor the charms of solitude; he often has to endure moments of sadness and ennui that make him regret the society of his fellows. One day, when I was in that situation, and I was passing over in my imagination the agreeable objects that I had seen in the world, I felt myself keenly pressed to abandon my desert; however, as I was accustomed to it and I loved it in the depths of my heart I foresaw that that step would be a source of remorse for me, which would poison the pleasures of which I wanted to go in search in cities. In that state I even experienced a violent combat within me, which concluded with a profound exhaustion in which I fell asleep.

I thought in a dream that I had found a talisman that had the virtue of attracting the amity of all those I wished. I thought my fortune was made; it was only a matter of deciding which amity would be the most advantageous to me.

I gave preference to that of a king. Immediately transported to the court I found myself in the greatest favor with the prince. My talisman was an emerald on which the image of fortune was engraved; I wore it suspended on strings immediately over the skin of my stomach, for fear of losing it; but all the care that I took to preserve the talisman could not render my happiness durable. One seeks it in vain in courts.

The favor I enjoyed made people envious. Courtiers threw over all my actions a varnish of blackness and malevolence. Although the protection of the prince was a rampart for me against their impostures, I could not help dreading it. The racket of affairs, ceremonies, ostentation and rumor was a burden to me. I reproached the great expenses that my position required; it seemed to me that I was snatching them from the needs of the people and that I was making the poor shed tears.

That idea bore disgust, bitterness and remorse into my soul. My agitated senses no longer knew any repose. I regretted the calm and peace that I had enjoyed in my hermitage.

Finally, the cabals of my enemies burst forth. The king took umbrage regarding my fidelity; I was disgraced. I congratulated myself on my fall; I found myself happy in no longer languishing in the midst of terrors and ennui. By an unpardonable inconsequence, of which, however, I have heard that there are many examples in the world. I made my talisman serve my ambition once again.

I desired and promptly obtained the amity of a distributor of benefits, and it was not an idle amity; it procured me immense wealth. I was appointed to several rich abbeys and also I had a house furnished in the best taste, a multitude of valets, a sumptuous table, perfumes, music, brilliant carriages, etc.

I swam in riches, but my pleasures were soon troubled once again by remorse. When I was alone and I examined my heart, I felt covered in confusion; I could not think without blushing that I possessed so many ecclesiastical benefits without being of any utility to the church or the public. Chagrins and cares were combined with the remorse. I was overwhelmed by the weight of sadness. In vain I tried to resist; I could only recover peace of mind by quitting my benefits.

Having become free, I was no wiser. I sought other friends for a motive of interest, and my talisman was again very efficacious. I had them of every sort of age and estate, but I did not have the power to render amity durable, because my talisman did not have the power to change the character of those I chose for friends. I was therefore even more unhappy his time. After a week, a young man who liked me tenderly picked a quarrel with me inappropriately, and laid me out on the tiles with a sword-thrust to the abdomen. Other friends carried me to a house and assembled a troop of surgeons and physicians around me.

The money I had was soon spent on remedies. It was necessary to have recourse the purses of my friends, but at the first word I said to interest them in my favor I saw them flee. I was abandoned, and the physicians, seeing that I was unable to pay, gave me a remedy that put me on the brink of death. I was taken to a hospital, where I was finally healed, but with difficulty.

I had had time to reflect on the infidelity and folly of the majority of men, and I believed that there were no more true fiends in the world. When I was able to walk I went to throw my talisman in the river, firmly resolved not to emerge from my hermitage again.

Dream II

I dreamed that a frightful storm had almost overturned my cell during a night on which all of nature seemed to be in upheaval. Dawn dispelled that sad chaos and the sun, more brilliant than ever, dissipated the storm clouds. A fresh and tranquil air succeeded the unleashed winds, and the birds, resuming their chirping everywhere, announced the most beautiful day. I got up, my heart full of joy, on seeing calm and serenity returned to nature, but anxious nonetheless about the ravages that the tempest had made in my garden.

My dread was only too well founded; I went out and I saw sadly that the carnations I cherished particularly had been very badly treated. Some were hanging their heads sadly, others were completely broken. I was afflicted, when, bearing my gaze further away, I saw that the tempest had spared the narcissi and violets that did not rise far above the ground; they even had a new charm, for the round drops of water formed on their leaves and colored by a bright and ardent sun resembled beautiful pearls, with the consequence that the little plants were embellished by the same cause that had broken my carnations.

Similarly, I saw that the humblest leguminous vegetables in my garden had remained intact, without sustaining any harm. I understood by virtue of that circumstance that the elevated stems of my carnations had exposed them to the fury of the storm and had caused their ruin. Then I remembered my philosophy and I thought:

It is thus that heaven is pleased to strike elevated and superb heads; it is thus that fortune makes a game of knocking down the proud colossi that she has heaped with favors, while modest men, like those violets and legumes, are sheltered from great reverses. In my hermitage, I am like the herb that is spared. The storms of fortune rumble over my head without descending as far as me. They cast down Ministers and favorites, but only give a new value to my solitude.

That thought filled me with a real joy, which did not vanish with sleep.

Dream III

Having sat down in the afternoon in the shade of a tree in my garden, I was amusing myself rereading an old book of theories regarding the structure of the world. While reflecting on the astonishing discoveries of the human mind, I went to sleep, and my imagination, struck by what I had read, enabled me to travel among the heavenly bodies. I thought that a natural weight was drawing me. I felt myself falling toward the planet whose orbit is said to be closest to the sun, and which is named Mercury, I believe.

I sensed myself approaching an excessive heat; my blood was boiling and I found myself in a vivacity and a petulance that astonished me. A numerous people had assembled to see me fall from the heights of the atmosphere; apparently, their astronomers had predicted my fall.

The inhabitants of the planet had figures similar to those of apes. Their eyes were sharp and fiery. Their limbs were continually agitated. They were light and dazed, which I attributed to the inflamed air that they breathed, for I sensed a great agitation in myself. At any rate, they were mild, sympathetic and affable, and they all spoke French, to my great astonishment.

Scarcely had I set foot on that new world that I was carried in triumph to the palace, where the chief of the nation resided. He was quite tall, with an entirely human figure, and appeared grave and serious. He was on an elevated platform, sitting on a stool garnished with gold cloth. Lower down were other creatures, half human and half ape. They were all considerable individuals, as it was easy for me to judge from the gilded paper stars that each wore stuck to the pit of their stomach. One of the most apparent was holding an ivory cane in his hand, another a set of scales, and all of them had different marks of dignity.

The rest of the courtiers and the crowd that filled the palace were entirely simian. As soon as the prince made a movement, it was immediately imitated by the entire assembly. In his presence they all quit their dazed appearance and took on their master's gravity. I also saw that they were impressed by new fashions, for, in less than an hour, the entire court was filled with boxes, half black and half white, which were labeled: *In the manner of the man fallen from the moon*, and of which I was the occasion.

Meanwhile, the Prince having considered me with a cold eye, all the apes, who had thus far given me many caresses, were no longer looking at me with anything but indifference. That determined me to leave the court in order to go and observe the mores of that people.

I was treated everywhere with humanity. I wanted to witness a marriage, if that was permissible to me. I did not find the gaiety there that I expected. An old ape, who gave the impression of being a person of importance, was marrying his son to the daughter of another ape, whose appearance was entirely ignoble, but who possessed great wealth. That wealth consisted of immense bags of Indian chestnuts, which are esteemed on that planet as gold is on ours.

The two young apes did not appear to be much occupied with one another. As soon as the ceremony was over, the husband, without thinking that he had a wife, carried away the chestnuts, gamboling, and for her part, the she-ape formed a court of young apes, all anxious to please her, and apparently untroubled by the absence of the new husband.

A rumor went around that the King had become devout, and immediately, I saw the principal inhabitants marching with their backs curbed in an attitude of great compunction. They all carried long chaplets in their belts, which hung down to their feet. The next day, however, further news having destroyed that one, the apes resumed their stupidity and threw away their chaplets.

While I was admiring the mores of the planet, and thinking of making other observations, an overripe pear fell off the tree under which I was asleep and, having fallen on my nose, woke me with a start.

Dream IV

I was thinking, after having dug my garden for some time; I put my hands on the handle of my spade and my chin on my hands. I was resting and meditating in that posture when I suddenly saw asparagus tips emerging at my feet, which grew as I looked at them. That event caused me great joy because, not having seen any for a long time, I tried to pick one, and I perceived that I had severed a finger.

In my surprise, I felt mine; I counted them, and, perceiving that none of them was missing, I did not know what to think.

I leaned over in order to look more attentively, but I recoiled in fright at the sight of an entire hand that emerged from the ground. Reassured, however, and wanting to know whether my eyes might have deceived me, I put the index finger of my right hand against that singular plant, which immediately seized my finger forcefully. I fell backwards, uttering a cry of fright, and remained for some time in a cruel perplexity, without daring to make the slightest movement.

I got up gradually, only opening my eyes partially, and thinking about running away. When I was on my feet, however, I saw that I was surrounded by human limbs and entire bodies. Here I saw feet, there hands, elsewhere heads, in other places noses and ears, and further away trunks with neither arms nor legs. The middle of my garden was covered by extremely small entire figures. The spectacle amazed me.

What's happening to me? I said to myself. *Where will I find nourishment for so many people? What shall I do with the separated limbs? If men of law come to my solitude, won't they think that I'm a murderer?*

In that extremity, I remembered a skillful physician I thought I had seen in Amsterdam when he was commencing a great work on natural history. I went to consult him about the phenomena in my garden. Being a prudent man, however, he did not want to decide anything without having examined it for himself.

He therefore came to my solitude, and, at the sight of the new productions that had frightened me so much, he did not testify the slightest surprise, which caused me to judge that he was accustomed to seeing marvels.

He had brought several instruments, in order to make his observations, including a microscope, by means of which I saw the finger I had severed as large as my body. He dissected it, and found inside the bone a little molecule that he called a mold.[5] Then he examined all the limbs and all the bodies, and the quality of the terrain that had produced them.

---

[5] The French *moule* is ambiguous, meaning "mussel" as well as "mold," but Mercier evidently means the latter. It is unclear which writer's theories of reproduction Mercier had in mind in this satire, but a possible candidate is Charles-François Tiphaigne de la Roche, who publicized his ideas in visionary fantasies such as *Amilec, ou la Graine d'hommes* (1754; tr. as *Amilec*, Black Coat Press, ISBN 978-1-61227-033-3), although he was an agriculturalist, not a physician.

After he had made his observations he turned to me and told me that there was nothing surprising in the spectacle that astonished me, that everything was simple and natural. As I did not understand the causes, however, because I had not studied the new philosophy, I begged him to explain how human bodies had been able to grow in that place, and he continued thus:

"Vegetables and animals are composed of an infinity of organic parts that are similar to them; thus, in removing several layers from an onion, one still finds an onion, until one finally reached its seed, which ought to be called an interior mold; for nature is filled with living organic molecules, analogous to all the bodies that exist or can exist, and these molecules have the property of assimilating themselves to the animal or vegetable that they want to form, provided that they find an interior mold to which they can attach themselves and penetrate, by means of an admirable power with which they are endowed.

"Thus, one can consider all the parts of an animal or a vegetable as so many interior molds, to which the little organized bodies that are analogous to them assimilate themselves; in that manner, one can conceive clearly that nature, without it costing her anything, can produce in a very short time an infinity of living beings that already exist, but are not visible. The interior mold nourishes itself on the parts of aliments that are analogous to it, by the intussuception[6] of the organic particles appropriate to it and it reproduces itself because it contains organic particles that resemble it and which come to it by nourishment. That is why your garden is producing human bodies. All the marvelous disappears as soon as one supposes that this patch of ground was once a cemetery, and that is what I did first, because the thing speaks for itself."

---

[6] I have transcribed this term directly, although its modern meaning in medical science is more specific than the more general Latin-derived implication intended here. It refers to a kind of infolding like that of a collapsible pocket telescope.

I remained in admiration at this profound reasoning for some time. I wanted to ask him afterwards whether, by means of interior molds, it might be possible for a man to have twenty arms and as many legs, or even whether nature, to amuse herself might make a single living being out of all the human beings and all the animals that exist and have existed.

To my great astonishment, however, he was not in a condition to answer my questions. All his organic particles decomposed and, forming a ray of dust, went to assemble in a corner of my garden. I followed their direction and saw that they formed a nightingale, which amused me with its song; that enabled me to understand that in that location there was an interior mold of a nightingale, able to assimilate the living molecules of the savant naturalist.

Dream V

Would you believe that a poor hermitage could become the object of the ambition of a rich and powerful man? It is, however, only too true that in a dream I was expelled from my cell and obliged to abandon it to the sovereign of the country in which it is situated.

I had raised a ram, of which a shepherd has made me the gift; he was the faithful companion of my walks and my reveries. One day he went to join a flock of ewes that were grazing not far from my hermitage. The shepherdess gave him salt and took him to see her family. She showed him to her father, who wanted to have him. He came to ask me to sell him; I refused because I loved him like a child.

My refusal piqued him, and in order to avenge himself he accused me, in the presence of anyone who cared to listen to him, of having usurped a considerable tract of land and of having made a park of it in which sheep contracted diseases that did not fail to spread and infect neighboring flocks.

Those rumors reached the ears of the sovereign, and I was initially condemned to be exiled from my desert. Then I received an order to give it to my accuser. I obeyed promptly, darting a last glance of tenderness at the dear retreat that I was quitting, and my ram.

I had not covered a league when I received an order to return to my solitude and to receive there the commissioners charged with verifying on the spot the accusations brought against me. I returned, and I waited for the commissioners for a long time.

When they arrived they interrogated me to discover whether, since my condemnation, I had removed by illegitimate means any money furniture or livestock from my hermitage. I replied that I had no other future than my meager bed, a stool, a table, a wooden spoon, a pair of spectacles, a staff and a few old books; and that my livestock consisted of a very intelligent and very fat ram which kept me company.

They drew up an official report of all my responses, and after having measured my garden and examined the walls of my cell, they heard a number of witnesses and put seals on my spectacles and my other items of furniture, having forbidden me to make use of anything that was sealed. They enjoined me in addition to remain in my solitude and not to go further than twenty paces in any direction.

It no longer had any charm for me then. Ennui and sadness overwhelmed me. I drew up long and respectful petitions to obtain permission to quit the delightful desert where I had spent such pleasant moments. I had my plaints and my pleas brought to the ears of judges by means of a young shepherd, who came to ask me to teach him to read. For a long time, though, all my protestations were futile; my case was heard slowly. Finally, however, it was judged.

I received the verdict, which permitted me to change residence. The man who brought it made a very fine speech, in which he proved to me that I had been calumniated and that the sovereign master of the land was very satisfied with the regular life I had led in his estates thus far, but that he needed my cell, and that when I had quit it, in order to give evidence of his benevolence he would send me every year a sixth of the

revenue from my garden, and that, in addition, he would permit me to take away my spectacles.

Oh, I was glad, when I awoke, to find that I was tranquil
in my retreat.

Dream VI

Although I am very placid, I sometimes had heated arguments in my dreams. In this one I had become an antiquary,
and in that capacity, I had great quarrels with other scholars
over several objects of erudition, I wrote a folio volume to
prove to one of them that an ear of a colossal statue of
Faustina that had been disinterred a short while before had
been sculpted and added more than a century after the figure
and at the end of the empire of Alexander Severus, whereas
the statue had been executed under the Antonines, as was
proven by the character of the design and the chisel-work,
which were evidently of that century.

I cited so many authorities that I thought my theory regarding Faustina's ear was beyond all contestation, but my
adversary combated it with a work even more ample than
mine.

I was then taken as an arbiter between two other anti-
quarians whose sentiments were divided regarding an inscription engraved on a severely mutilated marble that had been
found while repairing a road. One claimed that it as a prayer to
Aesculapius, the other the tomb of a Druid, and each of them
sustained his opinion with a great deal of heat, citing authorities without number. Having studied the marble attentively,
however, I discovered these words in Gothic characters: *Road
from Chalons to Vitri*. The two scholars did not want to abide
by my decision, and their dispute became even more heated, to
such a point that after being heaped with insults, one threw the
marble at the head of his adversary and knocked him out.

After that bloody scene, I thought that I had amassed one
of the finest cabinets in Europe, in which I have employed
immense sums. I possessed unique specimens, among others

painted clay vases, one blue and the other red-brown; they were admired and envied by all collectors. I had a multitude of canopic jars, antique statues, medallions and bronzes.

One day, when I was sitting in my cabinet, contemplating my riches, an Egyptian mummy that was lying in is box facing me stood up. I was penetrated by fright and threw myself on my knees. Then I heard words emerging from the cadaver's mouth in a low and sad voice:

"Insensate, why put into objects that have neither taste not utility sums with which you could relieve a province? Know that the science of antiquaries is as obscure as it is vain. You believe that I was one of the ancient Egyptians whom their relatives embalmed and conserved carefully; know that I was a murderer. It was only three years ago that I was hanged in Marseille. A surgeon of that city, knowing how avid travelers are for mummies, after having me embalmed, and covered in bandages and hieroglyphs that he invented, sold me to the German who sold me to you."

Having finished those words, the cadaver fell back into its box.

Dream VII

In order to extract myself from the misery to which I believed that I had been reduced in a dream, I imagined that I might become an author, but as that profession has several branches it was necessary to choose the one that could give me bread promptly without obliging me to study a great deal.

After a few reflections, I decided to make a commentary on a Greek author. In consequence, I rented a garret and a lot of dictionaries, and in very little time I had composed a stout volume on the retreat of the ten thousand reported by Xenophon. I sold my manuscript and my surprise was extreme when I saw it printed, for I must confess that I did not have the slightest idea of the military art or the least knowledge of Greek. I trembled that someone might ask me for explanations of a few points in my book, which, fortunately, did not emerge from the printer's warehouse.

However, as the printer was not reimbursed for the money he had given me, nor for the expenditure he had made for the printing of the Commentary, he charged me with insults. On the other hand, I had not paid the rent on the garret and other debts that I had incurred while I was working, for in hope of an assured product I had nourished myself and dressed myself well. As a result, my creditors, seeing that I was unable to acquit myself in their regard, had me put in prison.

A charitable man clad in religious garb came to visit me; I told him the story of my unfortunate adventure, and he consoled me, telling me that my misfortune was not hopeless.

"The scant success of your book," he said, doubtless comes from the fact that you did not put anything in it against the government or against mores; undertake another work, insert in it a few voluptuous pictures, gallant adventures, jeers against religion, exclamations against the prejudices of the human race, a few thrusts against the sovereign and magistrates; finally, take precautions to have your book banned, and your fortune will be made."

"But Reverend," I said to him, "can I in all conscience take that advice?"

"Employ a part of the profit you make in pious works," he replied, "and take my words for it, be tranquil in that regard"

I came out of prison—I have no idea why, for I certainly had not found the wherewithal to pay my debts—and I tried to become an author in the manner that my friend had explained to me. I set to work, but, by virtue of an error of imagination, it turned out, when it was finished, to be a treatise on genealogies. It was very profound; that is why it procured me honors and wealth.

Everyone, believing me to be a skillful genealogist, asked me for titles of nobility, and I made them for people of all sorts.

A barber who had become very rich by way of inheritances came to beg me to find him a genealogy and a coat of arms. I discovered an illustrious ancestor for him killed at Cérisoles, a crown of pearls, a Constable's sword and an escutcheon with three sable flamboyants on a field of gold.

At the same time I received a letter from a merchant who had made a large fortune in Cadiz. He was the son of a stone-carver and asked me for a nobility of at least four centuries. I surpassed his hopes by far. I made him a descendant of Froila I, the fourth king of Asturias; I put among his ancestors saints, generals of orders, cardinals and other qualified persons.

A great Seigneur wanting to marry an actress, I was charged with finding suitable parents for the woman, and I acquitted my commission honorably. As I continued dreaming, however, I became an actor myself. I had the most fortunate dispositions for the theater; I was firm in the principles of effrontery and incapable of allowing myself to be put off by booing and whistling. I was a joker. Young Seigneurs sought my acquaintance and amused themselves therein. Soon, however, I felt the bitterness of that estate. My first trials in the theater were not successful and I was beaten with blows of canes and the flat of swords at a supper during which I took it into my head to make fun of a fop who was present.

Those setbacks and the dolor that I thought I felt made me dream of another métier. I was engaged to serve as maître-d'hôtel in the house of a gentleman. In a short time I became very rich and my master very poor, but what is incredible is that he became my steward in his turn, and we soon fund ourselves back in our original estates.

That last disgrace determined me to quit society; I loved solitude and repose, and I became a Carthusian, but I had not been in that holy retreat for long when I found it impossible to emerge from my cell, because of the excess of my pot belly; it seemed to me that when I was next to my fire I felt myself melting like a lump of wax. I made efforts to move away, but in vain; I became liquid.

You cannot imagine the anguish in which I was found, and how weary I felt when I woke up.

Dream VIII

The smallest objects become very valuable when they more necessary, and one only separates from them dolorously. Such are spectacles for an old man. I hope, therefore, that no one will find it ridiculous that, having lost mine one day, I was grievously afflicted by it. Alas, what would become of me if Heaven did not return my dear spectacles?

But I have them, and I shall not repeat here the sad plaints by which I was retained in my desert while I lacked them. I shall only say that in the sweet sleep that the joy of seeing them again procured me, I was able, without bring perceived, to discover the thoughts of men; they were presented to me through those spectacles, almost as one sees objects in a dark room.

I cannot express the pleasure that that discovery gave me. I hastened to put it to work without telling anyone. While I was deliberating as to with whom I ought to commence my observations, I perceived that I was in a very gallantly furnished boudoir. I saw a coquette leaning on a writing-desk, who appeared to be dreaming,

I put my spectacles on and I saw her imagination filled by ribbons. A spaniel came next, and was replaced by a negro, then by little shoes, and the shoes by all sorts of pompoms. All of that was succeeded rapidly by an opera hall, a carriage with lilac and silver varnish, two striped horses, a mall filled with people, a small parakeet, a church and a seller of trinkets.

Then I saw a small human figure appear, whose submissive and respectful attitude and frequent sighs enabled me to deduce that he was a maltreated lover. The beauty started to laugh merely in thinking about that man, who was soon chased away by another small figure who seemed more at ease. He gave the impression of one of those pretty fellows who possess the art of sweet talk and flirting with all women. After he had whistled and pirouetted, he disappeared and was replaced by an exceedingly ugly little man who was carrying two bags full of money in his hands. That one appeared welcome but the second took the stage again and remained there for almost six minutes. The little spaniel and the trinket-seller expelled him and returned momentarily. Then I saw a little monkey and bracelets garnished with diamonds, and shortly afterwards, a very agreeable young woman.

When the latter arrived the dreamer took on an anxious and jealous attitude, biting the tip of her finger. She stood up, made a tour of the boudoir two or three times, and then sat down at a dressing table and stated to try out facial expressions in her mirror. I saw her sometimes smiling languidly and sometimes open her eyes with all her might in order to find expressions of vivacity. At another time she put on a cold and disdainful expression. Finally she put herself in her imagination beside the young woman.

Thinking that I would be bored by seeing them together for very long, I went to make my observations elsewhere. I went into a beautiful but eccentrically decorated house. There I saw a man dressed in an extraordinary manner who was sitting next to his fire with his feet on the fire-irons. He was watching, attentively, pieces of meat that were roasting.

I looked into his imagination with my spectacles, and the first object that struck me was a frangipane tart, which I saw for quite a long time; then I perceived a lamb stuffed with truffles, a map of the world, English soldiers, a naval battle, a pâté, a portrait of Sully, salted tongues, smelts on a skewer, a jet of water, bookshelves, and the cataracts of the Nile; after all that, the roasts were cooked, and he had nothing else in his mind but them.

I left him to eat in order to hasten to further discoveries. I introduced myself into a rich and comfortable apartment ornamented with porcelains, paintings and old lacquer. There I contemplated a fat abbé clad in lilac velvet, with golden olives and lace. Good cheer and health shone in his face. He was alone in front of a big fire next to a little table on which there was a pot of tea. I stayed there for some time without discovering anything in his imagination. I thought that dust had tarnished my spectacles; I cleaned them but still could not see anything except a space devoid of objects. As I was about to go elsewhere to seek out a more occupied heart, however, I saw a red cap appear, a crosier, a papal cavalcade and a large sturgeon. At that sight, my spectacles fell off, and when I picked them up again I found myself in the bedroom of a fop.

Everything was in disorder. I perceived on a table a broken fan, a box of pills, a few books whose titles scandalized me, reminding me that I was a hermit, lists of merchants, a portrait of a woman, a broken sword, several ripped-up playing cards, pots of ointment and other similar objects. He was lying on a chaise-longue, looking harassed; he had a pale and downcast face, and pulled down one of his socks, gazing at his leg with satisfaction. I tried to bring his ideas into focus, turning my spectacles this way and that, but all I could see there was himself in miniature.

I went into the house of a jurisconsultant, but thought I had made a mistake, because all I could see in the head of that man in a simarre was a theater hall, a freemasons' lodge and a few pamphlets.

From there I transported myself into the home of a miser. It was night and I saw him, by the light of a little lamp, in a room whose walls were hung with cobwebs. The door was locked by several bolts. He appeared to be deeply engrossed in calculations, but the slightest sound made him turn his head, with an anxiety that was painted on his face. I saw nothing in his soul but a strong-box and a few sheets of paper filled with figures.

I made a slight sound and immediately, I saw five or six men armed with pistols enter precipitately into his imagination. The miser went pale, but after having listened for a long time without hearing anything more, he resumed calculating and I saw the thieves leave; but when I made another slight movement, they returned even more precipitately than the first time, and stayed for longer. I left them there.

I wanted to see the soul of a courtier. I went to his house, and found him with one of his friends. They were giving one another touching marks of esteem and the most tender affection, but having looked into their hearts, I saw in the first his tender friend hanged, and in the friend's heart, the courtier broken on the wheel. After having embraced, they separated, and the imagination of the courtier was filled successively by a Saint Hubert hunt, a red sash, and a numerous court, in which he appeared himself, base and crawling.

Then I saw the house of a Minister, and the courtier walking outside the door of one of the secretaries, who received him some time later with a disdainful expression, and sent him away promptly. Those objects gave way to a maréchal's baton, a dog-pack, and English horse and a little country house.

Dream IX

In this dream I thought I found myself at the entrance to a magnificent château. On the point of going in I was stopped by two doormen with bandoliers and large wigs, while a third domestic went to inform his master of my arrival. A moment later I saw a magnificent dressed man, puffed up with pride, coming toward me; I thought that it was the master, but I was told that it was only one of his officers of the third rank.

When he reached me he asked me where I had left my carriage and servants. I replied that I was a poor hermit, and had nothing similar. He did not let me finish, and withdrew scornfully. Immediately, I saw another emerge, covered in armories, who ordered me to follow him. He took me, via a back door, into a rather poorly furnished room, but which was nevertheless decorated on all sides by armories, in relief or painted. He had me brought olives, bread and cider.

After that light snack I asked to be presented to the Seigneur of the place. That proposition shocked him; looking at me askance, he replied that people like me were not presented. I was about to go away sadly when he shut the door and told me, while swearing, that no one left the house without giving a tip to the servants. I had good reasons for not giving them anything; I tried to open the door in order to flee, but I was suddenly besieged by fifteen or twenty lackeys, who spoke to me in the same terms.

Although I had nothing to give them, I nevertheless put my hands in my pockets; but when they saw that nothing came out for them, they decided to take it out on my person by means of ill-treatment. They took a large blanket, put me into it, and stated to toss me. With every thrust they threw me up to the ceiling, where I was cruelly bruised.

Finally, it seemed to me that I passed through it, and found myself in a magnificent drawing room where the Seigneur of the château was receiving his guests. He was sunk in an immense morocco leather armchair, with spectacles garnished with precious stones on his nose and an ample wig on his head. His robe was scarlet; he had one leg resting on a crimson velvet stool, which enabled me to understand that he was crippled by gout. His armories were on the stool and on two crosiers that he used in order to sustain him when he wanted to get up.

He was examining successively, one after another, long scrolls of parchment, which were presented respectfully by all those who came in, and he assigned them places around him in accordance with the nobility and wealth indicated by the parchment. I went out without him having perceived me, and, having introduced myself into another room I found a numerous company there, all occupied in joking about the master of the house and turning to ridicule his airs of conceit and the etiquette he made everyone observe in his house.

I encountered in a large hall an intimate friend whom I had left in society and had not seen for twenty-eight years. I had not ceased to think about him since I had been in my solitude, for the duties of amity have always been sacred to me; sometimes I thought I saw him and talked to him; he replied and gave me various signs of sincere and tender attachment; and that commerce had many charms for me. As soon as I saw him I stopped in surprise; he stopped too, and having stared at one another mutually in recognition, we threw our arms around one another and embraced tenderly.

"How delighted I am," he said to me. "What a joy, what a delight it is for me to see you again after so many years of absence."

I felt no less joy than him; I was about to make him party to my transports when a young man passing close to us asked him whether he was coming to dine with him.

"Yes, of course," he replied, "I'm coming."

He left, and I never saw him again.

Dream X

In the dream I was sitting by the edge of the sea. There, considering the waves that a slight wind was pushing toward the shore and the seashells that they were bringing and dragging away alternately, my gaze paused on an oyster that had remained dry and far enough away from the water for the waves, gentle for the moment, not to be able to reach it. It was slightly open in the sunlight, and I saw something shiny inside.

I opened it fully and I saw that what had struck my sight with its gleam was a little golden bell. The clapper was a pearl. It was covered with extraordinary characters. I made futile efforts to read them; I took it in my fingertips and, having shaken it, my astonishment was extreme to see a long file of men and women appear, of various ages and estate, who were walking two by two and passed before me as if in review. I understood then that the bell was a magical object, which had the power to resuscitate the dead; for all those composing that procession were dead people, ancient and modern.

Firstly I recognized Saint John Chrysostom, with white hair and pontifical garments; his countenance was grave and modest; the expression on his face was noble and imprinted with respect and veneration. He was leaning on a pastoral staff and walking at a slow pace.

Beside him, a modern prelate was walking on tiptoe; he was laden with jewelry, with a little mantle, his hat under his arm, and holding in his hand a box of pastilles some of which he was chewing complacently. After a few capers and pirouettes he took a piece of paper out of his pocket and presented it, in a light and agreeable manner, to Saint Chrysostom.

"Look, Monsieur," he said to him, "and see how nicely I've completed these end-rhymes."

Having darted a glance at them, the patriarch threw them away disdainfully. "It appears," he said, is a loud and majestic voice, "that you haven't studied my Homilies."

"What are Homilies?" asked the modern prelate laughing. "Have you, Monsieur, read my poetry?"

At that moment I sensed an odor, or perfume, which seemed pleasant at first, but obliged me to pinch my nose when it became stronger and sharper. Then I saw two military men appear. One was an old knight, with an extremely ugly face but a martial expression; he was covered in iron and carried a Constable's sword. I understood that he was Duguesclin, whose portrait I had once seen. The other was a courtier, with an agreeable face; he was the one who had brought the perfume; he was wearing rouge, and his wig, circled with laurels, was heavily powdered. He was dressed as gallantly as could be, and was taking snuff in an elegant fashion; he made the diamonds he had on his fingers shine; his gait was that of a dancer; sometimes he arranged the plumes of his hat, sometimes he removed any dust that might be on his coat with a little clothes-brush. Such was the difference I remarked between those two men.

They were followed by two magistrates who had lived in different times. The first was clad in a long black robe and seemed aged; his head was shaved and sunk into his shoulders, a high collar and a studious and occupied expression. While walking his was gravely examining a Code bound in parchment. I felt penetrated with respect for him, even before I even realized that he was President Janin. The other scarcely resembled him; he was a young man in hunting costume. His hair knotted gracefully; he was whistling a fashionable dance tone and affecting foppish airs.

After that I saw Jacques Coeur, that generous citizen, who only employed the immense wealth that his industry had acquired in helping his fatherland and its king. His attire and his countenance were modest. I sensed a sincere esteem for him born in my heart, thinking that he had been able to forbid himself pride in a distinguished position, and that neither his great wealth nor the favor he enjoyed had been able to make him forget his original estate.

I observed entire opposite qualities in a financier who had not been dead for long. That one was covered in gold. A prodigiously stout belly, a vermilion complexion a well-powdered wig and a great deal of jewelry concurred in giving him an opulent appearance. He was leaning heavily on a cane with a golden pommel. His physiognomy and his manners were vulgar and ignoble.

Those two men were talking to one another as they walked. Jacques Coeur was describing to the modern man the means he had employed to become rich and the usage he had made of his wealth. "Apparently," the new financier replied, "all the properties of the zero were not known in your time? A single stroke of the pen made two thirds of my fortune; I didn't have to go to as much trouble as you...."

I could not hear the rest of their conversation; they drew away, and the women who came immediately after them attracted my attention.

Some were of tall and majestic stature; extremely long hair mingled with several nets of pearls fell in large waves over their shoulders. Their features were very symmetrical, their bearing noble and proud; they were clad like our ancestors during the reign of Charles VII: an ample high collar, a great many pearls, short and split sleeves, their fingers laden with rings; a long hoop petticoat and a pearly robe announced the proud mistresses of our ancestors, who were able to awaken their ailing courage with generous reproaches. Beside them were walking, with bewildered expressions, several women clad in modern dress; it was difficult to distinguish their natural features, the varnish covering their faces rendering them all nearly identical; their speech was witty but libertine; they inspired joy and pleasure, but not virtue.

Then I saw a part of Henri IV's court pass by, followed immediately by a modern court, which was composed of a multitude of decrepit young men with pale faces and utterly deformed little men; but the adornments, and the richness of the costumes, effaced the ancient court, for the latter was only composed of robust and sinewy warriors covered in iron, who did not seem much occupied with their personal appearance.

At that point in my dream, the sun, which was already quite high, shone so brightly in my eyes that it woke me up and, regretfully, I saw the entire spectacle disappear.

Dream XI

One of my friends, who comes to see me from time to time, had brought me some new works in order to show me how the knowledge of men of letters had improved since I had quit society. Among those books there was one on natural history that was highly esteemed. I started reading it avidly, because I have always loved that genre of science.

I was immediately struck by the difference between the new philosophy and that of my time. It seemed to me that the modern was better, but I found things in it that shocked me. I was revolted to see that all the reasoning of the new philosophers tended only to seek physical causes for everything and to dispute with the Creator, inch by inch, so to speak, the production of those works. I believed that I saw the truth, however, in the manner in which the sentiments were exposed; I allowed myself to be drawn and convinced; I could not stop reading.

When night had fallen I lit my lamp and, having sat down on my bed, I continued to read. As I was not accustomed to staying up late, slumber weighed down my eyes, and I fell asleep.

Then I thought I was sitting in a dense wood, with my book in my hand, reflecting on the theories of the new philosophy. I saw a venerable old man emerging from between the trees. His age was only marked by white hair and a long bushy beard that hung down over his stomach. He did not show any sign of decrepitude. His broad and majestic forehead was imprinted with respect, his gaze was soft and his face full of grace. His head was circle by a crown of elm leaves and he was leaning on an ivory cane. I was struck by his noble and simple appearance. I got up and saluted him.

"What are you dreaming about, my son" he asked.

I replied to him that a book I had just read had give birth to afflicting doubts. He sat down on the grass and invited me to sit beside him.

"It was fifty years ago," he said, "that I quit the court, responsibilities and honors in order to come into these woods to enjoy my existence and study nature. That study is the most beautiful and the most interesting that a man can make; but profound and continual homages rendered to the Creator ought to be the fruit of our knowledge of that sort. I prostrate myself before the Supreme Being when I consider the magnificence of the universe. On the one hand, I lose myself in the immense extent of the vortices that move a thousand worlds, and on the other, in the infinite smallness of those animals for which a drop of water is a world. The slightest production is a subject of profound admiration for me.

"Oh, my son, what is the aberration of the human mind that has dared to attribute the marvels of creation to an effect of chance? Does not everything that we see in the universe rise up against such an absurdity? Does not our reason itself revolt against it? Are not that blade of grass and that acorn sufficient to make one sense that a powerful being has presided over the formation of the world and the tiniest objects? Consider yourself for a moment, my son, and see whether you can avoid seeing in yourself the hand of a God.

"Although thousands of people have made discoveries in nature and regarding themselves, do they know yet how they breathe, how they live, how they speak, and how they think? And yet, they pretend to explain everything, and they dispute with the Almighty the glory of having made everything. If at least they were of good faith, one could lament their blindness, but, to the shame of reason, they decide malignly against reason itself.

"If the reproduction of an insect escapes their feeble eyes, they conclude that hazard is its creator; all the other living beings raise their voices in vain; we cannot see, say the philosophers, how this takes birth; it is therefore corruption, the dust, an accident that produces it. As for us, my son, let us adore the hand that made us and sustains us; we only need ourselves in order to recognize his power. When I simply consider that at the first order of my will, that power inexplicable for philosophers, I put my body in motion, which is such a beautiful machine, I exclaim, full of glory and joy, that I am the work of a God."

I was listening with respect and interest to that wise old man's speech when the light that I had allowed to brighten, having set fire to the straw of my bed, woke me up with a start, and thought that I had set fire to my cell.

It was only with difficulty that I succeeded in putting it out, and having loaded modern philosophy, which had nearly caused me to burn alive, with maledictions, I lay down tranquilly and enjoyed a peaceful slumber for the rest of the night.

Dream XII

Nothing is more bizarre than the changes that arrive in sleep. Confined for twenty-eight years in a desert where calm and peace are the only things that touch me, where nothing can irritate my desires or inspire me with vengeance, I became in a dream the general of an army, and thought that the State had reposed on me the care of vanquishing its enemies.

Scarcely had I charged myself with such an honorable employment, however, than I sensed a great depth of timidity in thinking about the dangers of war. But a man who, like me, had the command of armies assured me that my life was not at risk, that nowadays the officers of the general staff have the right to take measures against perils so well that one only rarely hears mention any longer of a bullet inflicting the slightest scratch on them. I was very encouraged by that opinion and willingly accepted the command.

The prince I served liked conquests. It was decided in his council that I would go to subjugate a distant nation to the north, but, as a peace treaty had previously been made with that people, it was necessary to find some plausible pretext for breaking it, and we wanted to be able to impute the infraction to the enemy that we were attacking, because otherwise, right would not have been on our side, and the war would have seemed unjust. We deliberated for a long time and held several councils at the court. I took advantage of the intervals to raise troops, for in making me a general I had not been given any soldiers, doubtless because they wanted to leave me the liberty of choosing them myself.

I had read a great deal in my youth and I had noticed that historians, poets, orators and even some classes of philosophers reason marvelously about the military art. Some demonstrated clearly that winning a battle was dependent on some cause or other; that some maneuver, for example, would have saved the Imperial army at the battle of Bouvines, or that if Philippe de Valois had taken possession of the high ground at Crecy and if he had used his artillery appropriately, the English would have been beaten. Other learned men gave the tactical rules that suited various people of Europe. Geometers gave the means of reliably attacking a fortress and causing a bomb to explode at the precise point that one wanted to destroy. Finally, remembering that poets sang the praises enthusiastically of the courage, intrepidity and prudence of their heroes, I judged that they must necessarily have the virtues and sentiments that they celebrated so well.

With those thoughts in mind I resolve to form an army of all those scholars, so well informed in the métier of war. When I had enrolled them, I distributed to each of them the employment I thought most appropriate.

I took for my general a profound scholar who had just translated from the Greek the military art of Xenophon and who knew perfectly the manner of making war against Persians. I gave the employment of field-marshal to an illustrious poet who, in order to attract my esteem, had already begun work on an epic poem about my future conquest. In the most pompous style, he divided Olympus between me and my enemies, although I still did not know who they were.

I appointed a Geographer as adjutant because I had been told that the employment in question demanded an exact knowledge of the country.

Finally, I distributed the most distinguished ranks to the scholars whose names were the best known, and of the host of mediocre and poor authors, the quantity of whom was prodigious, I made soldiers and subaltern officers. After I had regulated everything in that fashion, I learned that war had been declared against Norway, and this is what had furnished the occasion.

My prince had instructed his ambassador at that court to request that he be sent parrots native to the country; it had been replied that the birds in question were only found in America and the southern hemisphere, and that Norway could not furnish any. With that, war was declared. A manifesto was published in which my prince explained the indispensable reasons that obliged him to trouble, reluctantly, the peace of his estates and to shed the blood of his dear people.

Having received the order to depart, I made a review of my troops, although I knew very little about military discipline. The majority of my cavaliers did not know from which side to mount a horse. A few became tangled up in the black cloaks that serve them as a uniform; almost all of them had lorgnettes and wigs that got caught p in their weapons. They seemed to be in the most ridiculous embarrassment.

I departed at the head of that savant army. On the second day, however, the captain of the Guides led us astray. He was a professor of Hebrew to whom I had given that employment, because of his profound knowledge of languages. He was able to speak Hebrew, Greek and Syriac to the people we found on our route, but he could neither understand the guides nor find the route.

We found ourselves in a marsh and, to complete the misfortune, the commissioner of food supplies having applied himself to composing an ode in my honor instead of proving instead of procuring provisions the army found itself famished. The soldiers, humdrum authors accustomed to dying of hunger, were not greatly afflicted, but the officers murmured loudly.

However, as dreams are inconsequent, I found myself a moment later within one day of the enemy. Those people, who had good spies on the ground, were informed about the progress of my army and the disorder that reigned within it, marched in haste in order to take us by surprise. I received the news from a dozen tall, thin men, starveling authors who served as scouts.

I immediately summoned the Geometers to order the construction of a camp fortified in accordance with the rules, which would be able to rest the efforts of enemies. They soon brought me a plan drawn on paper. It was a plan of an impregnable camp, but they all assured me that they could not execute it on the terrain. Then I ordered the soldiers to fortify themselves as best they could with palisades. Those poor fellows had a great desire to put their lives in surety but, being unable to overcome their customary idleness, the work went slowly.

Meanwhile, I saw a deputation arrive of the principal officers of a corps of physicists. They had come to propose to me a means they had discovered of giving a violent electric shock to the entire enemy army simultaneously. They assured me that by attacking vigorously at the moment of the shock, I was certain of victory. I liked that idea, but it was necessary to take a steel chain all the way to the enemy retrenchments, and none of my soldiers had the courage to do it. I was obliged to abandon the enterprise and began to fear a rout.

My lieutenant-general had even less hope than me. He regretted the chariots armed with scythes and cavalry of Cyrus the younger, and did not believe that one could be victorious without such aid.

With time pressing, I set about arranging my army in battle order. Then everyone let me know that he would be very happy to be in the rearguard. The philosophers, most of all, showed a great desire to be in a safe place. They displayed fine humanitarian principles, and made sage reflections of the short duration of human life and the blindness that led to making war. All the other scholars appreciated those reasons. Poltroonery spread through the ranks with rapidity.

Promptly, in order to deter desertions, I had a scaffold raised in the middle of the camp. I had an eloquent orator climb up on it, who, by means of a harangue full of energy, erudition and solidity, gave a species of valor to my troops. He spoke pompously about honor and love of the fatherland. He reminded his listens of the intrepidity of their ancestors, the Gaulish and German people who had brought Rome to within an inch of defeat.

At the most animated point in his speech, someone came to say that the enemy would soon be within the range of cannon fire. At that news, the orator leapt lightly from the scaffold and fled. The philosophers had preceded him. My lieutenant-general shouted loudly that a retreat, like that of the ten thousand, would be more glorious than a battle; in consequence he took the lead. All the rest of the troops disbanded, and, remembering myself that a general had to preserve his life, I did my best to run away.

Dream XIII

In my childhood, my mother and aged relatives had filled my imagination with tales of sprites, the resuscitated dead, and other similar absurdities. Those traces, profoundly engraved in a tender brain, scar over, so to speak, with age and reason, but are never entirely effaced; one cannot criticize too strongly those who give or allow children to obtain those injurious impressions, which influence their mental health and way of thinking throughout their lives.

In order to get to my subject, one of those tales that had struck me most forcefully was that of certain dead people who come by night to suck the blood of the living and desiccate them by filling their own veins with it. I remember that in my childhood, they caused me to pass bad nights. I believed that I felt myself being sucked by those maleficent cadavers, and in truth, I became visibly thinner, but it was an effect of the fear.

I do not know how my imagination, that night, represented those objects to me in a dream, which had faded from my memory long ago. I believed that I was among sepulchers in a cypress grove. There, I saw desiccated cadavers emerging from their tombs, which, in standing upright, appeared in the attitude of someone imbibing the foam of a wine or some other liquor. It did not take me long to divine what they were doing.

I saw a vast plain where a large number of men were occupied in different kinds of rustic labor. Some were harvesting, others planting, cultivating vines and fruit trees; some were sowing the ground with seeds for the following year; they were all covered in sweat and dust. From those men and the fruits that they were picking or planning, I saw rays departing composed of little particles of their substance, which went to render themselves into the mouths of the vampires.

As those specters sucked, I saw the unfortunate cultivators diminishing, losing their strength, becoming dry and sick, and finally falling into weakness. The fruits of their efforts, the crops and flocks, all went into the avid throats of the phantoms, which, meanwhile, acquired full faces, with fresh and brightly colored cheeks, and a squat and replete stature. While

I considered them, their stoutness became more excessive by the minute; finally, they all appeared to my eyes with ample wigs, golden crutches, and padded and embroidered garments covered in jewels. The majority were in large armchairs, and seemed to have a taste for it.

I asked someone who those men were and whether they were not the same ones that I had seen emerging from the ground a little while before. I was told that they were called superintendents, controllers, tax-collectors and provincial stewards. I considered with surprise the change that I had just seen overtake their figures. However, they were still sucking as avidly as at the beginning; their pot-bellies were prodigious. Finally, they were almost all gripped by a horrible indigestion, and I saw them with horror vomiting up the aliments with which they were filled.

Dream XIV

In society I often felt sorry for those women delivered to idleness, who make their happiness depend on an infinity of particular objects, the loss of which afflicts them sorely. I judged that they could never be content, or that their contentment was as rapid as lightning. Those ideas, although very ancient, returned to me in a dream, which had been caused by another that was rather singular. I had seen the heart of one of those women laid bare; it was linked to different places by an innumerable multitude of threads, the other ends of which were connected to everything that she loved.

The object to which the tightest thread was attached was a little parakeet of the rarest species. Every time it seemed a little sad, the woman was heartbroken. Other taut threads, which were linked to very sensitive parts of the heart, were those of a porcelain mantelpiece garniture, a writing desk, a elegant carriage, a little jonquil monkey and a cluster of precious stones. Ornaments, jewelry and slippers that enabled her to sense the smallness and elegance of her feet clung as strongly to the heart by means of threads whose slightest vibration was painful. Threads thinner than the rest, and very slack, ended in her husband and children, and by virtue of an inconceivable singularity, the further away the husband was, the more the thread relaxed, only becoming inconvenient for the heart when the object was nearby.

However, the monkey lost an eye fighting with a cat. That accident broke the thread rudely. The lady's heart bled and her eyes shed tears. Soon afterwards, that affliction was followed by another, no less bitter. A group from the garniture of the mantelpiece fell off, and was cruelly mutilated by the fall. The heart was then scarcely able to breathe, but, the parakeet having unfortunately swallowed a perfidious piece of candy, its chain carried away a piece of the heart in separating therefrom, and the lady fainted completely. When she recovered consciousness, she continued to receive other wounds. A few threads still tugged forcefully at her heart, but several were detached, tearing it.

I felt sorry for her, having fallen victim to so many accidents, and I was beginning to reflect philosophically on the misfortune one has in being too attracted to the vain objects one possesses when I perceived her beside a young village girl. She had a lively and cheerful expression; I could not see on her face the anxiety and regret that disfigured the lady's.

Her heart had only five threads, and I remarked with satisfaction that the principal one was attached to her husband. He was a vigorous young peasant with a pleasant face, who seemed very content with his wife. A second thread was very tightly attached to a pretty little child; a third ended in a well-stocked chicken-run. One of the others, which were less sturdy, was attached to two oxen and the last to herd of goats. I did not see any of them break while I was looking at them. I judged that the peasant woman was happier than the lady. Her heart was at peace, the objects of her affection were legitimate, and Heaven was watching over their conservation.

Dream XV

I have heard it said a hundred times that dreams are only bizarre games of the imagination and an extravagant accumulation of thoughts and objects devoid of connection. I have, in fact, often experienced that myself since I have become a dreamer by estate, and my reader will not have failed to notice it. However, there are exceptions to the rule; here, for example, is one that bears such a striking character of verity that it surprised me when I wanted to recall it in order to write it down, and when I reread it, I could scarcely believe that I had had it while asleep. This is the naïve recitation.

From the window of my cell, where I was leaning on the sill, I thought I could see the most beautiful landscape in the world. The sun was rising, the air was calm and serene. The principal object that struck my sight was a mountain, at the summit of which was a temple in the form of a rotunda, made of alabaster of the greatest whiteness. The roof was covered in sheets of gold, and that metal shone on the cornices, the friezes and all the ornaments. That beautiful edifice was surrounded by a dazzling light.

At the foot of the mountain I saw a vast plain that it was necessary to traverse in order to reach the temple. The part of the plain that was to my left appeared to me to be a place of delights. Meadows dotted with flowers were cut across by lines of poplars and willows. Silvery streams flowed slowly there, which sometimes changed into sheets of water bordered with moss and violets, presenting warm and perfumes baths, and sometimes fell noisily from elevations, forming cascades with a thousand charming effects. With the chirping of birds, a fresh and embalmed air, everything attracted me into that valley; everything there respired pleasure.

On traveling there, however, one drew away from the temple considerably, and eventually ended up in a frightful marsh, the black and stagnant water of which exhaled a noxious odor. Instead of reeds it was covered with dead leaves that the wind brought there; poisonous plants grew on its edges, and a thick black vapor rose continually from its surface.

I turned my eyes away from such a sad object in order to examine the rest of the plain, which was to my right. It was cut into four parts by lines parallel to the plane of the mountain. Of those four parts, the one nearest to me was the most agreeable. It was a meadow covered with nascent grass and trees in flower.

The second zone was a rapid river that went to flow noisily into the marsh. There were several delightful islets in the direction of its mouth, and those islets hid the danger of being abandoned to the current.

Beyond the river, in the third division, there was a beautiful region similar to an orchard. It was planted with trees laden with fruits and large oaks that bore their crowns up to the clouds.

Finally, a fourth, very different, canton was part of the mountain. A continual autumn reigned there, and the trees were shedding some of their leaves; I even saw snow and ice there. In order to reach the temple it was necessary to cross that zone.

In the first, furthest away from the temple, the path was broad and beautiful, but it ended at the river, the passage of which was extremely narrow and dangerous. There were, in truth, small boats and oars on the bank to assist travelers, but he current was so rapid that it was difficult to cross it in a straight line. The path from the other bank of the river across the third division was less difficult, but arid and rugged. Finally, the path frayed through the fourth zone was the easiest, and arrived at the summit of the mountain by means of a gentle slope.

That entire country was populated by an innumerable multitude of persons of all ages, both sexes and all estates. I saw all of them depart from the first line and direct their steps toward the mountain. At first they followed the path that led there directly, but they had scarcely reached the river than, enchanted by the deceptive beauty of the valley that presented itself to the left, they forgot the goal for which they were headed. The majority, without even deigning to get into the boats on the river's edge, threw themselves into the river in order to swim and were carried away by the rapidity of the current into the gulf where its waters were discharged.

A large number of those who went along the bank into the enchanted region allowed themselves to follow the natural slope that led them to the edge of the marsh. A few, frightened by the peril in which they had placed themselves, tried to re-join the path to the mountain, but the paths they were obliged to take were very difficult and full of obstacles.

Those who traversed the river in boats were the wisest; however, I remarked that very few traversed it in a straight line. Almost all yielded, to a lesser or greater degree, to the current. Thus, I saw that a large fraction of the multitude perished in that dangerous passage.

In the third zone the attrition was less. Nevertheless, several of those who had traversed the river courageously allowed themselves to be seduced by the brilliant spectacle of the valley; a few came back, but a large number lost courage because of the difficulty of the paths. Finally, in the very last division, a few, disgusted by the length of the journey, threw themselves toward the left, but they were few in number, and, in general, all those who had traversed the river and the third zone arrived at the temple.

Suddenly, I explained that allegory to myself; I saw it as a faithful depiction of human life; but, considering how great the number was of those who perished and how many escaped the perils of the journey, I was sorely afflicted, and, abandoning myself to an excess of sadness and my blind judgment, I said to myself: "Do so many people have to perish, then? Has the father of nature only given them existence in order to render them unfortunate? For every one that reaches the goal, how many lose themselves on the way? How many yield to the obstacles that oppose their happiness and go to hurl themselves into the gulf?"

While I was plunged in those black thoughts, the most dazzling spectacle suddenly struck my eyes. A ray of sunlight descended from the orb of that star all the way to my feet. It was accompanied to either side by clouds painted with all the colors of the rainbow. An angel slid rapidly over the flat surface that the ray presented in coming toward me. I prostrated myself, hiding my face with my hands. I had only been in that posture briefly when a soft and majestic voice called to me.

I lifted my head, and only saw a handsome young man. His blond hair was tied back gracefully on his head; an azure headband covered his forehead; a dazzling whiter robe was tightened by a golden belt. He spoke to me in a grave and imposing tone, but full of mildness.

"The Ancient of Days," he said to me, "who can measure the ocean in the palm of his hand, had deigned to send me to you in order to dissipate the doubts into which your blind imagination is drawing you. Admire his goodness. He created humans in order to be happy, but he wants them to tend to happiness freely and by the usage of their will. That is the prerogative that distinguishes them from brutes. Every man senses within himself that he is free, and it is that intimate sentiment that gives birth in him the mild contentment that he feels in doing good, or the piercing cry that frightens and lacerates him when he violates the laws of nature and the Creator.

"If humans were not free, their hearts would not experience pleasure or remorse; they would be mastered by a blind instinct and would lose the residue of the august resemblance they have to the Divinity, which is their glory.

"It is on human liberty that all divine and human laws are founded. Should the Almighty have ordered his creature to be virtuous? Would humans imitating the Supreme Being have established rules for good order if virtue had been impracticable and the passions invincible?

"Know that the Eternal covers with his wing everyone who has recourse to him. His arm sets aside vice and leads to virtue. Those whom you saw perishing were the proud who scorned and rejected his aid. His bounty will serve as a support for temerity, although it abandons the presumptuous. Cease, them, to murmur, feeble mortal, and adore the justice as well as the bounty of the Almighty. He permits vice to have its attractions in order to make virtue shine; but he gives arms to vanquish it to those who ask him for them sincerely."

Scarcely had the celestial envoy finished speaking than his stature became more than human; his robe fell majestically over his feet; his wings, whiter than snow, whose tips were gilded, covered a part of his body. Then I saw him quit his material substance, which he had taken on in order not to frighten me; his body took on the colors of the rainbow, in the brightest hues, and, rising up perpendicularly into the sky, he disappeared from my sight.

Dream XVI

I thought while dreaming that I found myself in a gathering of high society. As I was timid, I took up a position in a corner where, without being troubled by anyone, I could observe what was happening and make reflections.

In addition to several tables where people were playing cards, there was a circle of women and two or three men who were listening with interest and good humor to an abbé who was playing the joker and reciting with satisfaction many platitudes—in my judgment, at least. Suddenly, however, I saw him fall from his perch on the arrival of a young magistrate, who took possession of the audience and started talking more loudly and in a more pompous tone than the abbé. The latter placed himself behind the ladies, biting his fingernails while his triumphant competitor forestalled by bursts of laughter the applause of the audience. But he was soon supplanted in his turn by a third joker who appeared. The president came to keep the abbé company, but they did not say a word to one another.

One of the things that had struck me most in about the assembly was the extraordinarily animated complexion of the ladies. I asked someone I thought I knew what the cause of that was. He drew me to one side and told me that the complexion was artificial and that it was an adornment necessary to ladies in order to distinguish them from damsels, who did not make use of it while they hoped to marry. He added that at a certain age, women ceased to ornament themselves in that way because then they became devout, but that the age was not fixed and he had known women of sixty who still had rouge in their wrinkles. He also told me that ladies with rouge were divisible into two classes, the ill and the discontented.

After that instruction, I thought I saw the entire assembly disappear, and having retired like everyone else, I found myself at the evening toilette of one of those ladies. First I saw her spit out on to a table two rather large ivory balls, which caused her cheeks to become prodigiously hollow. The beautiful rouge that had surprised me so much remained upon two wads of cotton wool with which she rubbed her thin face. A moment later I saw two small strips of moleskin fall, which served her as eyebrows.

Her complexion then seemed quite pale; but that beauty did not take long to disappear, because the woman scraped her face with a small ivory knife, which caused a species of plaster to flake off, which had covered her wrinkled skin. I confess that she was beginning to frighten me. But the destruction had not finished yet. She pulled a thread of brass wire from a corner of her mouth, and in an instant I saw all her teeth rain down in the table.

Her hair was also false; a chambermaid took fold of it at the top, along with the headdress and carried the whole to a wooden head. I could not help being frightened then: a jaundiced complexion, withered and desiccated skin, a toothless mouth, blue and livid lips, a bald head with only a few scattered gray hairs: it does not need as much as that to disconcert a man who has never seen it before.

I tried to flee but could not; it was necessary to remain in order to see the face of that phantom change for a third time. A jar full of grease as brought, and after having steeped bandages in it she was packaged like a mummy; she disappeared, and I no longer saw anything but a hideous skeleton. Her table and her dressing table appeared to me to be a sepulcher full of bones, her dressing room a crypt from which groaning voices emerged. I uttered a cry of fright and woke up covered in a cold sweat.

Dream XVII

I amused myself during the day remembering the preceding dream, which was the cause of my having another of the same genre the following night. I was no longer timid; I felt free and cheerful, and it seemed to me that in a beautiful apartment I was bringing forward an armchair for a woman who was standing up and who appeared to me to be very uncomfortable, or very discontented, to judge by her rouge, for I thought that the rouge was a remedy and not an adornment, and that the worse a woman's malady was, the more she put on her cheeks.

I said to this one, therefore, that I was very sorry for her woes, that I had experienced a similar condition myself and that I knew how much one suffered from it. She interrupted me with a burst of laughter that disconcerted me; I tried to speak to her in a different tone, but I was suddenly transported into another house, whose mistress had natural colors; I knew by virtue of that fact that she was in the age of devotion; there was no doubt about that, in consequence of what I had been told in the previous dream, for that is not impossible.

I said nothing to that one, but another, younger woman appeared to me to merit a compliment of condolence, because rouge was still a remedy in my imagination. I began by opening my mouth, when a small child that she was holding on her knee held out his arms to caress me; I have always liked children, and I took him by the hand, which I kissed. I amused him with little tales, and then I returned him to the lady, saying to her: "One can easily see, Madame, that you're his mother; he resembles you perfectly, anyone but you would not have made him so lovable."

At those words the entire company blushed and lowered their eyes. I hastened to leave, and when I was already in the

132

antechamber someone called me back and told me that I had offended the lady, who was not married and was a canoness. The speech troubled me and woke me up.

Dream XVIII

I had become a J***,[7] and at first, in order to make the most of that savant quality, I began by speaking ill of the Pope, cardinals, bishops, etc. I found the change very singular, because I have always had a horror of slander, but something, I know not what, in the depths of my heart told me that I was not doing anything wrong and that, on the contrary, I had the efficacious grace of following my vocation. I also thought that a young man, no matter how meek he might be, suddenly learns to swear energetically if he becomes a soldier, a carriage-driver or a river dweller, so I reassured myself.

My charity and my ardent zeal did not take long to give me the reputation of an enlightened Casuist. My decisions were oracles; I was consulted night and day. Among others, a lady came to open her conscience to me, not in confession—I never mingle those in my dreams—but in conversation, as one does when one wants to have the advice of a doctor to counterbalance that of a confessor.

She had a great deal of difficulty explaining herself, but as Jansenists have a great penetration and know the human heart so well I saw clearly that it was a sin of the tongue and I told her that doubtless she had spoken ill of someone.

"Yes, Monsieur," she said to me, with a sigh. "What troubles me is that my confessor claims that I'm obliged to make great reparations."

I asked her of whom she had spoken ill.

"Alas," she replied, "firstly it was my husband, and after that a few priests, bishops and our holy father the Pope."

---

[7] It is not obvious why Mercier uses asterisks here, as he spells out the word "Jansenist" in full subsequently.

On hearing that declaration I forgot that I was a J   , and I told her that her confessor was right, that nothing could dispense her from the reparations that he demanded, that slanderers were veritable thieves of someone else's property, and of the most precious property of all, and were in consequence were obliged, at least as rigorously as other thieves, to repair the wrong that they had done to their neighbor; that in addition to that, there were aggravating circumstances in her crime; and that the quality of the persons of whom she had spoke ill augmented the malice considerably.

She dissolved in tears while I was speaking to her in that fashion; I did not know what to say to console her. I had a desire to weep too, for I have a tender heart; she left my study murmuring the word J***; that word put me back on track.

"Oh, Madame," I shouted. "I beg your pardon a thousand times; I was distracted when I decided our case. I forgot to ask you whether your husband, the priests and that bishops concerned are J***?"

"No," she told me, "they're all constitutionaries."

"In that case, Madame," I told her, "it's necessary to console yourself; the case is different. Not only have you not done any harm, but you have carried out a work of justice. In fact, it's a received principle that all constitutionaries are small minds, people who have no common sense, veritable imbeciles; in consequence, you'll sense clearly that ne ca say anything one likes about those people with a clear conscience. In any case, all the Appellants, even the women, are great men. I ask you, can great men sin in speaking ill of imbeciles and false devotees?"

I was about to give her other profs to support my decision when I was brought a letter, which I opened immediately.

A suck nun was consulting me to know whether she would do well to obtain permission to have herself taken to the tomb of St. P***. The question embarrassed me; I thought about it for a long time, and finally I seemed to me that I answered very nearly this: that great man had never claimed to be a saint; if he had been made one involuntarily, it did not seem to me that he could have performed miracles involuntarily; thus, the nun who was consulting me ought to admire the great Deacon and not invoke him.

Scarcely had I finished that response that I received another letter, but this one was a *lettre de cachet*, by which I was condemned to exile. I was delighted to see myself treated like great men; you cannot imagine how self-satisfied I was, and I understood better than ever how elevated my spirit was.

I obtained a few days in order to prepare for my journey, during which I received visits from several female devotees of great quality, who clubbed together in order to procure me a abundant subsistence in my exile. I departed for Brussels, only accompanied by two domestics, who announced me along the route as a martyr, which obliged me to lead a penitent life.

Having arrived in Brussels I put myself at ease with other J***s that I found. I cannot express the pleasure that I savored there; I sometimes sighed, however, in thinking about Port-Royal; the memory of that precious solitude drew tears from my eyes. In those moments of affliction, I asked Heaven for the convocation of the future council, and I finally thought that it had been assembled and that I could have faith in it. But I soon realized that I was in an assembly of young women, who had an old coquette talking to them about fashions. They were all so attentive and so animated that they did not pay any heed to me.

I listened to their discussion as best I could, but very little of it remained in my memory, because they were often all talking at the same time and the terms that they were using were, for me, detached from any idea. I understood, however, by dint of the reflections that I made, that there were three questions at stake. The first was whether something they called a toquet was or was not the veritable coiffure of a demoiselle; the second whether it was not time to finish uncovering the arm in its entirety; and the third whether there was not more charm in showing the lower teeth when laughing than the upper ones. The session lasted two hours without them being able to reach any conclusion.

Dream XIX

When I wanted to quit society and bury myself in solitude, my relatives opposed that design for a long time; but since I have been here they have forgotten me entirely. That indifference has often afflicted me, and one day, when I felt more chagrin than usual, having gone to sleep, I believed in a dream that I had found a treasure while digging my garden.

That discovery did not please me as much as you might think. I no longer had any ambition and I cherished my hermitage, which fulfilled my desires; what value could a treasure have with such dispositions? I took it, however, and I filled wooden jars that I had made a little while before.

Continuing to dream, however, I saw two of my nephews arriving at my home, who had learned—I have no idea how—about my good fortune. They made me the most urgent caresses; in order to please me they initially found my cell agreeable and my garden charming; then they represented to me that I ought, however, not to fix myself irrevocably in a desert; that I had a duty to my family and society, and that, finally, I was wrong to deprive them of the pleasure of caring for me in my old age.

I allowed myself to be won over by their insistence; I made my adieux to my cell, to my spring and my garden; I climbed into a carriage that my nephews had brought for my treasure and for me, and they took me to the city where they were established. I was received by my family with demonstrations of joy that penetrated me. I was delighted by the cares and attentions they had for me.

However, I soon perceived that I was kept out of sight, and that the friends with whom I would gladly have been on familiar terms were kept away. I also learned that they only talked about me with amity in my presence. All that made me understand, although in a dream, that my relatives' enthusiasm related to my treasure rather than me. In order to be more assured, I put myself to bed and I paid a domestic to spread the news of my death in the house.

As soon as it was announced, I saw my nephews running into my room, who, without thinking of me, threw themselves precipitately on my coffers. After having smashed them they began to fight, each of them wanting to have it all. At the moment when the combat became most animated, however, I got up indignantly, and they both fled.

Then I assembled a few old friends that I had in the city, I distributed my treasure to them, and, having recovered my satchel and my staff, I came to confine myself in my heritage forever.

Dream XX

I saw in a dream a small society composed of three or four women in the age of devotion, and, in consequence, devoid of rouge, and a young woman to be married. The older women were giving the young one advice, all that the same time, on how to curl and arrange her hair, and the rest of her adornment. One wanted the hair to be swept backwards, another was teaching her to make expressive gestures with her fan, a third to lower her voice, to smile in an agreeable manner, and a thousand other affectations. They criticized her harshly when she did not succeed at the first attempt.

For myself, I found her very pleasing without all those instructions. She interested me by virtue of her air of decency and candor. I saw that she was taking lessons from the matrons reluctantly, and that her complaisance cost her a great deal; she had tears in her eyes, but as soon as the old women perceived her irritation they overwhelmed her with an insupportable babble. It was necessary that ridiculous grimaces take the place of natural naivety.

In the end, after having almost reduced her to despair, and having exhausted their knowledge and maxims on the art of dress and behavior, they changed the subject of their conversation. They talked about malicious gossip. The dowagers protested against the bitterness, the divisions and the hatreds that the vice in question spread through society and the atrocity of blackening the reputation of one's neighbor. They made the most heated reflections on that matter.

"Look at Madame such-and-such," said one of them, "who slanders everyone right, left and center, as one throws stones."

"Truly," said another, "I think she's a fine one to talk about others; people also criticize her, thank God. To talk as she does, it's necessary that one's own conduct is better, or less known. How does she dare tell contain stories in front of people who know the part she played in them?"

"My word," added the first who had spoken, "there's a vestal who isn't worthy to guard the sacred flame. It's said that she's been in devotion for several days; if it's not a sham, she does very well, for after the life she's led one can't do too much penance."

"And our neighbor," said another, "what do you think of her? Have you ever seen anything so gauche, so crooked? She'd like to play young, as if we didn't know her age and her life. And her good friend? There's a woman of horrible malevolence. The other day she tore up five or six people of my acquaintance, in front of me, with an unequaled dexterity; it's necessary to mistrust that little monster; what a crime malicious gossip is!

"But," she continued," do you know anyone more slanderous than my cousin? Personally, I don't. She comes here sometimes, you can judge for yourself. What a fake! And her face, isn't it agreeable? Isn't she well dolled up, with her teeth, which she takes out every evening for fear of wearing them away in her sleep?"

They continued to tear apart that absentee, who came in while they were saying black things on her account. As soon as she appeared the old women got up hurriedly and embraced her.

"How charming you are," they cried, "not to forget us entirely. We were just talking about you, and saying a lots of nasty things, as you can imagine."

Dream XXI

I found myself, in this dream, in the home of a sworn connoisseur of all the productions of the fine arts. He was a man of distinguished birth, and in a placement that put him in a position to render service to artists; that is why I saw a crowd of them around him who had come to consult him and request his approval for their works.

He judged them in a trenchant tone, excusing himself when he did not approve by virtue of the rule he had made of not allowing artists to stray from the paths of good taste by a slack condescension. He only talked decisively. All those who applauded him looked at one another, laughing and shrugging their shoulders. In fact, the verdicts he pronounced with so much assurance seemed to me to be absurd. However, a great number of authors flocked to obtain his advice; one read with enthusiasm a freshly rhymed ode; another asked him to examine a partly-engraved illustration, pretending to be having some difficulty finishing it; a musician asked for his sentiment regarding a work of his making that he was about to give to the public.

The connoisseur replied to them all briefly and decisively, in a cold tone. Each artist, after having praised his taste loudly, withdrew, and I remained alone with the art-lover.

It seemed to me that I had more knowledge than he did. He showed me proudly some very bad verses he had written, and detestable music that he played on a perfidious violin, which occasioned shudders and grimaces that it was not possible for me to disguise. Fortunately, he took all that for marks of applause, and looked at me with satisfaction.

"Admit," he said, precipitately, "that this passage is pretty," and continued to rip my ears.

Finally, he granted me mercy with the violin, in order to enable me to admire a bad landscape in water color, which he copied, he said, a hundred times better than the original.

His apartment was in chaos. Heaped on the parquet, one saw books, manuscripts, models of machines, prints, antique bronzes, plans, musical instruments, medallions, marine plants and fragments of crystal. He had specimens of all the arts; one could scarcely move around in his study. On one armchair I saw a piece of old mosaic, seashells and a portfolio; and on the other hand, a canvas on an easel. Everything was covered in dust and cobwebs, which seemed natural to me, for I understood that no hand had dared to touch that savant disorder.

The master himself was in an extraordinary state of undress; he pointed out to me with pleasure the neglected appearance of his person and his study. "This is how one is obliged to be," he said, "when one directs the taste of an entire capital and also works oneself."

After that he made me remark the choice of his library, but I only saw dictionaries and elementary texts there, from which the man who had the insanity of believing himself to be a scholar had only extracted a partial understanding more pernicious that ignorance.

He also showed me a work he was composing on agriculture, but waking up prevented me from reading it, and I was very glad, for I suspected that, like so many others, he had never seen a single arpent cultivated.

Dream XXII

I went to knock on the door of an old friend. As soon as he saw me he delivered himself to the delightful transports of amity that can only be felt, and would only be weakened by more vivid and energetic expressions.

When the first moments of our pleasant agitation had passed, I told him that all his caresses had not made me forget what I was, and I begged him to remember that.

"I remember that you're my friend," he said, pressing my hand to his bosom, "And my heart will never forget it."

"But fortune has taken everything from me," I said. "I'm reduced to poverty."

"You're my friend," he said, again, "And in consequence, you can't be poorer than me; everything I have is yours, and from this moment on, I establish you as master in my house."

He lodged me in a very comfortable apartment and gave me a domestic whom he ordered to furnish me with anything I desired. It is not possible to savor on earth a happiness similar to mine. That tender friend had nothing hidden for me, and I could open my heart to him with confidence. Oh, what charms one finds in the effusions of a true amity! We withdrew into a small but charming study, and there we talked at our ease, without any other motive but hearing one another.

He had associated himself with three other friends almost the same age as him. They lived together in a mild and honest liberty. They communicated their enlightenment, their pleasures and their pains to one another. All four loved virtue and made it the solid support of their reciprocal attachment. They were well-meaning and had banished malevolence from their society.

The happiness of a dream does not last long. A sad objet came to trouble my pleasures. I dreamed that I had been condemned to perpetual imprisonment and that I had me to hide with my friend. I confided my misfortune to him and begged him to help me obtain mercy.

He set about it with a zeal and ardor that is scarcely conceivable, but, although he was loved and respected by several important people, he could not obtain anything by means of protections. It was necessary to spread large sums in various bureaux, and it was only by the loss of his entire fortune that he finally succeeded in abolishing my condemnation.

Alas, I wish to Heaven that he had not loved me so much. He seemed scarcely touched by having sacrificed everything for me. He even found a pleasure in the sacrifice that, he said, nothing could equal. But his heart, too sensible, could not hold against the cowardice of a false friend.

It was a man who had sworn him the most sincere attachment a thousand times, and who begged him in all his letters to give him the opportunity to prove it. He was then powerful at court, and could easily have obtained my pardon by mans of the Minister, but that Minister did not please him; he was never able to resolve himself to begging him in my favor, and my friend implored him to do so in vain in the name of the amity he had sworn; he got down on his knees but nothing could touch him; he replied that he was ready to do him any other service, but that one was beyond his strength.

My friend was pierced with the sharpest dolor; his generous courage sustained him until he had completed the task of my deliverance, but then, yielding to all his sensibility, bitterness gnawed at his heart; he died a few days later, leaving me in a situation difficult to depict, but which occasioned me sensations so dolorous that I woke up with a start, shedding a torrent of tears.

Dream XXIII

In the first moments of a light sleep I thought I heard a muffled noise near my head, which, not being loud enough to prevent me from sleeping, caused me to dream that I was witnessing a debate. The scene was in a large hall filled with people of all sorts. Two men in long coats were at odds. It was a matter of what is known in the schools as the contingent future. One said that there was one thing that had to happen, and the other sustained that it was something that might happen. Each one supported himself on the authority of all the ancient scholastic doctors. The entire audience was excited and took part in the heat of the debate.

One of the combatants, having made an effort to utter a cry of victory at the end of an argument, dislocated his jaw and remained open-mouthed, making a very ugly grimace. Then two members of the audience got up at the same time, each claiming the right of replacing the crippled champion. They both alleged in their favor the time they had spent on the benches and the doctoral letters that had been given to them. One said that he had received the doctorate in the month of April and his adversary in the month of May, and that, in consequence, he ought to have priority. The other, on the contrary, claimed the month of May was better for scholars than that of April, and proved it by means of a quantity of observations on the various productions of the earth and on animals.

As they spoke rapidly, the two men gradually drew nearer to one another, raising their voices, although they ought naturally to have lowered them. When they were close enough, they struck one another, without meaning to, while making animated gestures. The first who felt his rival's hand, thinking that he had been outraged, tried to take off his bonnet in order to take those present as witnesses to the insult he had received, but as his hand was trembling, he dropped it, and when he bent down to pick it up his adversary stepped on his hand.

Instantly, confused cries went up; the entire hall was filled with tumult; fighting broke out on all sides, and having woken up, I discovered that all those doctors who had been making so much noise were only a fly buzzing in my ear.

Dream XXIV

I am always surprised when I think how many times I have seen myself in dreams in the din of cities, having fled from it when I was there, and only being able to breathe in the country. In this dream, I was in the middle of one of those great cities where a continual noise reigns. It was raining abundantly and after having been splashed by several vehicles I had the misfortune of being knocked over in the mud by a carriage hitched to six spirited horses. I was quite sure that it was the fault of the insolent conductors, who, having seen my simple and slightly rustic appearance, had taken pleasure in maltreating me.

I got up very crumpled, and, seeing one of those public houses that are called "cafés" I slipped inside in the midst of the crowd that was going into it. I put my back against a stove in order to dry my clothes. In the meantime, I examined the company. I saw on one side passionate gamblers who went into a fury when luck did not favor them; they threw cards and candles at one another's heads, seemed to want to cut one another's throats, and, after having exchanged numerous insults, resumed their game with an admirable composure. Their table was surrounded by people who took sides in favor of one or other of the players.

Near there, I noticed a man sprawled in an armchair who was not fixing his gaze on any object and who was expressing his ennui with frequent yawns; I judged that he was one of those men one sees sometimes in society, who, being a burden to others as well as themselves, wanders from one café to another without any other purpose but getting to the end of the day.

Elsewhere, a man in a black coat was reading a newspaper intently and frowning. A young soldier, holding an advocate by the lapel, was demonstrating to him heatedly that it would be easy for him, with six hundred men, to beat and put an enemy army to flight by surprising them in a particular place. Several others were quarreling over political arguments and setting the courts of Europe to rights by shouting at the top of their voices.

What caught my attention more, however, was a group of fops whose extravagances were attracting the admiration of the entire café. They came in whistling, jumping, pirouetting, embracing one another, giving one another slaps of the cane and punches, singing, performing entrechats, saying all the stupid things that the language has thus far been able to furnish, showing ne another love-letters, reading them aloud, and then going to fight one another after having paid someone to come and separate them. With that, several young men barely out of school threw punches at one another very awkwardly, covering themselves with an inconceivable ridicule.

One of the principal actors of the café was a coarse joker who kept the audience in stitches by means of spicy obscenities, insipid gibes and revolting impieties.

While I was most occupied with these observations, however, I saw all those idlers metamorphosed into cockchafers, which, emerging from the doors, the windows and the chimneys, went to buzz around a chestnut tree.

Dream XXV

In this dream I believed myself to be exceedingly rich, and in order to make an honorable employment of my wealth I bought nobility with a fine estate, which gave me the title of Baron. I had illustrious armories painted on the doors, the windows and the mantelpieces of my château. I had them put on the hats of my domestics, on their stockings, on my horses' shoes, and many other places, but I had them engraved particularly on the books in a very voluminous library, which I bought expressly for that purpose.

When I had a sufficiently passable household, I hastened to go everywhere, taking visiting cards signed in the name of my Barony. I had the most beautiful ones made for Madame la Baronne, my wife, who was very well brought up and always called me Monsieur le Baron. We were very well received everywhere, without anyone disputing my nobility, because everyone knew that I had paid very dearly for it. I hosted great dinners, which disturbed my business affairs somewhat, and thus caused me to make the resolution to go and spend some time in my Seigneurie.

I wrote to my steward telling him to put all my subjects under arms when I arrived, in order to honor Madame la Baronne, but I had not taken the precaution of consulting her on my project; I only communicated it to her on the eve of the

145

day fixed for the departure. She flew into a violent anger, asking me whether I had married her in order to drag her into the country in the midst of peasants. She told me that she was not made for that, that a woman of her rank ought not to lie in slavery in the midst of fields.

That speech surprised me so much that I fell over backwards. I woke up and saw that I really had fallen out of bed. I got back into it, feeling bruised all over, and, having fallen asleep again, I dreamed that I had become a surgeon in a foreign country.

I was summoned to treat a little girl who had a very short nose and an excessively pointed chin. I promised to cure her. I had her pass into a cabinet where I laid out magnificent implements. I took some scissors of circular form and with the same thrust, without meaning too, I cut off both the chin and the nose. She pointed out my mistake, and, without being disconcerted, I told her that it had been necessary to cut off the nose in order to have a place large enough to fit the end of the chin to it. She liked that reason. I stuck the piece on as best I could, and, believing that I was going away, I went back to dreaming that I was a great Seigneur, but without my wife returning to my thoughts.

My lands, although very extensive, were not proportionate to my desires—which appeared very strange when I woke up, because I had never been ambitious. I therefore resolved to augment my possessions, and for that, I thought that it was necessary to become a merchant. But, one of my friends having observed that trade was not becoming to my rank, told me that he would procure me a very skillful man of confidence, who would render me master of all the funds of my Seigneuries in a few years. He did, indeed, send me the man in question, of whom I asked what I ought to do in order to become a richer landowner.

"Nothing simpler," he told me. "For a few years, leave in arrears the incomes that you owe your serfs; lend to them at interests for their needs, and when the arrears, the sums lent and the interest are worth half the wealth of each debtor, you issue legal injunctions against them. The expenses they incur will augment their debts, they'll abandon their funds to you, and some of them will still be your debtors after you've acquired everything they possess. If any of them find it easy to pay you regularly, and you desire their wealth, you can institute lawsuits against them for having supplied you with eggs that are too small, for having talked about you with insufficient respect, or because they haven't fed your servants, and a thousand other things that might come to mind."

As he finished speaking the man began to yawn, and his mouth, which suddenly became prodigiously wide, appeared to me to be the lair of the filthiest animals. He yawned for a second time, and as the opening of his mouth widened, his head disappeared into that void and the rest of his body dissolved before my eyes.

Dream XXVI

Although a sober life like that of a hermit is an efficacious means of preserving health, it has not been possible for me to avoid maladies entirely in my solitude; I have often experienced slight ones, and I have almost always cured them with a decoction of the leaves of a arbutus that I found very near my cell. The day that I made that discovery, I indulged in profound meditations on the art of medicine. I judged that it was impossible that the first physicians would have employed an infinity of harmful remedies before finding those that were not, and I amused myself by making a calculation with an awl on the bark of a tree.

I put in proportion the number of sick people and the number of physicians that there were per century in a certain area of land, and I discovered, by means of that operation, that each physician, living for sixty years, would have killed six hundred and thirty-six people. I went to sleep thanking God that I had not lived in those early times, and I became a physician myself in a dream.

I composed a great many soothing remedies, because I had for a principle that all maladies came from the overheating and effervescence of the blood. I particularly wanted to cure the inequality of humor that is in humans. I made my first trials in Holland on several women, who went mad, which surprised me greatly, because the plants I used contained a great many sedative and anodyne salts. I was not discouraged, however, because I explained to the husbands of the women that their wives had had an imminent disposition to rabies for a long time, which, thanks to my remedies, had been changed into simple madness A few even supported my sentiment with very good arguments and they all paid me very well. But as I had only been a physician for two days, I felt some remorse, which made me anxious and rendered me pensive.

I often went to visit my madwomen, as much to perform the duty of my responsibility as to examine what they said, for it sometimes only requires a word to make good observers change their theory.

One of them seemed to merit my attention particularly. Her mania was cleanliness, about which she never ceased talking to me. She always had a magnifying glass in hand, which made a grain of dust seem an enormous soiling to her. It was necessary to dust the furniture continually. She changed her clothes all the time. Her parquet, in which I could see myself as if in a mirror, seemed to her to resemble a hayloft.

I felt sorry for her and tried to make her change her way of thinking, but I was even more attentive to trying to extract from her folly some consequence useful to medicine. I therefore considered that, since dust appeared to be such a considerable substance to the woman, that substance must have particles susceptible of being magnified, and that those particles must contain others that necessarily had some virtue. Considering, on the other hand, that a very slight dose of certain poisons caused great ravages in the stomach and the entire human machine, which is a very large body, I concluded that the stomach magnified objects, and that, in consequence, dust might be a specific against all maladies.

It is a great advantage for society when it finds courageous men who put into practice the speculative verities that they have discovered by means of their meditations. That is what I undertook to do. I accumulated a great deal of dust, which I collected myself in several houses in order not to be deceived, I preferred that which furniture upholstered in silk caused to emerge, because the worm that produces that material contains a great deal of volatile salt, phlegm and oil, which it communicates to its work; the dust that has remained for some time on silk must be impregnated with the same substances and beneficent qualities that they contain.

I changed the color of the dust and formed it into pills, not in order to make it more efficacious but out of condescension for the patients, who would not have liked to make use of it in its natural state, and I mingled a preparation of antimony with it in order to render it diaphoretic.

I made the first trial of it on the madwoman that I mentioned, and the success surpassed my hopes. A few envious individuals published that, in spite of my remedy, she was still mad, but reasonable men rendered me justice. In fact, she no longer showed any sign of her original mania, and the one of which people continued to accuse her consisted of believing that her feet were so small that no one could persuade her to stand on them.

However, I do not know how it happened that, at that moment, I thought that the pills had become a poison that was doing a lot of damage, and by virtue of a contradiction of which one only sees examples in dreams, it seemed that I had embittered other physicians against me, who ought to have been singing my praises, since I was procuring them work and profit. In that extremity, I composed a volume of letters which were supposed to have been written to me by invalids that my pills had cured. That book caused the physicians to shut up, or at least prevented anyone for believing them. I also took the precaution of making a present of several boxes of pills to communities of monks, nuns and country priests. My liberality and my book spoke loudly in my favor, and in very little time

I received as many genuine letters as I had previously made false ones. People wrote to me from everywhere to tell me about the miracles worked by my pills, and I must confess that I saw something supernatural in that.

One country bourgeois told me in his letter that his wife had gone twelve days without opening her bowels, and having made use of my remedy, the effect had been so sudden and powerful that she had died of an extraordinary evacuation. He added that the death was not due to the pills but to too great an abundance of matter, which is very probable, since the patient would have been perfectly well if she had only discharged herself by degrees; but precipitation spoils many things, and, as Hippocrates observes, in order to be cured in a day, one is often ill for a month.

A monk who could not apply himself to study without being overwhelmed by drowsiness, was completely cured by the use of the pills, and he assured me in his letter that he no longer slept by day or night—which, he added, "is an inestimable advantage for me because I can now do as much work as two of our monks put together and thus make up for lost time." He then consulted me about terrible stomach pains that he had been suffering since his cure. I replied to him that he had the remedy in his hands, that it was necessary to continue its usage, and that if, by chance, the malady got worse, he should double the dose.

I was called to the bedside of a woman of quality who was dying, and I found six physicians there who were deliberating as to the manner of enabling her to live for one more day but who could not reach agreement. They received me coldly at first, and did not appear to think much of my knowledge, doubtless because my face did not prejudice them in my favor.

One of them harangued me, staring at me and making gestures analogous to his punctuation marks. When he had finished, I made my apologies for not having understood him and asked him to repeat what he had said. He recommenced in a louder voice, and, having listened more attentively myself, I understood that he was speaking Latin. I was very embarrassed, for I had forgotten that language. I replied with a few phrases in an Alpine dialect, which he mistook for an Oriental language and judged me very knowledgeable in consequence. Then he asked me for my opinion on the lady's malady, and as I did not want to decide lightly I approached her in order to take her pulse, and, having found that she was dead, I said that I had been summoned too late and that it was impossible to make her live even for ten minutes.

The physicians debated my response for a quarter of an hour, at the end of which they saw that the patient was no more, which gave them a high opinion of my skill; but I did not take it any further.

Dream XXVII

Everyone knows that hermits have to lead a penitent life and sometimes endure the dolors of hunger. I have followed that rule since I have been in my solitude, but it is not always duty that has been the motive for my penitence. I sometimes fast by necessity, and often out of idleness, because I prefer sleeping and dreaming in the grass to going in search of nourishment. So I often dream about meals, which only leaves me with a greater appetite when I wake up. This is a dream of that sort.

I believed that I was in the home of a rich Dutch merchant, whom I imagined that I had known once, and who was very fond of good cheer. My surprise was extreme, when the time for the meal arrived, having gone into the dining room, to find nothing but a hot stove. I went to the kitchen, and did not find anyone there. I went back to the master of the house and asked him whether we would be dining soon.

"We no longer eat in my house," he told me. "We warm ourselves."

I thought that he was joking, but he invited me to sit down beside him. "I'm speaking seriously," he added. "I've dismissed my cook and my maître-d'hôtel because I considered that everything one eats in a pure waste, and one is often

151

inconvenienced by it. I saw clearly that it was better to employ my money in my fireplace than my table. A good fire is better than a big meal. Besides which, while ne is warming oneself one can work, one can play, and do a thousand things that are impossible while ne is eating."

I could not appreciate his reasoning, because I was hungry. "I beg you," I said to him, "to have something brought to me, for I'm ready to fall in a faint."

"No," he replied, "That can't be done; no one here has dared to eat since I instituted my reform. Can one regale oneself better than being next to a good fire?"

I do not know what change occurred in my stomach to change the object of my dream. Doubtless I ceased to feel hungry, for I was no longer thinking about that; but I believe that I experienced a keen sensation of cold.

I asked him for a place near his fire, and, thinking that I was drawing nearer to it, I felt pinched by an extremely bitter air that struck my face and seemed to be arriving via the channel of a fireplace devoid of fire. I shall not pause here to combat those who do not want to believe these contradictions; I shall only say that while I was asleep, and doubtless at the moment when the Dutchman wanted to warm me, the window of my cell was open to the most violent north wind, which covered my meager bed entirely with snow.

Continuing my dream, I said to my host that I was very cold; and, by a bizarre effect of my imagination. I was speaking to him at the table. He served me in abundance the finest dishes of the meal, but I could not eat; I was shivering and blowing on my fingers. The master did not appear to pay any attention to my veritable need, and as I could see other guests who were sighing after a fire as much as me, I did not dare complain.

Finally, the meal ended, to my great satisfaction. I ran in order to be the first one at the fireplace, need causing me to forget politeness; but I was no more fortunate than those who came after me. Instead of the good fire for which I was hoping I only found a lamp suspended from the mantelpiece by a silver chain. I thought that I was mistaken, and was about to go out to look for another room when I saw everyone coming into that one.

I did not know what to do; I rubbed my hands and stamped my feet. Coffee was brought; I took a cup promptly, which I held in both hands in order to warm them a little, but they were so numb that they could not hold it; I dropped it on a magnificent parquet. At that accident, the mistress of the house railed at me with an anger whose like I had never seen, and made me all the insults that can emerge from the mouth of a furious woman. She summoned I know not how many domestics to wipe the parquet. Some brought sponges, others cloths, and potions that were unfamiliar to me. I notices that they all had swollen hands, and red noses, for I was still thinking about the cold that I felt, which rendered me insensible to the insults.

I left that room, I don't know how, and I went to the kitchen, but in the same way, I only found a lamp on a shelf there. I asked the cook whether the fire was already out; he replied that it was on the shelf, and when he saw my expression of astonishment he told me that in order to work in that kitchen one only made use of the lamp that was on the shelf, and that he had a secret for rendering its heat excessive. He explained it to me but I did not understand any of the explanation, and, imagining that the master of the house doubtless had the same secret for augmenting the heat of his lamp, I went back to the room promptly.

"Where have you been?" he asked me. "We've had an infernal fire; I sent someone to look for you in order for you to take advantage of it, but you couldn't be found, and you've arrived just as it's gone out."

I had more desire to weep than to respond to him, but I told him that I had not gone very far and that his wood burned with a strange rapidity.

"It burns all too rapidly," he told me. "I'm ruining myself in wood. My domestics cause me a horrible consumption. I protest, and hit them with a stick, but nothing works."

I could see so little wood that I could not understand where he got sticks with which to beat his domestics. A host of confused and vague objects filled my imagination until I woke up.

Dream XXVIII

One evening, on a fine summer day, I was sitting under an oak tree, contemplating the beauties that the author of nature lavishes on his works. That consideration delighted me and caused a sweetness and abundance of peaceful joy to flow into my soul, beyond anything that can be conceived of the most delightful. I went to sleep in that state and was transported in a dream to the summit of a mountain, which I believed to be very close to my cell.

I found on that summit a very extensive plain, planted with all sorts of trees and watered by various channels. In the middle of the plain stood a château, well constructed but of simple architecture and devoid of ornamentation. I went into it confidently, although I was ignorant of the character of those who inhabited it.

Scarcely had I taken the first step when I saw a young man coming toward me, who embraced me in a tender and cheerful fashion and introduced me into a beautiful apartment. He was tall and well made, and an air of candor and innocence heightened the beauty of his face. It was legible in his eyes that he was benevolent. He was wearing a long robe of smooth, light and clean fabric, with a blue ribbon around the waist. I admired him, and could not understand how a mortal could cause me all the satisfaction that I savored in gazing at him.

Soon, however, his wife having appeared, my admiration increased. As soon as I saw her, an involuntary movement made me prostrate myself at her feet. She lifted me up in a kindly fashion, telling me that so much ceremony was unnecessary for a woman who lived in mediocrity. I did not know where I was. I dared not look at her, for fear of diminishing the veneration that the first glance had inspired in me. She was the same age as her husband, and, like him, very simply dressed. She was weaving in wool. The husband was occupied with ivory, with which he was making the most beautiful things in the world.

He invited me to sit down and told me that one lived in greet liberty in his house; that he exempted all those who came to see him of the embarrassing conventions of high society, on condition that they exempted him from idleness. His dexterity occupied me very agreeably, as did his conversation. His tongue did not distill any malevolence; he spoke about his fellows with the interest of a brother for his brethren. He felt sorry for the nobles who buried themselves in idleness and deprived themselves of the delightful pleasure of benevolence.

"They make use of riches," he said, "to buy good cheer, beautiful furniture, fine carriages, and sometimes brutal delights that vanish when one has hardly savored them and give way to constant remorse. Why not seek happiness where nature has put it? One is only happy when one is content; it is the heart that decides on that point; it is, so to speak, the organ of happiness. Now, nothing pleases the heart as much s benevolence; it is the quality most analogous and most natural to it. External goods only appear to content it, only being a veil that hides its indigence; as they cumulate the veil thickens, and becomes a burden that fatigues it and prevents it from making its plaints heard.

"Oh," he cried, "if the rich knew how happy one is when one is benevolent! There is not one of them who would not want to spread his riches in the bosom of poverty. For myself, I bless Heaven for having put me in a place where I can enjoy a pure and solid felicity every day in making others happy.

"When I see that with a small sum I can dry up the tears of a desolate family; when I perceive that my presence dissipates sadness and spreads serenity over the face of an unfortu-

155

nate, and that a slight benefit charges cries of dolor into cries of joy, gratitude and benediction; when a tender child, snatched from the arms of death and returned by my care to his parents, comes with his mother to embrace my knees and tell me that I am his father, can similar spectacles not delight my heart? Can I stop the delightful tears in which the well-born soul finds is happiness?

"I would be less happy," he went on, "if I were alone, but a virtuous wife redoubles my pleasures by sharing them which me and enabling me to share hers. I go with her to the sick who appeal to her for help. We go together into somber and disgusting huts, which we render an abode of peace. I see her hastening to the bedside of a dying man, who recommends his children to her, who bless her. And when I receive the effusions of her benevolent soul, when she recounts to me the charms that she has savored in relieving misery, my stirred heart experiences the purest joy, the most perfect contentment that one can conceive down here."

Such was the conversation of that divine man; such were the sentiments of the two spouses for the poor inhabitants of their lands. They wanted to associate me with their excursion, which thy directed toward a hamlet where they told me that there were sick people. As soon as they approached, all the little children uttered cries of jubilation, which moved me. They hastened around them like lambs surrounding a shepherdess who gives them salt.

The husband went into a cottage in order to dress the wounds of a young man who had fallen from a tree and had broken his leg. The lady remained in the midst of the children, and taught them; she took account of their conduct, and recommended them to sincerity, obedience and avoidance of idleness, and caressed them all in order to animate them to practice the advice that she gave them.

While she was thus occupied, waiting for her husband, a young woman came, her eyes lowered and bathed with tears, to ask her to be kind enough to come and see her mother for a moment, who had a favor to ask of her.

The woman was reaching her final moment; her husband and all the members of her family were weeping around her bed. When she perceived her benefactress, joy reanimated her face, and gave her the strength to put her hands together as a sign of gratitude.

"My dear friend," the lady said to her, "have you some subject of anxiety that I can remove from you? Have you not entrusted me with the care of your little children? Are you not assured that I will serve as their mother?"

"Oh, Madame," the sick woman replied, "I know your good heart too well to be anxious about the fate of my children; I can quit them without regret, because I know that you will be more useful to them than me; you have already rendered services of which I would never have been capable; you have instructed them in their duty; it is to you that I owe the pleasure they have given me by their mildness, their obedience and the attachment they have for me; I am dying in peace, thinking that you will finish the task, and they will be even dearer to you when they no longer have a mother. Nothing attaches me to life but the pleasure of seeing you and loving you, but since it is necessary I will make that last sacrifice; I shall separate from you without complaint; I would only like, in dying, to kiss our hand."

The lady threw her arms around her, and I lost sight of her.

I found myself in the midst of a large number of reapers who were singing the pleasures of the country. They mingled the names of their masters, whom I had just quit, with their songs, and celebrating their benevolence. I listened to their rustic airs with an inexpressible satisfaction.

The time for the meal came and they all sat down on the grass; to begin with, each of them drank to the health of their Seigneurs, wishing them a thousand benedictions. I asked the oldest of them what he thought.

"May God preserve them for as long as Methuselah," he said. "They have only been living in this land for a few years, and they have already taken us all out of misery."

At the same time, he offered me a bottle so that I could also drink to the health of the worthy Seigneur, and all the reapers began citing different instances of his generosity, but I woke up, regretting bitterly that my dream had not continued, and that it was only a dream.

Dream XXIX

One of my old friends, having learned the location of my dwelling, had brought me some black puddings; I ate too many of them, and that was the only sin against temperance that I have committed in my retreat. I went to sleep with an indigestion, which occasioned me dreams analogous to the heavy nourishment that was inconveniencing me. I beg the physicians not to call that analogy into doubt.

I was transported, I have no idea how, to a frightful island called the Isle of Blood. No expression can render the horror that the land in question inspired in me. It was governed by a chief known as the Sansudourph, who was its absolute ruler; he had other chiefs under him, distributed between the villages and those chiefs, known as Sansuminadourphs, each had a great authority in his own canton. All those important persons nourished themselves on human blood, but only the Sansudourph had the right to drink it pure; the Sansuminadourphs mixed it with goats' blood.

All the inhabitants, men, women and children, were obliged at every full moon to draw from their veins the blood necessary to the nourishment of the chiefs of the nation; the tax was in proportion to age, and from the the of forty until death it diminished.

In addition to that tribute there was another. The Sansudourph and the other chiefs assembled their subjects to occupy them with various labors; they were animated with blows of an iron rod until they fell, bathed with sweat; that sweat belonged to the masters, who appointed officers to collected it with sponges, and those officers had the right to three quarters of it. The liquid was particularly for the usage of the women of the country; they distilled it and made use of it in the composition of a kind of lotion for reddening the elbow and the heel. They also made a beverage with it to animate the color of their flesh.

The wives of the foremost chief wore in their ears the hearts of two little children garnished with precious stones, and that was a third tribute that the inhabitants owed to their master after a certain number of moons.

Unfortunately for me, it was on the very day that the Sansudourph demanded the rent of hearts that my deranged imagination took me to that execrable island. I saw him emerge from his palace, licking his lips, dripping with blood, of which he had just drunk a large bowl. The officers were drunk on it.

He sat down and the child was immediately brought to him whose heart was to be given to him. It was a little girl, twelve years old. I had never seen anything so beautiful; her hair delighted me; the skin of her face resembled white satin painted pink; she smiled as she looked at her mother, who was holding her hand, and that smile caused me to shed a torrent of tears.

The Sansudourph was asked whether he wanted the tribute of blood at the same time as the tribute of the heart; he replied yes, but that, by an effect of his ordinary benevolence, he only wanted half the tax of blood. Then a vein was opened in the child's right arm, and the Sansudourph, throwing away the bowl in which he usually received the blood, took a kind of siphon, inserted it in the open vein and drank thus, in such a way that it was impossible to know exactly how much he had taken.

I had not ceased weeping, and yet I could not turn my eyes away from that spectacle. The child fainted; she was rubbed with her own blood in order to bring hr round, and her beautiful face became horrible, as if a rosebud had been dipped in bud. When she recovered consciousness and the apparatus had been placed over the wound, the executioner approached; that was the name given to the man who was responsible for extracting the heart. When I saw him taking out his implements I tore my hair; I would have liked to tear off his arms. Wretched black puddings, what a cruel night you made me pass.

The little girl was in the arms of her mother, who was washing her with her tears, and her father was holding her head. All of that was part of the obligation. The first blow that as struck caused her to utter one of those screams that have so much effect on mothers.

I had the good fortune at that moment to lose sight and hearing; that is why I do not know how the operation finished. I recovered my senses when it was over, and I saw the unfortunate tottering parents carrying away their daughter, doubtless dead, but who would live again, because the executioner, under penalty of losing his position, was obliged to restore life to the children who perished at his hands.

The black ideas to which the black pudding had given birth in my brain did not end with that spectacle. I went into a cabin inhabited by a numerous family. The nasty odor that it exhaled made me nauseous. I counted twenty individuals, men, women or children; they all resembled cadavers; they all tottered as they walked and had almost lost their voices.

An old man was lying on the ground, ready to render the last sigh. He was the father of the family. He saw around him his little children of the fourth generation; he wanted to embrace them before dying, but he did not have the strength; he begged his eldest son to lift his arms and put them around the necks of his children.

At the moment when he was holding two of them against his swollen breast, I saw three officers of a Sansuminadourph come in. They had bronzed faces, and grim and barbaric expressions. They told the unfortunate old man that they had come to collect the arrears that he owed their master. The sum was exorbitant, because the man had not paid anything for ten years, either for himself or his family, because of several maladies that had exhausted them all, and the Sansuminadourph had given him credit.

The dying woman was unable to reply. He made a sign to uncover his arms and show them to the officers. Then all the family members threw themselves at their feet; a younger daughter spoke, begging them to spare a life that could not last more than a few hours.

"The blood you take from my father," she said to them, "will not be worth the trouble of opening his veins; only a few drops will come out, and they will be tasteless. Leave us the consolation of seeing him expire without violence. If you kill him, several of us, already desiccated by sadness, will die of dolor, and those who survive us will be in no condition to give you anything for a long time."

The impatient officers imposed silence on her. "Give us your children," they said, "We'll begin with them. It's time that our master was paid, he's waited for you for too long."

Immediately, they opened the veins of the children and the mother, and left them motionless. They approached the old man, but he had rendered the last sigh when he had seen his family's blood flowing. They continued their execution on all the others, only leaving one young man, eighteen years old.

I remained alone with him; I did my best to console him, and I dared, in spite of is grief, to ask him for enlightenment regarding the credit or loan of blood, and he had the courage to satisfy me.

"Our Sansuminadourph," he said, "is a delicate man; he only wants good blood. When he finds a few families in his canton weakened by maladies or poverty, he waits a few years without demanding any tribute from them. But he has slaves that he maintains expressly, and from whom he takes the blood that the exhausted families can't pay. That's the blood that is called loaned blood. It's necessary to return it, when one is able to do so, and the tax is double for as many moons as have passed without payment. When the head of a family is on the point of dying without having settled the arrears, they run to him in order to take all the blood he might have, and that of his children; but they leave one person or two in each cabin to perpetuate the race and the rent of blood."

"What horror!" I cried. "What injustice!"

"No," he replied, "There's only injustice in a few cantons of the island, not in this one. Our priests have made laws in order that the interest on loaned blood should be legitimate; otherwise, the Sansuminadourph wouldn't accept it, because he's religious and has a delicate conscience. We're very fortunate that he left us for a few years without demanding anything. The measure of blood that we owe him at each full moon belongs to him; it's his property; when doesn't demand it, that blood circulates to our profit in our veins; so it's only just to return to him what he has lent us and the advantage we've obtained from it. The weaker one is, the more considerable that advantage is; because leaving a dying man the only drops of blood that are keeping him alive is leaving him his entire life; that's why he owes the Sansuminadourph his life and something more."

"And that," I said to him, "is also why you have just seen your entire family expire."

Dream XXX[8]

In this dream I had become a lax Casuist, and I was only able to comprehend when I woke up what the cause had been.

I put at the head of all my decisions these words from the gospel: *My yoke is easy and my burden is light.*[9] From that principle I drew the most consoling consequences. I dispensed all men of what they found too inconvenient in the law of God, and to anticipate their scruples, I preached everywhere that it was necessary not to read the gospel, because that book

---

[8] There is no dream XXX in the original, this one being numbered XXXI; however, the number XXXVI is subsequently repeated. I have therefore renumbered this dream and the next five in order to restore a coherent sequence.

[9] *Matthew* 11:30.

was capable of disturbing everyone, and that the morality that it contained was old and could not be in accord with present customs. I was universally applauded. I only found a few devout women who seemed a little surprised by my morality, and I excused them in consideration of their not having studied philosophy.

What brought my reputation to a peak, however, was a work that I wrote on loans and the matter of interest. While I was working on it, I received a letter from a prince very distant from the land where I lived, in which he consulted me on that matter. As I was in the heat of composition I think that I overlooked many inaccuracies in the response I made to him, but this is the gist of it:

"In order to respond categorically, Monseigneur, to the letter with which you have honored me, and to decide the question in a precise manner, it is necessary that I set before your eyes as summary of the explanation you have given me.

"The country of which you are the master is populated by very poor subjects who owe you large rents; these rents are a considerable part of your wealth. Your charity engages you not to demand them when poverty makes it impossible for your debtors to pay you, and then you give them credit. There are even some to whom you lend considerable sums in order to help them support a numerous family, who would succumb to indigence without that aid.

"When your subjects become less poor by virtue of the prosperity of the harvest, you demand the current rents, the arrears and something more, for having shared their temporary misfortunes. You add that famine has never left you hungry, having only deprived you of certain pleasures. On that subject you make the very just reflection that your wellbeing is a great advantage for the poor, because it puts you in a state to console their woes, which you could not do if you were inconvenienced by the general misery. Finally, you add that after several years of sterility, your debtors, having lost all hope of ever being able to reimburse you in full, have come to beg you to accept their property and to give their children passports to allow them to beg on your lands without risk.

"After reading this consultation very attentively, the undersigned adviser is of the opinion that the charity of the consultant is a heroic charity, since it appears from the above narrative that it has conserved the lives of a large number of people almost crushed by debts and the misery of the times. One cannot understand how such conduct can occasion scruples, unless one fears taking vanity from it, which it is necessary to avoid carefully. As for what is demanded in excess of the sums due, it appears that it favors the debtors a little too much, which is a small injustice, for one can see by the consultation that those debtors have drawn an inestimable profit from arrears and interest that they cannot pay, since that is what prevented them from dying of hunger. With regard to the funds, houses and other things that the insolvent abandon to their creditor, or which the latter takes from them—although it does not say that in the letter—there is nothing in that by justice and reason, although it is necessary to observe that if the property abandoned or taken does not have as much value as the debt, the passport that is given to the children of the debts ought to make mention of that inconvenience, and bear an injunction to the beggars to save from the alms they receive the surplus value of the debt."

Such was my approximate reply, and I completed my book on usury, but when I began to savor the pleasure of the applause that it attracted to me I woke up from the nightmare. Perhaps I did not wake up entirely, because what happened to me appeared to be another dream. This is what happened.

I was lying on my back. I felt my stomach pressed and almost crushed by an enormous weight. I could neither speak, nor breathe, nor make the slightest movement. I had no doubt that it was an old witch about whom I had heard my nurse talk when I was a child. She had assured me that she had felt her a thousand times, that she had seen her climbing on to her bed, that she had spoken to her and had often warded her off by means of the virtue of a certain root. There are impressions that reason does not efface. I thought, therefore, that the witch had charged me with a mountain.

In my fear I raised my eyes to Heaven. Then I saw my cell bright with light, and immediately, a forceful voice cried to me: "Wretch why do you also want to kill us? I've come to demand of you that you retract your decision, or to stifle you in my arms."

I no longer felt the weight on my stomach; that is why, being able to respond, I said, tremulously: "Who are you? And what decision is it necessary to retract?"

"I am," said the voice of the old man, "the man you saw die on the Isle of Blood. I died blessing you, seeing the interest you took in our misfortunes; I have not ceased, since my death, to recommend you to the Sovereign of the other world, who loves you, and who has permitted me to come and threaten you and punish you on his behalf. He has shown me a barbaric reply that you have made to our Sansuminadourph, who had begun to feel some remorse for his tyranny. Your decision has confirmed him in his cruelty; the inhabitants of the Isle of Blood will be more unhappy than ever, and will heap you with malediction."

"What!" I cried, weeping, "I have been capable of authorizing the barbarity of a Sansuminadourph! I have been able to contribute to the misfortunes of those poor inhabitants that I took to my heart! No, that isn't me."

"It is you," said the voice. And at that moment, I saw something like a finger of light, which, running over lines that I recognized as being in my handwriting, obliged me to confess my sin.

I turned to the wall, and I extracted a nail from it, with which I made several incisions, and I wrote in my blood at the bottom of the response these words:

I retract, I abjure, I detest, I abhor the present decision, and I wrote it without meaning to, in a moment of dementia. I declare anyone who approves of it and follows it to be barbaric.

165

Scarcely had I finished the last word than the light disappeared.

Dream XXXI

In a malady that I thought I had in a dream, I went to consult a physician who, by virtue of a strange bizarrerie, turned out to be the inventor of pills that I had invented myself in another dream, as you have seen. He spoke to me about them at first as the most powerful remedy that had been imagined since the origin of medicine. But all his words were punctuated by profound sighs that pierced my heart. I asked him the cause of the dolorous tone that he adopted in talking about a discovery so flattering for him.

He took some time before replying, and then uttered a cry. "Yes," he said to me, "the invention of the divine pills ought to have caused statues of me to be erected all over the world, but—would you believe it?—I have just been publicly hanged because of them."

I begged him to explain that mystery to me, and he continued thus:

"The initial successes of my remedy were very flattering; out of a thousand people who made use of them, only eight hundred died; then, having opened several cadavers, I saw evidently that they had died of poison. My reputation extended throughout France, where I was regarded as the restorer of humanity. I received letters of praise from everywhere, and often very considerable bills of exchange; in a short time I became exceedingly rich, and you know that nothing excites as much jealousy as wealth. I did not take long to have the proof of it. Certain charlatans, whose credit my pills had caused to decline, inundated the public with defamatory libels against me and against my remedy.

"The vulgar, always inconsequent in their march, lent an ear to the calumny, and, forgetting that they owed their health to me, turned against me. They all abandoned me; the fermentation of minds had begun in the north of France, and the fire spread to the coast of the southern provinces, only becoming more violent and more difficult to extinguish. I tried in vain to oppose the conflagration. I retired with two friends to the small town where you see me, in order to wait for the end of the misfortunes that threatened me.

"Rigorous information was fabricated against me; witnesses were suborned who deposed that my pills had depopulated I don't know how many villages. Several monks and priests attempted to support my cause, but they were not heeded; they were regarded as interested parties who enriched themselves by means of the sepulchers of the dead. I was hanged in effigy in twenty different places. I was sensibly afflicted by that, because I considered that the sick would be without resource and delivered, as before, to the ignorance or ordinary physicians.

"My two friends consoled me, enabling me to hope that the storm unleashed against me would die down, and that I would be elevated as much as I had been cast down. They reminded me of many great men who, after having been the victim of fanaticism, had become the admiration of posterity. Their speech could not dissipate all my sadness; I feared being really hanged in the end.

"Alas, chagrin brings about very humiliating revolutions within us. By virtue of dwelling on the sad idea of human ingratitude, I became ingrate in my turn. A benevolent man, touched by my woes, had given me hospitality and supplied my needs while sparing me the shame of having to expose them to him. In my somber reveries I imagined that the man in question was deriving vanity from his benefits and that he regarded me as a beggar. That idea revolted my pride. I became his delator. As soon as he perceived that he made me very mild reproaches, attributing my fault to the excess of my bitterness. But I took that conduct badly again, and, no longer being able to look at him, I quit his house.

"Scarcely had I lost sight of him than I was arrested and put in irons. I had no protection and I was accused by a large number of persons, so the very next day I was condemned to be hanged and dissected by the Faculty of Surgery. I asked to be permitted to swallow a few of my pills, and having taken them I died before arriving at the scaffold—which did not, however, prevent them from hanging me."

"You're dead, then?" I said to him.

"Yes, undoubtedly," he replied.

Dream XXXII

I believed that I was sitting under a leafy oak on a beautiful spring day. I saw a channel of pure and tranquil water in front of me, and in that channel an island covered with flowering linden trees.

In the middle of the island was a pavilion, closed in part by crimson curtains that were attached by cords and golden hoops. I perceived a prince there, asleep on a bed. Around him, silence reigned, and everything appeared to be respecting his sleep. A nymph was rocking the bed with her foot, in a playful manner, as nurses do to send children to sleep. She was leaning over slightly, and I saw mice emerging from one of her ears, with which her brain appeared to be filled. As soon as they reached the ground I saw one of them acquire a cardinal's hat, another a baton of command, and others sashes, medals and various signs of dignity. Then they became proud and disdainful men. Soon the island was full of those transformed mice, which all came to bend their knee before the nymph that had created them.

On the banks of the channel, meanwhile, I saw a numerous people who were extending their arms in a desperate manner toward the island, where no one was paying any attention to their gestures. Several wanted to pass over in small boats in order to expose their plaints, which would undoubtedly have been heard by the prince, but the new inhabitants of the island were agitating the water so much with their breath that it seemed to be impossible to land there.

Nevertheless, several old men, at the peril of drowning, threw themselves into a boat and attempted the crossing. Then the transformed newcomers threw themselves face down on the shore and immediately started blowing with all their might. A frightful tempest rose up over the channel; the boat was in constant danger of sinking, and the waves often hid it entirely from my sight. Sometimes I saw it plunge into an abyss, sometimes tossed by the waves. But those who were guiding it were so successful in their sage maneuvers that they reached the shore and disembarked. All those who had opposed their passage so vigorously were obliged to allow them to approach the pavilion, because they feared the justice of the prince.

Then the gravest of the company advanced in a respectful manner, and, after having made three profound inclinations, took a long scroll of paper from beneath his simarre, and began to read.

The prince rubbed his eyes, raised himself up on his elbow, yawned three times, and went back to sleep involuntarily to the sound of several instruments played by courtiers.

The old man, seeing that no one was listening, rolled up his petition, set fire to it, and blew the smoke respectfully up the prince's nose.

Dream XXXIII

I was traveling in a dream in the environs of my hermitage. I had taken a staff in my hand, put bread in my satchel and hung a large water-bottle from my belt.

I stopped in the first hamlet and went into a house with a thatched roof, where I found fourteen or fifteen little children clad in rags, but charming in their gaiety. The oldest of them was not yet ten years old. I addressed myself to that one and asked him several questions, which he answered very well. I gave him something to drink and amused myself helping the smallest ones to drink too.

A mother arrived in the meantime, one of two in the family. She was young and beautiful, although sunburned. Candor, innocence and tenderness were painted on her face. All the children threw themselves upon her and seized avidly a few fruits that she had picked for their nourishment.

When they had finished I took the bread out of my satchel and gave it to them. Then I entered into conversation with the woman; I sympathized with her poverty and asked her how such a numerous family could subsist, for I saw nothing but sad signs of indigence everywhere.

She replied to me that Providence was great and that, in spite of her poverty, she did not find the family too numerous. "God has given us good health thus far," she told me, "By dint of working we live, frugally, in truth, but in peace, and sometimes in joy. For when we're all together and everyone has bread, we savor a pleasure that can't be imagined.

"It's true," she added, "that the taxes, the Seigneurial rents and the tithe cause us a great deal of chagrin. When we've sweated all year long, and in the end we see the greater part of our harvest taken away, our hearts bleed and we spend a few days in sadness."

When she finished speaking she went out, and went to pick vegetables in a little garden in order to prepare the dinner.

I went to sit on the grass in the shade of a tree. There, thinking about the moderation of that family, I felt my heart constricted at not being in a position to do anything for the people of the countryside. *They can be rendered happy at such scant expense*, I said to myself. *What a pleasure it would be for me if I could go from cottage to cottage spreading joy in each family. What a delightful use of my riches I'd be making, if I had any!*

After I had occupied myself with such thoughts for some time, the peasant woman came to tell me that I was expected at dinner. A large plate of vegetables, water and black bread composed the meal. It had more attractions for me than the most sumptuous feast. The good humor and good appetite of the children, the unity and reciprocal tenderness of the two mothers and their husbands, were giving me an inexpressible pleasure when I suddenly saw sadness spread over all the faces of those good people. A bleak silence succeeded the joyful speech. I went pale with the others without knowing the cause.

"Don't you hear that noise?" one of the women said to me. "That's the Seigneur's mules, which the domestics are bringing here to take the wheat that we owe him, and which it's just to pay. But alas, what can we do? The hail has ravaged our fields."

While she was still speaking, the Seigneur's servants and soldiers sent by the exactor of the tally all came in at the same time. They were invited to sit down and one of the husbands ran to buy wine for them. Lowering my head, pensively, I listened sadly to the insolent speech of the valets and the soldiers, and, thinking that they had come to afflict the honest folk that had given me hospitality, my bile stirred, fire rose to my head, I stood up abruptly, and struck the ground with my staff.

"Wretches!" I said to them. "Have you no shame, to come to take away the nourishment of this poor family, who are going to die of hunger?"

At those words I was seized. The Seigneur's valets wanted to tie me up and take me to the prison of the château, but the soldiers took me from their hands, saying that I ought to be punished on the king's behalf.

I thought that I was going to be taken to prison then, but instead of going there I saw myself at the foot of the throne. I was not disconcerted at all, because I felt animated by zeal for the cause of the poor; I stared at the monarch and, seeing that he was not saying anything to me, I addressed him myself. I made a long speech to justify myself, and to prove to him that my fault ought to please him.

"Oh, Sire," I said to him, emotionally, "your heart would quiver as well as mine of Your Majesty saw the needs of the people of the country, and the barbaric manner in which they are treated on your behalf."

At that exclamation, the king softened and ordered that taxes be reduced. I woke up in that pleasant hope.

Dream XXXIV

For three days a violent fever had prevented me from writing down my dreams, but the delirium that it caused me had made me experience somber and extravagant ones, of which these are some.

In my first fit, I thought that a specter clad in white took me by the hand. Having made vain efforts to free myself, I followed him into a subterranean aqueduct, where the damp and the lack of air gave me the impression of choking. After having wandered on that somber route for a long time, I arrived in a vast space, but almost as dark and even more lugubrious. Vaults of a prodigious elevation closed it up above; the bottom could not be perceived.

That immense edifice only obtained illumination from three lamps suspended at a great height. The walls of raw stone were patched with sad branches of cypress and stalactites, produced there by the damp. Bats and a thousand baleful birds were fluttering in the vaults. Everything there inspired terror. On lowering my gaze I saw nothing but sepulchers, bones, niches filled with cinerary urns, and mausolea so disfigured by moss and earth that one could scarcely make out their form.

Meanwhile, my guide disappeared, after having led me into the middle of the edifice. Seeing that I was alone in that vast silence, fear took hold of my heart more than ever; a cold sweat ran over all my limbs. I uttered a piercing cry, which woke up all the dead. Immediately, I heard the rattle of bones that were reassembling precipitately. A host of specters stood up and advanced toward me.

I fell in a faint on to a tomb; but, having recovered the usage of my senses, I saw myself surrounded by several light shades with pale and fleshless faces. One of them started speaking to me in a low and extremely faint voice, although it was making efforts to cry out.

"Why have you come among us?" it said to me. "Who brought you into this abode of the dead?"

"My unfortunate fate," I replied, "for I'm still alive. An importunate phantom dragged me here, I don't know why." Afterwards, I told him who I was. I talked to him about my hermitage and the life I led there.

"You're wiser than us," the shade replied to me. "You'll return among the living, since you're able to enjoy life."

I began to familiarize myself with the shades. I asked the name of one who was speaking to me.

"I am," he said, "one of the men who had most ambition on earth, and consequently the greatest folly. You see the remains of Charles XII, King of Sweden. It was me who depopulated my estates in order to ravage those of others. This is where those endeavors that were the admiration of my century have ended. If I were able to return to earth and I were free to choose an estate, I would not prefer that of king, let alone that of conqueror.

"You see this shade beside me; it is his lot that I envy. He was an honest gardener who spent sixty years of peaceful life pruning trees, cultivating vegetables and savoring all the pleasures that country life offers in abundance. He was able to enjoy his being, while I, allowing myself to be dazzled by the false gleam of a chimerical glory, spent my days in a sterile agitation and cruel difficulties, always eaten away by desires and anxieties.

"Now that I am no longer prey to ambition, I laugh at the extravagances that it causes men to pursue. I admire, however, the providence that has permitted that malady to take possession of the human heart. The order of society would no longer subsist if conditions were equal. It is necessary that some men should be more powerful than others. Where would souls be found generous enough to take charge voluntarily of the cares, difficulties and agitation that government demands? Ambition causes all that to be passed over. One gives oneself the most violent movements, one employs the most costly maneuvers, often even crime and perfidy, in order finally to succeed in charging oneself with the embarrassments of command.

"But whatever the effects of ambition are, they are all abolished by death, everything ends with the tomb. These heaps of ashes that you see are the remains of the men who shifted the world and filled it with the noise of their name and their projects. When the fatal hour has sounded, it is necessary to quit everything and descend into the tomb.

"Do you see that sad shade? That is the superb Charles Quint, who wanted to unite the world under his scepter; that is what has become of his power. That other is Julius Caesar. That skull covered with moss that you struck with your foot is that of the famous Guido Alberoni, the adroit minister who guided Europe at his whim. These bones are the remains of Elizabeth, Queen of England. There is the dust of Mohammed, the ambitious impostor who gave laws to Asia. If I named all the dead that this lugubrious abode contained, you would see that nothing distinguishes here those whom the earth feared from the most unknown of men."

I woke up at that point; and, going to sleep again a moment later, I dreamed about tombs again. I believed that I had been charged by a prince with finding relics for a superb chapel that he was having built. I sought directions to a charnel house, which, I was assured, was filled with holy corpses.

I descended into it alone, and, after having searched for some time, I found that one inscription named Saint Aigrefin.[10] That name pleased me, and the skeleton was also entire and in good condition. I loaded it on to my shoulders, but I had only taken a few steps when it slapped me hard on each cheek with its dry hands, and simultaneously jabbed me in the back with its knee. I threw it on the ground promptly, thinking that a saint ought not to have so much malice.

Having started to reflect on the pains I felt, it occurred to me that I had a sure means of locating the true relics, but ap-

---

[10] An *aigrefin* is a cheat, or trickster.

proaching to each corpse the bruises that the first had inflicted on me. But I presented my face and my back to all the dead in vain; my wounds remained; from which I concluded that I had nothing for which to hope in that place and that I ought to make my research elsewhere.

I went into another subterrain nearby; I thought I perceived a monk on his knees before the sepulcher of a saint. I wanted until he had finished his prayer, and as soon as he had gone I lifted up the relic. As I fled precipitately, however, I fell a few paces from the sepulcher and I immediately found myself surrounded by seven or eight phantoms of evil appearance, each of which demanded a few limbs in a menacing manner.

The first was a Jew who demanded, in an insolent tone that I return his shoulder-blade. A French Guard demanded his skull; an old churchwarden with a halberd and a bandolier claimed that I had taken one of his legs. In sum, they all wanted some debris on my relic; I abandoned it to them, and the specters, having taken what belonged to them, commenced dancing an extravagant ballet.

I was extremely surprised. I was thinking sadly about the lack of success of my research when one of the specters approached me and told me that I had just visited the cemeteries of hanged men; I understood then why I had not found veritable relics, and, believing that my error was a punishment for the criminal design I had had of sealing them, I resolved to go to Rome and obtain one by prayer. As soon as I thought that I was at the gates of the city, however, I woke up.

Dream XXXV

I had just been reading attentively the mysterious visions of Saint John, known by the name of the Apocalypse, and those astonishing revelations had struck me vividly, for that which only slides over minds obfuscated by the multitude and the din of objects remains and is profoundly engraved in a placid soul. Sleep weighed down my eyes while I was still reflecting on that reading, and I thought I saw in a dream the destruction of the human race.

It seemed to me that good faith no longer counted for anything on earth, that people were only occupied in deceiving one another and supplanting one another; that impiety, seduction, broken promises and the most shameful crimes were only regarded as games, and that it was even fashionable to be blackened by them.

It was resolved to chastise the human race and afflict the earth with scourges appropriate to its destruction. I saw a carriage covered in gold plate and precious stones set forth, drawn by six horses; the individual inside it was named Luxury; the power was given to him to ravage the earth and to absorb two thirds of men, in order to charge the rest with an excessive superfluity. The carriage departed with an astonishing rapidity and marked its route by the indigence it left in its wake.

Another carriage, even more brilliant, followed close behind; the individual inside was named Finance; his stature was short but monstrously fat and heavy; his appearance was ignoble, his fingernails hooked and stained by ink. He snorted while he talked, and noisy hiccups showed that his digestion was laborious; rapine, pride ignorance and bad taste surrounded the carriage. Some held on to the straps, others were on the seat of the imperial.

The power was given to Finance to starve half of Europe, and the carriage set forth. I saw a troop of vagabonds who started trotting after it suddenly transformed into men stuffed with opulence, who, after having stripped everything in their passage, died of apoplexy and were replaced by other emaciated vagabonds, who suddenly acquired prodigious bellies, gouty legs and apoplectic necks, and died of indigestion.

I lost sight of them, and that scourge was replaced by another even sadder. I saw a one-eyed mule set forth, laden with canvas sacks full of old papers. The individual mounted on the mule was named Chicanery. She was an old woman, small, stiff and squinting; her cheeks were hollow, her eyes sad but ardent; she made efforts to hasten her mount, and seemed anxious. Her following was composed of a large number of meager and skeletal men with pale faces in flat wings and threadbare sleeves.

She was given a great power extended over almost all the civilized states, and departed at a gentle trot; those composing her cortege ravaged and exhausted everything in their passage, but they did not grow fat in consequence like those I had seen in the previous scourge; on the contrary, I saw them getting thinner as they spread misery, and they ended up dying of hunger.

For the fourth scourge I saw a kind of brown carriage appear drawn by a poor nag; the individual inside it was clad in black and had two blue lenses before his eyes, which caused him to see everything in that color. His name was Systematic Medicine; death was mounted behind his carriage. The last scourge killed a great many of the people that the others had ruined and impoverished.

Here I lost the thread of my visions; I thought that all men had cataracts, but with the result that the pellicles that covered their eyes did not deprive them completely of sight. Those pellicles were of different colors; I saw some that were jonquil, blue, gray, black, green, etc. Almost all young people had ones that were rose-tinted, and old people brown ones. Everyone thought that objects were the color of their cataract, and that disease was contagious. I noticed one man who saw everything crimson, and who had a brilliant and persuasive eloquence. He changed the cataracts of a thousand people in a moment, and rendered them the same color as his own, with the result that they all judged as crimson things that were not at all.

Everyone criticized and turned to ridicule others who did not see as they did. One of the band approached me and asked me what color I saw things; I noticed that his cataract was green and I replied, in order to please him, that I saw everything green. At that response, he embraced me enthusiastically and said: "Finally, I've found someone who sees things as they are. How unfortunate our species is! Everyone you can see," he added, "is blind; it's only the two of us who have good eyes." I understood that the man imagined that he was a philosopher, because he set about reasoning at great length about the various cataracts of his fellows; he criticized them and felt sorry for them because they were unable to see things as green that were not, as he did.

In the end, as his philosophical discourse never ended, I thought that I fell asleep, and ceased dreaming.

Dream XXXVI

I had once read with pleasure the works of a man named ; I liked his pleasantries. He had many admirers and novice authors valued his suffrage and benevolence very highly. Personally, not wanting to become an author, I contented myself with reading his works without seeking his amity. Once I was in my solitude I heard no further mention of him, and I thought he was dead, or would be before long, but I conserved a high idea of his merit and his taste, with the consequence that when I had written down the dreams that you have just read, I greatly regretted not having made his acquaintance, which would have been great help to me. Because, I said to myself, if I give this work to the public without some man of reputation having seen it, I shall be whistled everywhere, whereas, if Monsieur had been one of my friends and he had been kind enough to give me his approval, I would have been sure of a fortunate success.

I went to sleep on those thoughts, and I perceived the great man in a dream. Overjoyed by that encounter, I ran to him, but when I was close enough to speak to him, I saw that he was motionless on a tree trunk and covered by a swarm of little insects who were sucking his blood avidly. I chased them away with my handkerchief, and, having removed a few leeches that were attached to his body, I found that he was diaphanous and that one could contemplate all his interior parts, because they were magnified by the transparent surface, which had the effect of a magnifying glass.

As I moved closer in order to examine that singularity, a troop of all sorts of men in turned-down collars and flat wigs, whom I judged by their appearance to be minor authors, shoved me away, saying that they alone had the privilege of judging A***[11] As they persisted in opposing me, however, the philosopher blew on them and annihilated them, leaving me free to contemplate him at my leisure.

His blood, which was flowing loudly in his veins, was like a torrent of fire; it deposited a red powder in the heart, which, after having fumed for some time, caught fire and caused a rather powerful explosion, followed by a an odor that was very agreeable but caused those surrounding him a kind of delirium.

The heart, in addition to its ordinary ventricles, had three other cavities, each of which was connected to an artery and a vein; and as those cavities were very thick, that part of the philosopher had little depth.

Beneath the liver, in the place occupied in other men by the gall bladder, there was a singularly dilated vessel. Instead of bile, I saw a great spongy lake, brown in color, into which a bitter humor was brought by a stout artery, and taken away by other vessels into the sinus of the brain.

Like the heart, the brain had several cavities or ventricles. I noticed that in one of them there was a gland cut across in all directions by an infinity of exceedingly tangled lines, and I recognized that it was the gland of memory. I could see hardly anything in the others. The ventricle of judgment con-

---

[11] The author/philosopher in question is evidently Voltaire, whose baptismal name was François-Marie Arouet, hence A***. Although Mercier had no sympathy with Voltaire's freethought and his allegiance to the theatrical traditions of tragedy, he obviously took some inspiration in the present work and its predecessor from the great man's *contes philosophiques*.

tained a species of gland that was slightly weakened in several places. That one, which dilates greatly when a man reflects in order to know the truth, was partly closed by a desiccated and very hard pellicle, which often prevented the exercise of that organ.

That structure appeared to me so extraordinary that I wanted to study it with a particular attention; in consequence I examined it at close range; but how astonished I was suddenly to hear the following words:

"Groan over the weaknesses of celebrated men, but do not criticize them severely; distinguish the productions of different ages, never pronounce in accordance with the same principles on the fruits of passion and those of reason."

"When I had reflected on what I had just heard, I looked for the body of the celebrated man who had occupied me, but I could not recognize him; I only saw in his place a magnificent phosphorus, which, in consuming itself, only left me a dark gray stone, triangular in form. As soon as it had cooled down somewhat, I put it in my pocket to protect it from the impressions of the air, and, having started to reflect on the usage I might be able to make of it, I suddenly found myself in a chemistry laboratory.

I saw a man, black and sweating, who appeared to be dreaming attentively next to a stove on which there was a red copper vessel. He had bushy hair and a long unkempt beard; a glass mask covered his face and he was wearing a dirty loincloth. As soon as he perceived me he took off his mask and ran toward me, transported by joy. He embraced me, crying: "I'm the happiest of men! I've just found the regime of the supreme degree of chemical fire for the distillation of the black oil of colcothar."

I congratulated him and begged him to explain the usage of all the utensils that I saw. He did so with an urgency that delighted me, but I think I ought to spare the reader the description of the laboratory. After he had shown me everything and explained everything, I told him that I had picked up a stone in the place where I had seen a man disappear, consumed like a phosphorus; that if he believed that he could make use of it in his art I would offer it to him gladly.

He asked to see it. I showed it to him. He placed it on a block of porphyry, and, having put on his spectacles, he examined it for a long time with a touchstone, often chancing is facial expression and making gesture that expressed the various movements born in his heart. Finally, looking at me intently, he said to me, with an expression of surprise mingled with joy and admiration: "Is it really true that it's you who have found this sublime stone?"

"Yes," I said, "It's me, and furthermore, I saw it made by the fire that decomposed a human body."

"Oh, my friend," he cried, "let us bless Heaven; we no longer have need of anything; it's the philosopher's stone."

"I'm not far from believing it," I replied, "because the man who furnished the matter was a philosopher."

"Yes, my friend," he added, "I swear to you that it's the great work, for which people have been searching for a long time, and which can only be found by the sudden and instantaneous decomposition of a man. Chemists have not yet been able to capture it, but we have it, and it's necessary to enjoy it."

Immediately, he approached it to the cross of my rosary, which was made of copper, and which was suddenly changed into gold.

Such a fortunate experiment completed transporting my chemist; in his enthusiasm, he set fire to his laboratory, and I ran away, with the philosopher's stone in my hand.

I established myself in a great city, where I set about making gold. I changed the entire stock of a boilermaker's shop into that precious metal, and in a very short time I had prodigious sums. Then I saw everyone paying court to me, and although I had neither talent nor charm, people found me witty, possessed of good taste and charming, with all the qualities imaginable. I had a beautiful house, a superb carriage, jewels, and an infinity of other luxury objects; all that took the place of merit. I attracted the esteem of the public by the livery of my domestics, the suppleness of the springs and braces of my vehicles, the horses that drew me with rapidity, and the rich snuff-boxes that filled my pockets, which I changed continually.

Women, above all, were touched by my rare qualities. I saw them hastening around me. Mothers made their daughters exhaust all the resources of their toilette in order to please me. A prodigious number of those daughters wanted to marry me. Some employed affectations or coquetry to succeed in that aim, others played the ingénue. As soon as I appeared in a gathering, all the other men could no longer aspire to a word or a glance; all eyes were on me.

I allowed myself to be dazed by the pretended happiness that my riches gave me. Unfortunately, I thought about taking a wife. However, as gold had not troubled my reason completely, among all the young women who were seeking my hand, I wanted to chose the one who seemed the most modest and the least brazen. I soon saw, however, that it is in vain that one put one's eyes and judgment to work in discovering the natural in women of high society.

The day after my marriage I discovered how I had been deceived. My wife was quarrelsome, jealous, a coquette and a gambler. As soon as she had attained her goal she quit the deceptive mask, the tender and natural appearance that she had imposed on me. From then on she seemed to take it as her task to desolate me. She only sought to cause me anxiety. I could not go home without being criticized; she had only disdain in my regard, while she gave all the others a very honest welcome. Her expenditure was enormous, and I was continually obliged to make gold in order to pay her debts.

I was greatly surprised, however, one day when she had lost immense sums gabling, to discover that my philosophical stone had lost its virtue. That event, the insults I received and the bad manners of my wife drove me mad. Scarcely had I given the first signs of it than she had me put in an asylum. I believed in my madness that I always had her on my shoulders, scolding me as usual. I made continual efforts to get rid of her.

Finally, awakening enabled me to see that I was not mad, since I had no wife.

SEMIRAMIS

I dreamed that I had become an antiquary and that I had formed one of the finest cabinets in Europe. I was particularly devoted to mummies, and I bought them in all direction.

I had learned to distinguish the true mummies of Egypt from the counterfeits that the Jews make in order to catch Europeans. By chewing a little bit of the mummy I had succeeded in distinguishing an Egyptian skeleton from the skeleton of a hanged man put in an oven by the counterfeiters, then embalmed and covered with bandages and hieroglyphs and sold by clever rogues who make fun of profound scholars.

I was not a dupe of those impostors; I could almost recognize by the shape of the head the ancient Egyptians aromatized by a particular secret, who have transmitted their desiccated figures to us jealously.

They were lined up in my cabinet, and I rejoiced in saying; "All of them spoke three thousand years ago; they scarcely suspected that they would emerge from catacombs near Great Cairo to travel to Europe and come to Paris to satisfy my curiosity Here I am, surrounded by people dead and not buried, who had no suspicion that their bodies would belong to me one day in all propriety."

That idea pleased me, and I walked in the midst of those embalmed bodies that no longer had names, and to whom I lent the ones that pleased my imagination.

Making a review of my ancient black riches one day, I picked up the head of a mummy and studied it attentively.

"Who are you?" I said to it, in a low voice. "Who are you?"

Suddenly, the head made a movement between my hands and said: "I'm Semiramis."

"You? Were you beautiful?"

"Yes. I appeased a sedition by showing myself with my breast bare and my hair scattered."

"Did you build those superb gardens so greatly praised?"

"I had Babylon built; I built with magnificence on the Tigris and the Euphrates."

"You did truly extraordinary things."

"I reigned like a great man; I combined talents and courage."

"And what of your military expeditions?"

"I made several conquests in Ethiopia; I penetrated into India."

"You must have loved glory, Madame, with passion?"

"I was born for it."

"And those weaknesses of which history speaks?"

"What does it matter? The duties of the empire did not suffer therefrom. I rendered Assyria happy; I merited the honors of Apotheosis."

"All your ideas are elevated, Madame; I respect you greatly. But something causes me chagrin: you were a despot."

"A woman is very well-seated on a despotic throne."

"Why is that, Madame?"

"Because the harshness of the government was always softened by the pity natural to my sex, and by the ascendancy that heaven has wanted to give women. Pride blushes less in humiliating itself before her; and then, I love the arts and those who cultivate them; they were not assimilated to the rest of my subjects."

"But Madame, did you not refuse to hand on to your son Ninias the scepter of which you were only the depositary?"

"The scepter that I bore was not a deposit."

"But once again, dare I ask, did you, in fact, put your husband Ninus to death?"

"No."

"History says so."

"History lies."

"But Monsieur de Voltaire has written a tragedy about that, and credits you with remorse."

185

"Tragedies are fiction."

"And the voice of the world, which accuses you?"

"The world will be disabused."

"When?"

"When the day necessary for the truth arrives."

With those words the head became heavier again; it dropped from my hands and fell back into its box.

THE IRON MAN

I dreamed that while traveling in the valleys of the Swiss mountains, I discovered, in the midst of a chain of very high rocks bordered by precipices, a lair carpeted by blackened verdure. I do not know what curiosity, which tormented me night and day, told me to enter it.

I climbed with effort toward a sheer and steep place, aiding myself with my hands and feet, and I saw that someone else had been as curious and as bold as me; for there was an iron crampon and a large pulley attached to the rock that served as a dome to the entrance of the lair.

The entrance was difficult to reach, but I pulled myself up with the aid of the crampon and the pulley, and immediately found myself under a low stony vault, which formed a long corridor.

The juice distilled by the rock was petrified as it fell, and formed columns, seats and tables. I advanced, and I heard a muffled sound in the distance, like that of a torrent precipitated from the top of a hill.

I was not mistaken, for, having advanced, I saw the source of a great river that was running impetuously through a narrow space. Immediately, a loud voice shouted to me: "Temeritous individual, what has given you the audacity to come to this redoubtable place? If you want to avoid death, plunge into the foamy torrent."

And suddenly, I perceived a giant armed with a heavy club, who rose up in front of me, and the voice repeated: "Plunge into the foamy torrent."

Scarcely had I dived in than I felt my entire body hardening by degrees, and that I was becoming iron from head to toe.

A being whose grandeur and majesty were above the human, clad in an azure robe, crowned with amaranth, said to me: "You have the strength; travel the world. You are justice personified; act. I have endowed you with all that is necessary to exercise august functions."

My muscles of steel had retained their suppleness; my brazen arm was endowed with an extraordinary strength. With one blow I knocked over a wall; my hand was a catapult that launched enormous darts into the distance; I shook prodigious masses, and nothing resisted my impulsion, which was increased by any contrary effort.

Although made of iron, I felt the movements of pity and commiseration beating more forcefully in my breast. My heart was even more warmed by my love for my fellows; the sentiment of equity had become more powerful there, and my head appeared to be illuminated by a new understanding.

I marched through the streets, and, seeing one man striking another, I struck him in my turn. Any man who did not lift up his comrade, fallen by accident, I laid on the ground with instant correction. I punished insults and violence, and went in all directions redressing order everywhere that it was wounded.

All absurd, abusive or cruel usages I attacked without mercy, and my arm, although iron, was weary in the evening of redressing that host of ancient abuses. The prelate, the courtier and the royal valet, obtained no favor from my rigid equity. From the courtier who obtains charges and lucrative posts by trickery, to the pickpocket who steals handkerchiefs, everyone received a salutary reprimand to his face, and sometimes an expressive gesture, if the case required it.

The rogue, the knave and the scoundrel ran away as I approached; but I had their descriptions, and in my fortunate velocity, I seized them in order to punish them.

I encountered a tax-collector with a hydropic belly, carrying a sack of paper, for which he demanded a thousand louis. I took an equal volume with which to pay the insatiable

188

leech who dared to murmur, and I delivered the full settlement to the discretion of his famished clerks.

The usurer also had his share of my distributive justice. With the tip of my finger I erased the note of the young wastrel who had promised to pay double what he had received, and when I encountered in the street one of those succulent dinners prepared for libertinage, prodigality and hypocrisy, I took pleasure in taking it to attics where indigents without bread were awaiting the help of charity in order to eat.

I saw a man who had betrayed the fatherland; I made him get down from his carriage in front of his numerous domestics and I marked his forehead. I engraved three letters on the cheek of another, who had delayed a fortunate epoch by criminal insouciance. The poltroon received a kick in the rear and the dastard who had counseled lucrative infamies saw his ears hang down over his broad shoulders.

I opened the prisons suddenly; any murderer was put to death in an invisible instant; I fustigated thieves rudely and sent him to the public works; the calumniator was punished in the same way.

My metamorphosis had given me justice in spirit, rectitude in the heart and firmness in the soul. I was the prompt redresser of the most inveterate abuses, and consequently, I had a great deal to do; for my justice was simultaneously remunerative, punitive and civil.

But as it was often the law that committed the sin, I effaced all the old edicts already struck by public scorn, and which even the tribunals dared not reawaken for fear of attracting universal criticism.

No lieutenant of police, I assure you, ever did his duty better; my elastic arm took the place of sixty assistants; I did my own spying, for my legs were as indefatigable as my arms, and I ran from the gilded drawing-room to the obscure tavern. Here I snatched the cards from the frantic hand of the gambler, there the bottle from the drunkard's mouth; no sentence was belated, the punishment following the crime swiftly; one of the flicks of my fingers was worth the hundred blows of the stick applied to a Chinaman on the command of a mandarin.

My ears were endowed by an exquisite sensibility. I could hear three leagues away when anyone appealed to me, and arrived more rapidly than mounted police at the gallop. My flashing eyes caused the guilty to pale; he was half punished by that devastating gaze.

When I crossed the streets, I distinguished the idle man who was walking to consume time, and I imposed a task on him.

Whoever passed by was obliged to look me in the face and tell me what his employment was. If he had none, he was fustigated severely.

I approached a fortress containing prisoners who were neither murderers, nor thieves, nor seditious. I saw a man for forty who, delivered to his reflections, was detained in profound idleness, and more insupportable than all the rest. I asked him what the reason was.

"It was for having moved the tip of my tongue," he told me, "Which did not cause a single hair to fall from all the ample wigs that decided my captivity."

Another had moved three fingers of his hand, one of which was slightly stained with ink, which had not occasioned the fall of a single tile throughout the kingdom, and he was guarded under thirty bolts.

I let them both out of their cells, shrugging my shoulders in pity because the pride of men in high places dared to take liberty away from citizens on such frivolous pretexts.

I perceived the palace of the Law, and attached these verses to it:

Justice is of kings the most noble sharing,
Of their grandeur it is the firmest support;

The true image of God enters into their bearing,
And other virtues, without which they are naught.

Having entered a house with columns, I saw little wheels and men in robes and turned-down collars surrounding them. I asked what it was.

"It's a game," I was told, "Which is played before that which is most serious."

Immediately, children with rounded cheeks appeared, who had cakes and a great appetite. They were about to eat them when a voice cried: "Don't eat your cakes, my friends; give them to me; because, for one cake I will give you back fifteen; for two, two hundred and seventy; for three, five thousand five hundred; and for five, a million cakes."

The children opened their eyes wide and repeating "A million cakes!" fought and overcame their appetite. That magnificent promise was so attractive that they glimpsed in that game the prospect of a splendid meal for that day, the next and all the days of their life.

They sacrificed the pleasure of the moment, therefore, and having clubbed together they had a hundred cakes. Their gaze was attentive to the movement of the wheels, and shone with the keenest hope.

The wheels turned under the reflective and composed eyes of the grave magistrates, and all that was returned to the poor children, standing on tiptoe in order to see better was four cakes; so that pitiless egotism, the motor of those perfidious wheels, had devoured arithmetically ninety-six of them.

As the children wept, the magisterial voice, to console them, said: "Play constantly five or six hundred thousand times in succession, and you will surely be lucky; keep playing, my little friends, in order that you will be permitted to play."

Alarmed by the inequality of that barbaric and dangerous game, I broke all the wheels, in order that there could be no more question of that wicked custom, which stole from poor children deceived by hope the cakes that they would have eat-

191

en with a sensitive appetite, which would have enabled them to grow for the service of the fatherland. They remained stunted, their legs frail, and the ninety-six cakes passed on to tables where men were sitting who nibbled food with superb and disdainful teeth, who did not feel the need of hunger, and who gave the stolen cakes to their valets and their dogs.

I went to a famous sepulcher where royal cadavers lay; I said, like the Egyptian, "Emerge, impious cadaver, that you might be judged."

He got up, trembling. The people present, who recognized him, thought he had been resuscitated and uttered a long cry of pain.

I said to the cadaver: "Standing, do you hear the maledictions that you have merited. You might be buried in the superb pyramids the Egyptians have built; you might be surrounded by obelisks and monuments charges with trophies, and your memory would be the same. Fall back into death with the opprobrium that ought to accompany your name. Would you not give, presently, all your past grandeur for one single virtue?"

The cadaver uttered a long moan, and fell back into death and eternal opprobrium.

I became, above all, the enemy of all the multiplied bureaucrats that hinder and vex commerce, fatigue the traveler and cause him to curse the beautiful roads of the kingdom.

I expelled those hirelings scribbling on ruinous paper, with a rare sensuality, a mocking contentment and an inexpressible satisfaction. I broke their pens, more maleficent than daggers; I dried up their detestable inkwells, and there was no more question of those idle and voracious scribes, *omnes sedentes in telonio.*[12]

To signal the triumph I gave a meal to forty peasants on the same green baize where those insidious systems, so fecund in rapine, had been meditated.

---

[12] "Everyone sitting in toll-booths."

The unfortunate who, for a handful of salt or a pound of tobacco, had been treated as one of the great enemies of society, had salt and tobacco, and the monarch was richer for it.

The tribunals that had rendered these strange sentences no longer existed. I did so well that there was more money in the royal coffers, and no one went to the galleys for having sneezed, or salted his cooking-pot.

I took against other self-important clerks whose slender knowledge was flaunted in a host of equivocal operations.

They all had despotism in the head and in the heart. Absolute in their futile ideas, they took a malign pleasure in weighing upon all merit the hammer of the power that was sometimes at their disposal momentarily. They would have liked people to believe them the depositories of all political enlightenment, and took a puerile pride in having operated very petty things with enormous means.

Jealous of everything that did not emanate from their Minerva, they were determined that everyone should believe their works the ultimate effort of a profound and mysterious science, and their ignorance of true principles was veiled by a mass of words with which they complimented themselves, in order to complete their ridiculousness and ineptitude.

How I detested those frivolities, the insolent luxury of a few individuals whose superfluity was subsidized by the necessity of so many unfortunates, that troop of artistes useless to the whole world. I put to flight those petty architects, those painters, those decorators, etc., who had made fashionable those varnished cages, those filthy boudoirs, those rotundas, and, in sum, all those trinkets of futile ornamentation veritably made to scandalize the gaze of any sane person.

At the sight of all the foundations of various kinds, laid in various places, which are waiting for, and will wait a long time for, the final touches of the architect, I realized that patience was the rarest virtue, especially among the French. The science of great men has always been estimating the execution of works in accordance with their grandeur, and their grandeur in accordance with time.

I reminded the men in place of these principles, for projects no longer have either depth or maturity when one wants to hurry everything and does not give anything time.

And I engraved on a slab of marble: "Whoever you are, do not start anything unless you are certain of being able to finish it; be jealous of finishing rather than undertaking."

The slightest reform occasioned the strongest clamors in the part of interested parties; one, subjugated by his idleness, did not want to examine the question. It would have been necessary to ascertain the facts, which he did not want to do. Another had heard his grandfather say that all novelties were dangerous. A third examined everything with the telescope of personal interest. Then ignorance, malevolence, envy and avarice heaped upon any proposal the titles of ideal and chimerical projects, and the terms innovator and visionary were not spared.

But my brazen arms remedied everything. I expelled from his place the apathetic and indolent man who saw nothing but the revenues of his position, who was only afraid of losing them; his inaction, further prolonged, would have augmented the corruptive ferment, and everything would have been vitiated, when his belated retirement had exposed the exposed the wounds inflicted by his negligent timidity.

A man having said that the creditors of the State had no other debtor than the King, and no other guarantee than his will, I gave him a slap, and cried out: "A contract made to the profit of the state and founded on public faith must be national and bound to the state that it has alimented as the entrails to a human body. Anyone who contradicts me on that will feel the strength of my arms."

I distributed in large quantities the following quatrains; I put them in the hands of everyone; I gave them to passers-by in the same profusion that certain charlatans spread their deceitful and self-interested advertisements.

Men, to aid one another, received the supreme law.
Who wants to live for himself must live for others.
The ingrate can forget what he owes to his brothers,
But generosity is generosity's own reward.

Against the conscience there is no refuge;
It speaks in our hearts, nothing stifles its voice,
And of our actions it is simultaneously
The law, the accuser, the witness and the judge.

We obtain everything from God, including virtue.
What do we not owe to that supreme Being,[13]

---

[13] Author's note: "I sense that there is a God, and I do not sense that there is not. I conclude that God exists, because that conclusion is in my nature. I hold in my heart and mind to the doctrine of Socrates, who said that: 'God is unique and simple in nature, born of himself, only veritably good and unmixed with any matter or conjoined with anything temporary.'

"The infinite Being who preceded time, who exists by virtue of himself, cannot emerge from his sublime grandeur to allow himself to be grasped by our thought. Our thought cannot know that which is above itself, and we can only glimpse God under the features of the intelligence and wisdom imprinted on the globes and on the atom.

"Cold materialist, who calumniates human beings, do you see them taking pleasure in their state of abjection and misery, embracing a voluntary ignorance? See, on the contrary, the immensity of desires that is fermenting in the human bosom; see the features of grandeur on the face surrounded by misfortune; see the elevation of human thought alongside the weakness of the human arm.

Who, for love of good and verity,
Deigns to associate humans with his divinity?

No, humans do not die; that is a gross error,
It is a frightful blasphemy to believe them mortal;
Once one day, freed from their vile dust,
The unexpected guest will possess the heavens.

Do you think you are alone, a solitary being?
No, God follows, hears and sees you everywhere.
Dread that in your heart some shameful mystery
Might insult his presence and wound his eyes.

It is not to us alone that our life belongs;
Of the brief moments that Heaven afford us,
To holy amity we owe a part,
And the rest to the fatherland.

"And what attests their sublime origin is that they adore and prostrate themselves before virtue, while their determination for good is depraved by the lure of a feeble sensation.

"Can the man who contemplates in the silence of the night all the circling worlds—the host of heavenly bodies sown in the expanse, the foundation, the grandeur, the immensity of that marvelous edifice, all those brilliant stars—prevent himself from rising higher to the hand that fabricated and sustains that magnificent dome?

"Does not the soul sense the divinity distributed in the animate world? A leaf of a tree is the abode of a republic of tiny beings that savor the pleasures of life and reproduction. And that profusion of existence accorded to that infinite multitude of insects is only an effusion of the inalterable bounty that forms pleasure and pours it into the heart of an earthworm as into the human heart.

"See the article on God in my work entitled *Mon bonnet de nuit*, vol. 4, Lausanne edition."

Of our wealth and woes the uncertain measure
Is in opinion more than in nature.
Which is the most beautiful color? That of modesty,
Which engraves the innocence of the heart on the face.

Frank in ambition and desire,
Poor mortal, spend a life
Close on whose heels death follows.
A little suffices for the wise;
And to make a short voyage,
Few preparations are necessary.

One is a king when one masters oneself,
When one subjugates one's passions,
When of foolish ambitions
One does not sense the smitten soul,
And when, of a vain people, one scorns
The vain acclamations.

"The more delights the senses receive, the fewer ideas the soul has. Those vivid and frequent pleasures rob reason of fine and profound perceptions. A man requires a frugal life in order for his understanding to remain healthy. The man who eats too delicately can no longer eat after a few years. If sensual pleasure dominates you, you will soon be its slave, and you will no longer able to experience anything but ennui...."

That is what I said to a prince, who did not understand me; I was annoyed by that, because he was likeable.

Another prince confessed to me that in the midst of sensual delights he had encountered frightful voids. I advised him to set about doing good throughout the extent of his domains. He was disposed to do it, but, alas, he did not have sufficient substance to be veritably sensitive, to be able to weep, to be able to savor the keen and sweet joy that follows and recompenses a good deed, to be able, in sum, to sense the intoxication that accompanies the condition of a sublime sentiment.

When it is reflection, and not sentiment, that informs certain princes that there are unfortunates, their virtues are completely wasted and they do not feel that generosity and benevolence have something divine about them; that can only be felt by souls exercised in benevolence, for whom goodness of soul in not a phrase devoid of meaning.

A poet once said these beautiful lines to a prince:

Pleasures and grandeurs cannot fulfill my desires;
An instant of virtue renders me happy.[14]

I saw a very astonishing phenomenon; it was a minister of war fully occupied in making peace. All that was lacking then was to see a controller of finances finally renouncing loans, which ruin future generations.

My power did not extend as far as that; people abuse as long as they have the scope....

All the laws were enunciated in clear and precise terms. "It is necessary that laws by brief," said Seneca, "in order that the ignorant can easily grasp their spirit."

On seeing the host of nubile damsels that populate society, whom one sees everywhere, silent and cold, in the presence of their mothers, that idle regiment displeased me, and the hindrance and constraint that they experienced went to my heart.

Nothing seemed more ridiculous to me than those fully-grown damsels attached to their mothers' skirts, going around with her. Those white mummies bore on their faces the imprint of dissimulation. The endless slavery imposed on nubile young woman, so frequently victims of their complexion, appeared to me to be unjust and contrary to the laws and advantages of society. Whoever thinks himself able to study the

---

[14] The lines are from *Le Diogène d'Alembert, ou Diogène décent* (1754) by André-Pierre Le Guay de Prémontval.

character of his mistress under the eyes of her mother is absolutely mistaken. Damsels do not dare anything, while their mothers permit themselves everything. What is more likely to give birth to falsity and the very dangerous idea of only regarding marriage as an open door to licentious liberty?

I took those amiable creatures under my protection, to whom the usage of sentiment is refused at the age went sentiment develops, and which is the most active and most fecund in virtue. I stole from those jealous and arrogant mothers the sensible slaves of whom they made a display and over whom they exercised their countless caprices. I wanted those interesting creatures to cease to be useless to themselves and to others.

I brought in a law that liberated all young women at the age of twenty-one and which, at that epoch, which is no longer childhood, rendered them independent and absolute mistresses of their person; for nature has given women, in a short span, so much suffering, that pleasure belongs to them in their youth, which goes by so rapidly for them, alas, and which, as one philosopher has said "they are, in a sense, forced to live urgently,"[15] because soon dolor, the loss of their charms and the solitude that is a consequence of it, will consume a life that it has pleased nature to abridge. That rigor of fate can only be corrected by at least giving them the fine days marked for their enjoyment, temporary days that it is inhumane to immolate to arbitrary conventions, when their sensibility is in full flower and spreads its perfumes around them.[16]

---

[15] The quotation is attributed elsewhere to a Dutch physician named Walter Vandoevren (1730-1783).

[16] Author's note: "The role of the young woman, in the midst of modern mores and institutions, is the cruelest role in the world. If a young woman is melancholy, it is said that she is tormented by the need to have a lover. If she is cheerful and frivolous, that enjoyment scarcely touches her reserve; she can neither laugh not sigh. She is required to be young and not to be.

Young women of twenty do not have our ambition, our business affairs, our speculations, our voyages and our fatigues. It is therefore necessary to leave them free in the sentiment that occupies them. Their imagination is more lively and less distracted than ours; it is, in consequence, concentrated on a sole and unique object. The conjugal bed is almost the only place where an honest woman has enjoyment without danger and without remorse; it is her empire and her throne, from which she only descends with regret. Let us not criticize her; she buys pleasure dearly enough when she fulfills her duties. All fully-grown damsels, whose youth—which is to say, their life—had been pitilessly stolen from them, who were slowly drying out and dying of chagrin and ennui, thanks to me, would have the liberty of loving as they wish and transforming, in accordance with their choice, a lover into a husband. Happiness would be within their reach while the insouciance of youth permitted it to them. Those interesting crea-

---

"The sentiment that departs from a new heart is better than the sentiment that dissimulates, and these young women, who can never say a word of what they feel so strongly, are nearer to their fall than those who make naïve confessions of the pleasure they have in seeing their lover.

"The countless damsels who cover the whole of France and who can neither marry nor live in celibacy, whose still in habit and overload the parental house at twenty-five, as if they were only ten, form a spectacle that is simultaneously saddening and risible. What are those grown women doing with their mothers when they could be mothers themselves? What figure do they present to their father? They sense themselves how out of place they are. All morality senses the necessity of a law or a custom appropriate to reform our civil institutions, which, foolishly amalgamated with religious and narrow ideas, renders half of all women invincibly unhappy. There is, therefore, a piquant, curious and philosophical new book to be written entitled *Des Demoiselles*. Perhaps I will write it one day. In the meantime, let no one steal my title."

tures would no longer be seen wasting their best years displaying in society the petty and puerile ideas that give birth to an absolute slavery, for it destroys sentiment at length, and even virtues.

Pleasure enters into the essence of human being and the order of the world. Pleasure is the magnet of our nature, the soul of our actions. All animals seek it and deliver themselves to it. The appetite for regulated pleasure serves the interests of society rather than harming it.

I wanted the people to have fêtes and games. Refraining from troubling their recreations, I preferred to see them slightly turbulent that in the moroseness of constraint.

I made use of music and its distractions. Music is a fifth element for certain sensible souls; it given sensations to those who have none.

Dancing was not forgotten. The indolence of a muscle obliterates it and it is punished for its inaction by losing the solidity and play with which nature endowed it. All the muscles of the people went well—very well—and that animate tableau formed, under my gaze, the most interesting of all spectacles.

Many things related to public wellbeing are ordinarily neglected because they are possessed in common. *Communiter negligitur quod communiter possidetur*;[17] and the proverb says:

The community's donkey
Is always the most beaten.

I appointed an inspector who gave me advice of all the degradations that a public inconvenience could occasion, for the police are only made to confront all dangers.

---

[17] "Everyone neglects what everyone possesses."

Convinced that Nature has treasures of great value in her storehouses, which she reserves for us at the moment when we are thinking about them the least, that some of them are before our eyes although we do not see them, and that important discoveries have been the fruit of chance rather than experience, I recompensed all those who interrogated Nature, and the slightest well-designed or well-conducted experiment prevailed over theoretical volumes.

Who can explain the formation of the substance of the brain, which, soft and ductile, conserves in its folds and with the greatest order, the images of everything that we have seen heard and learned since our most ender childhood? Ideas, reflections and sentiments are all clear and distinct. The representation of an object comes after sixty years to strike us as vividly as if it were still present. The ideas that we try to chase away are those that return with the brightest colors. What is more astonishing than the structure of that organ, the seat of thought?

I made those reflections while seeing an anatomist dissect a brain. I made them to him, because he was searching for a fibril and was becoming impatient at being unable to find it.

Every human sense offers a tissue of miracles, and when one thinks of the incomprehensible enchainment that links them, there is no longer a language to celebrate it.

How pitiful a prince is when he seriously considers himself to be made of a finer clay than the rest of humankind! A vain individual of that sort is an ignoramus who can never be truly good. There are no generous souls but those that are sensible—which is to say, who have meditated on the nullity of grandeur and the reality of virtues; it is the practice of noble actions that teaches us to feel and think.

Intelligence purifies the heart, forms it, subjugates it to the truth, and removes arrogance therefrom, which is only a usurpation made by a depraved imagination over natural common sense. Heraclitus put it well: "Self-esteem is an epilepsy."

I put that little chapter in a safe place, strongly desirous that it might have its effect.

The more temples a religion builds, the closer is to its fall. A city only requires one temple, in order that it conserves the mysterious pomp that it imposes on the imagination. Enormous expenditures on sacred edifices seem to me to be ostentatious and onerous for the people, who ordinary bear the expense; and some temples were not yet finished, after half a century. There should be fewer temples, they should be simpler, and religious fervor would be augmented.

To give men the brake of religion is already an admirable institution; but to appropriate dogma and worship to the reform of the particular vices of a nation would by the masterpiece of the religious legislator.

Interior worship is the homage that every creature ought to render to the Supreme Being. It is religion par excellence, worthy to be offered to the one who is spirit and truth; but as humans are not isolated, they ought to publish their gratitude publicly.

The interest of the human species requires that a God be recognized and adored.

A joker said in my presence that he dearly wished that the controller-generals of finance resembled the king's librarians, because the latter, guardians of a great treasure, took great care not to make use of it for their own profit, which was not the case with those handling His Majesty's finances. I could not help laughing, and I made a small gift to the joker, for witticisms have their price.

I re-established in a public square the statue that Lycurgus had erected to Laughter. What is more innocent than the ingenuous laughter of a good man?

The function of Momus was to spy on the actions of the gods and criticize the absurd ones. How could they not be amused by what they saw? The Jester god sounded all his bells and it was permitted to everyone to laugh at their ease.

Yes, more excellent and rare things are said about a political affair that is hidden than those who think they know its secret imagine.

For the honor of the most considerable actions, as someone said, it is important that their motives remain carefully hidden.

"It is by means of printing that genius will speak to posterity until the end of the world. Who are you, then, enemies of printing? You fear it! You would be exposed by it; it would ferret out the truth from the depths of your entrails. Band together, rogues and impostors, form a league in the four corners of the world; printing will stand up to you; its annihilation is beyond your power.

"You cannot see the prodigious mainspring of the human mind, its slow but sure power, its perpetual tendency to amass from all parts the phosphoric materials of the truth; it might perhaps take a few more centuries, but in the end the maturity of ideas will destroy you, miserable adversaries of human reason, and the edifice of philosophy will repose on an unshakable foundation, while your names will be delivered to opprobrium."

That is what I permit myself to say to men who, for the sake of a despicable calculation of personal interest, inhibit all great brush-strokes and prevent the philosophical observer from raising himself to the sublime function of statesman and legislator, as if, by incessantly opposing the salutary activity of philosophy, one could rob a century of its energy, human understanding of its treasures and the virtuous man of his intimate enjoyments; for everything is great in a century and in a philosophical nation, and one cannot act with grandeur and dignity if one has not previously learned to think and speak with dignity.

Vile enemies of printed thoughts, it is you who annihilate national grandeur; you want everything to be paltry, small, hard and personal, like you, but you will not escape the pen that hollows out your ineptitude. You are already paling, you divine your history. People will be well avenged.

There was a time—and these prejudices of the Visigoths have not been entirely destroyed—when the profession of arms was the only distinguished one, when the arts that enable the ease, repose, commodities, glory, pleasures and nourishment of humankind were regarded with scorn.

I still see a residue of barbaric imbecility, subsisting in a few minds, which refuses to put the magistrate, the merchant and the renowned artist on the same level as the soldier. I compensated them, and I did so in such a way that sane ideas useful to politics would no longer encounter closed or calcined eyes.[18]

I fabricated a pipe of a new and rare structure, and I put it is the hands of those who contrived an interior profession of vanity; from all the prideful pretentions accumulated in the bowl nothing emerged, as from a cup, but the crests and

---

[18] Author's note: "A soldier risks his life, but it is only the affair of a moment. The man of law, depriving himself of all pleasures and devoting himself to the driest study, sacrifices his own continuously.

"What ridiculous ideas about nobility are still dominant! A gentleman will talk to you in a serious tone about his eight quarters; he will tell you that the emperor of the Turks is not a gentleman on his mother's side and that if he had a whim to be baptized and become a canon he would not be received in a German chapter. It is sometime necessary to hear such reasonings. "What does it matter from what blood one takes one's life? The noblest man is the one who serves his fatherland best."

plumes of peacocks. People saw all ridiculous or insensate projects flee and vanish in the little cloud of smoke.

Just as there are resemblances within families, so there are within the same nation. A custom cannot pass from one country to another without modification. Temperature, which influences facial features, can also influence the delicate and secret organs that envelop the thinking substance; hence the distinctive character of everything that lives and breathes; races respond to climates; their imprint is visible and sometimes insurmountable.

I wanted the sentiment of honor always to be the French soul, that no soldier should be struck down, and that no citizen be debased, without the precious sentiment being respected in them that leads to every species of glory. I wanted the nation always to be led by its own genius and not by foreign ideas that kill both courage and genius. I left the French vaudeville, song, and even the brochure, because they had no more bile once they had laughed, and nothing calms any affair better than letting good and bad jokers exert and exhaust themselves upon it.

One degree of industry is equivalent to sixty degrees of toil. Industry is nothing but the secret of amassing the greatest number of physical units with the fewest possible arms. It is therefore necessary to encourage the mechanicians who return to the culture of the land the host of arms employed in the arts of luxury. And that is what I did.

Rhymed sentences were born ready formed in my head and I verified those maxims exactly like Pibrac, because thought are retained more easily when they have a measured turn.

These quatrains were for people wanting to inspire in youth in good time the hatred of vice and the love of virtue;

for, although it is a vulgar saying, everything is contained within it.[19]

I saw an inexperienced young man slipping into the home of a woman who did not bear the name of prostitute, but who was a hundred times more dangerous. I gave the young man this quatrain:

> *The more profound vice is and the more it lures*
> *It always hits its mark, and merely by the feel*
> *It has spurs that come to light when it matures*
> *To inflict injuries that never heal.*

A statue that represented Time emerged from the studio of a sculptor; it lacked an inscription and I attached this one:

> *Time, by you the strongest are abased*
> *How propitious your rigor can be,*
> *While you take away delight run free*
> *You ensure that virtue is never effaced.*

A young painter had just finished a picture in which there was the heroic and holy figure of Temperance; I gave him these lines to put underneath it:

> *The laws that regulate our pleasures*
> *Are not inhuman chains*
> *Nature and heaven only set measures*
> *For fear of increasing pains.*

I saw a statue surrounded by deceptive inscriptions that insulted the credulity or the weakness of the people, and I effaced them; and as the man to whose adulation the statue had

---

[19] As it is asserted that the quatrains are rhymed, I have contrived rhymes in English in accordance with the same schemes employed in the original, retaining the spirit but not the precise meaning of Mercier's doggerel.

been erected had not merited the fatherland, I turned the head backwards, folded up the legs and rendered the face hideous; then it resembled his memory.

I came down heavily upon infidel depositaries of public funds. There were a great many powerful men who had a strong interested in the financial accounts of the realm being enveloped in obscurity. People in high positions distributed money with profusion, under the name of secret expenses, of which they did not render any account to their department, either in order to augment their personal fortune or in order to buy creatures. I examined rigorously the employment of funds that every man in place had to furnish to each of the departments. I defended the king's money as a lioness defends her cubs; I prevented disorder, waste, needles expense, frivolities and double employments, and my head required all its strength in order to delve into that frightful arithmetic. That mechanical part of the administration of the finances was what cost me the most. It was necessary to devote myself to stubborn labor, but I devoured that painful and disgusting toil for love of the interests of the prince and the fatherland, and at the end of that important task I gave incisive punches on the nose to all the rogues, which announced to the whole world that they had robbed the king and that state. Oh, how many bloody noses there were!

A man who asks another man for alms, and whose subsistence is, in consequence, founded on what he is accorded or refused, merits the attention of the government.

I did not have the cruelty to give beggars more cause for complaint than they had, for it was necessary to punish them, not make them perish in prison. I sent each of them to their parish, the place of their birth, and as people there knew, better than anywhere else, their setbacks or their vices, the officers in charge were able to impose appropriate tasks upon them. A severe correction obliged them to work, and any of them who left the district of his parish was brought back forcibly to suffer the punishment due to disobedience. By that means there would be no more vagabonds.

I had the laws observed that attribute to the head of a household empire over all the individuals composing it, for the sharing of authority seemed to me to be the greatest of errors, the most likely to foment discord. The physical power of women is already very considerable; if the law gave them as much authority as men, would not the latter soon be in the most abject dependency? Every husband ought to be the absolute master in his own house.

As my exhalation became devouring when I wanted to make it serve the good of humanity, with one breath I volatilized, more rapidly than a chemist's crucible, all the diamonds that infested France, and which require payment for all the evils that they occasion, for their extraction from mines and transport to Europe. That puerile and ruinous luxury excited my vigilance and indignation powerfully, and I believed that I was rendering an essential service to the fatherland in not leaving any trace of those perfidious gems bought with human blood, which only serve to aliment all known vanities, the most hollow and the most wretched.

"Baleful diamonds," I cried, loudly, "you must do all possible harm to men, because since the beginning you have caused all possible evils to humankind. In Brazil, alas, in order to conserve the monopoly on diamonds to kings, fifty square leagues around miles are desert, and anyone found in the vicinity is hung from the nearest tree if he cannot prove that he has business there. Lapidaries and diamond traders, I pronounce anathema upon you; let you and your merchandise vanish from the surface of the earth."

I forbade hunting to the gentry who made it a right to bear prejudice to country folk; it not just, merely for the pleasure of a hunter, for laborers or vine-cultivators to suffer any damage, and I tore up—with a sort of fury, I admit—the absurd and ferocious code of the penal laws that regulate hunting for the most powerful men of the region, who had dared to make the lives of beasts and men equivalent.

Hunting punishes, in truth, the man who makes it and occupation rather than a simple leisure pursuit. He becomes savage and grim; he loses moral ideas; he knows no other pleasure than wandering in the woods and the fields; he is no longer able to talk about anything else but the events of hunts, and he wastes the most precious days in that violent exercise, which renders his stomach robust, but weakens his head by as much and renders it unthinking; he ends up, that determined hunter, by living with dogs and beaters, by putting a wounded boar at the level of a prowess and game that he misses in the ranks of notable accidents. The enterprises of the day to come are slaughtering pheasants and massacring hares. Tell me, what need does a rational soul have to leap ditches, to climb hills, to brave cold and heat, to utter extravagant clamors and howls on the trail of animals, to be transported by joy when some capture is made and to slap one's forehead in rage and wrath if the prey escapes?

Are tearing apart innocent creatures as a pastime, and making a sport of their suffering, in order to hasten a slightly laborious digestion; and finding sensual pleasure in the terror and anguish of poor fugitive animals, without being pressed by need or hunger, games worthy of a man who ought to re-spect the creator of sensible beings even in the animals that he has subjected to torment?

"Opt, cruel hunters," I cried, "to embrace the theory of Descartes, which overtly contradicts reason, or judge your-selves fond of a ferocious pleasure. Live in the woods, pitiless and harsh hunters; cherish for preference the company of dogs and hares; forget all other affairs, and when you have wasted the most interesting hours of life running through the woods and the undergrowth, go in the evening to tell the story of a day that you have employed so worthily for yourself and the fatherland.

"Hunters, if, like Nimrod and Hercules you directed our attacks against the ferocious beasts that devastated your flocks and sometimes devoured the shepherds, you would be making noble war against monsters whom dread and weakness are forced to respect; but you do not kill those animals; you pursue the most timid, when they are gorged on the cabbages the lettuces and grains of unfortunate peasants, obliged to support that further imposition, deadlier than the intemperance of the seasons, and those victims often have to defend their lives against the voracity of a murderous gamekeeper who kills—O shame! O dolor!—with impunity."

Accursed hunting! The barbarians who inundated the empire at the beginning of the fifth century ennobled that exercise because they had a taste for it, and it required our fertile lands to be ravaged for the privileged amusement of a few idlers incapable of appreciating the value of time and the duties of humanity.

One man said to another: "You're a fool, with all your wit, you'll never succeed. Since I've known you, I've never heard mention of your talent once. People will soon cease to believe in it. Look at that fellow, he praises himself intrepidly to the periodicals."

"But it's a despicable vanity to talk about oneself," replied the modest man, "and I don't think it fools anyone."

"You're mistaken," retorted the other. "People begin by mocking the man who boasts of his merit, but they end up forgetting that the praise that they've heard emerged from his own mouth; they attribute it to someone else, and they end up praising, along with the crowd, the man they turned to ridicule yesterday. A repeated eulogy is like water that falls drop by drop, but which pierces, as Quinault says, the hardest rock."

I listened to that dialogue. They were two authors conversing, and each of whom had, as can be seen, very different character.

I stopped the vainglorious author and I said to him, before the entire audience: "You resemble a turkey-cock; when one stops to look at that animal, it swells up, sticks out its tail and makes its crest red, until it makes me burst out laughing."

"I am never cheerful when I listen to tender music," Shakespeare said.[20] "One is better than cheerful then, one is moved, touched, softened." One can say as much about a theatrical composition that stirs the soul. Whoever fears moving people, someone said, fears being good.

I shared Shakespeare's opinion; I gave the prize to sentimental music and dramas, of which one could say: *pectora mollescunt.*[21]

French tragedy makes me laugh a great deal, especially in the manner in which it is performed. I saw *The Death of Caesar* by Voltaire.[22] What a thin work! What a narrow frame! What wretched child's play substituted for the majesty of history! One could not disfigure Shakespeare's masterpiece more completely. Voltaire had not been able to read his superb, admirable original. Actors more ridiculous than the play brought into play a god humor that ended up with a sincere pity for the real poverty of the French theater.

The tragic poet, delivered to cold symmetry, almost always strayed from the historical tableau that, in its ensemble, had its truth. He had cut it awkwardly in order to make it enter forcibly into the frame of the rules. Thus, he deprived it of the newest and most interesting scenes, for it is the subject that ought to modify the theatrical action To tighten it when it ought to be extended, when it ought to expose great movements, is to lack artistry, interest and verity; it is to sacrifice the greatest beauties to desiccating rules that only destroy the illusion by removing a free effort from the mores and personality of every character.

---

[20] No, he didn't—but eighteenth-century French versions of Shakespeare's plays often bore little resemblance to the originals.

[21] "I soften breasts."

[22] *La Mort de César* (1735), not generally considered to be one of Voltaire's better works.

French tragedy subsequently was, for the multitude, an effect without a cause, and what is the point of a moral work whose purpose cannot be grasped, and which cannot say anything to the multitude? Speak to it about its mores, its fortune, and its present situation, and it will understand you.

What study is more worthy of a poet than to know well what he ought to inform his century, and to adapt his drama to that purpose?

Instead of a living and animate tableau, however, the tragic poet had metamorphosed Melpomene into a mannequin, whose attitude was perpetually bizarre and ridiculous. That strange caricature offered in addition the same dramatic mold for all peoples, for all governments, for all terrible or touching events. Servile adorers of what had been done and absolutely devoid of invention, the poets, forgetting the great destination of art, had made plays fake by virtue of wanting to adjust them to those of the ancients. Always the same protocol, always scenes of pure fantasy and the falsest taste that ever existed among a people, incessantly destroying historical truth and counting on replacing it with a vain elegance.

I expelled the pitiful tragic actors, with the eternal family of Atreus and Agamemnon; I made war on that bad taste, that emphatic declamation, cold and frantic, the most disagreeable sound that can strike a sensitive ear I put to flight, with the same order, those authors who went to pillage theater plays from old collections, in order to offer them subsequently with new and sonorous rhymes; and since they were impotent to give us a faithful depiction of ancient and modern mores and governments,[23] I forbade them to touch noble and grave sub-

---

[23] Author's note: "Cromwell and Guise have an entirely different physiognomy from Xipharès and Hypolite, and I think these new characters require another dramatic form than that of the divine Racine." Victor Hugo's unperformed *Cromwell* (1830) eventually became, thanks to its publication and its combative preface, one of the foundation stones of the new theatrical adventure for which Mercier was calling here.

jects emanated from history. The people, who were strangely irritated by all that nonsense, thanked me for having cased that grotesque cargo to disappear, which journalists and academicians had told them to admire. French tragedy and farce became synonyms; the national spectacle, entire changed and recast, offered interest, gaiety and instruction, and the employment of the dramatic writer, for the first time, was known to and cherished by the entire nation.

A man in an important position cried out as dolorously as my young author: "I want to annihilate all books—yes, all of them—because someone has written a pamphlet against me and is meditating another. Why are there books, since I don't read? What purpose do books serve? To make the people think, and I don't want them, personally, to think; it's up to them to follow the movement imposed upon them. Destruction to books! War upon books! An army of spies, agents and runners to prevent getting near a book, for these accursed books are the torment of my life and oblige me to measure my actions. Then too, books say everything, and reveal the most secret actions. One is never tranquil with these babbling books! To the fire, to the pillory and to the dungeon with all the books, if one can't put all the authors there. It's a crime to write."

"It's an inherent human right," I said, "since it's that of thinking. Now, thinking, speaking and writing are synonyms; for the intellectual operation is the same. Printing is a visible gift of the divinity, intended to counterbalance the evil that tyrants might do to the human species. Printing is an august and legitimate defense, which has neither violence not cruelty."

"But I fear satire."

"I can believe it."

"But I'm strong."

Hypolite is a French version of Hippolyte, but Mercier must actually mean Hippolytus.

"Strike, then, but know that there is no action without re-action."

I was the executor of a law that pleased me a great deal. It was appropriate to a century is which one devours one's capital, where a prodigal young man is scarcely in possession of his wealth than he dissipates in two or three years the fortune of his ancestors. That law imposed the prohibition of selling one's heritage. One had received it from one's ancestors; one owes it to one's descendants.

But if the government is prodigal itself, if it always wants to enjoy itself without measure, if it eats the future, destroys the past and dries up the present; if it has given individuals the fatal example of anticipating its revenues and devouring the foundation of its wealth...what will become of the law, the excellent law? I did my duty, I published it, because I felt sorry for the future generation; it will be poorer than ever, if money always goes to join the fatal mass of those who already possess a great deal of it.

Everything that concerns the labor of the countryside and the reproduction of vegetables was so well protected, honored and encouraged that the century was called the agricultural century. That title was as good as any other.

Distinguished agriculturalists wore three interlaced ears of wheat in the buttonhole of their coat.

The peasant, seen as an agriculturalist, a pastor and hunter, ought to be considered as the veritable Atlas, bearing the globe of the earth on his robust shoulders, for it is by means of him that the human race subsists.

I established a tribunal in which the judges of a point of honor took cognizance of those personal insults that put a citizen in the situation of breaking the law or bearing the consciousness of an unanswered affront. I extended that jurisdiction to all orders of citizens, because I wanted honor to be the foremost of treasures and for it to be secure against the multitude of misdemeanors that wound and offend delicate and sensible souls so sharply.

A man had committed an evil deed. He was getting ready to talk; I said to him: "You're going to offer a thousand bad reasons to palliate your fault; stick to the first."

I condemned an atheist to live alone. What is an atheist? He is a man who has isolated himself, who has made himself the center of the universe, who can no longer have any elevated desires or consoling thoughts; he is an egotist who has only destroyed a supreme being in order to be the being par excellence. It is necessary for him to live alone, as he will do one day, for Hell will be being alone, alone...the idea makes ne shiver.

I saw minds beginning to become excited for public interests and for the nation to devote its activity to worthy objects. "So much the better," I cried, "for forgetting the principle of morality and politics necessarily leads an empire to ruin. Let us approach nature as carefully as we can, she always makes laws more fortunate than those we give ourselves.

There are, says Montaigne, condemnations more criminal than the crime. I agree with him, and I had shameful procedures burned, because it is not good to retain the memory of certain iniquities.

Crimes committed by fanatics do not inspire any remorse in them. They sleep tranquilly on their sins; their conscience does not say anything to them; it is in vain that they have outraged nature. The religion they believe they have avenged assures them of a frightful, but real, peace for their heart. Is that not the most horrible sentiment that can denature the human heart?

All moral ideas are extinguished in a religious frenzy. The fanatic strikes blindly then; he becomes the most monstrous of beings.

I have been told that there are no more fanatics; I dug up a few, who did not lack the circumstances to frighten the world again. I punished them so harshly that, while calling themselves martyrs, they were obliged to summon to their aid someone who could close their scars, and that care deflected their atrabilious and cruel ideas for a while.

The responsibilities of the judiciary were no longer sold to the highest bidder which caused Seneca to say that magistrates, having bought justice wholesale, found it profitable to resell it retail.

I said to a man who had just made a dedication: "Poor fool, attaching yourself to praising the great; you're only making their self-esteem as blasé as their palate; they will no longer sense the finest and most delicate praise, any more than the exquisite sauce that their maître-d'hôtel will serve them this evening; you're wasting your time and your words."

I perceived a famous château; it lacked an inscription on the frontispiece; I put these lines there:

Eat under an awning, sleep under a baluster;
Be the descent of a thousand kings;
If you misunderstand the laws of humanity,
You will only be an illustrious criminal.

What a vast field of verities remains to be discovered in morality, physics and geometry! We are still on the edge of an immense quarry, and you give yourself the name of savants, Messieurs of the Académie. Savants! Oh, renounce that title.

I entered furtively into the room of a poet, a disciple of Voltaire; he was composing a tragedy, and reading all the tragic poets attentively; he took lines from them that he wrote down in a notebook, which he put in hidden drawer in his desk. I shouted "Thief!" in his ear, and then I disappeared.

I encountered another poet who had written twelve tragedies, not one of which had not been whistled. It was for that reason that he strutted and thought himself a great man, and joined in appreciating the faults of all printed works except his own.

I condemned him to speak from a pulpit on genius, on eloquence, on grace and the life of style; which is to say, everything that was foreign to him; which amused the public and generated laughter for some time.

I found that the price of seats at decent plays was too high. When people have become accustomed to certain enjoyments, it is a crime to abuse their taste by making them pay dear for them. There are habitudes that ought to be respected. And I included under the name of enjoyments tobacco, sugar, aromatics, perfumes, etc.

Forced labor was going badly; I got rid of it. I paid the workers who had previously worked poorly and done poor work, because they were working involuntarily and without profit. It was not the same when I brought a bag of money under my arm; I only needed half the workers then. Free and paid, they took less time and the roads were better constructed. It had previously been necessary to recommence the roads with further expenses; there was no longer any question of that. It is only good will that makes arms work well; as long as you constrain them you will not even have good diggers.

I perceived a wretched wall, a humiliating imprint of servitude, which cut across disagreeably and spoiled beautiful walks, intercepted the air and the view, and opened citizens in like sheep. The Chinese once built a wall against the invasions of Tartars; here it was the Tartars who had built the odious wall. Now, as a financial system is always petty, puerile and miserable, there is nothing as low and cruel as that species of men, who put the greatest obstacle in the way of national tranquility and prosperity, I condemned all the men of finance to demolish that wall, which chagrined a good people, who were submissive enough and gave enough money for them to be spared that humiliation; for they regarded it as a misfortune and an outrage. Now, why cause pain to a people who only ask to be loved and who pay gladly as long as the chains they carry are hidden from sight or decorated with a few flowers?

To cloister an immense and extremely populous city, the center and support of all royal power and all its grandeur, is to dishonor an ancient capital, spoil the monuments that it contains in its bosom, and diminish the admiration of foreigners, who would sigh like the natives on encountering in a circular line the eternal traces of the crushing customs duty. If it is necessary that it exists, why not at least hide such a sad sight from the eyes? Why give it such a frightful surface?

If a citizen goes out to respire the pure country air, he encounters an immense enclosure that one permits him to go into the fields after having found, with difficulty, the rare or narrow exit from which the rigorous customs duty still seems to be crying out through the mouths of its agents: "You're going out; when you come back you'll be searched."

I shared the affliction of the people, and not fruitlessly, thanks to my arm.

The man who had produced the plan and the project of that wall, having degraded the title of academician, his name became nonetheless an insult, and signified in popular parlance "the enemy of the good people."

A butcher killed a veal calf and his assistant raised a cutlass to disembowel a lamb. I stopped their arms and said to them: "Who has permitted you to kill that species-child? If you have been given permission, I forbid it; none of you will kill a calf or a lamb; can no one, then, read the future? Nature is not being given time to repair her losses. O foresight, foresight, how rare you are among men! They do not think about the propagation of the species, as if Nature could be sufficient for their avidity. The Carib sells his bed in the morning, not foreseeing that he will have need of it in the evening; man in society, stupid and devoid of prudence, does not take the slightest precaution to conserve species. He will eat veal, lamb and pullets, and will then be astonished to have no more oxen, sheep or hens. Does he not resemble the Carib who weeps in the evening because he was unable to foresee in the morning that he would go to bed at the end of the day?

Duty is sometimes confused with virtue, because it resembles it. A wise young woman was crowned in my presence because she had avoided young men; another had cared for her father; she was taken to see a play. There is no better proof of the morality of the century. A preacher even celebrated these virtues, unknown to those who possessed them, from the pulpit; virtue became a theatrical performance. Fine, if that is what you want, but it did not satisfy me. I respected the lord, the virtuous girl, and the people who surrounded her. That fête might reward duty, and that would suffice for it not to be interrupted; but virtue is beyond duty. I shall not say another word, for I confess that I do not have enough moral knowledge to weigh duty and the virtue in the eighteenth century. All that I know is that virtue is beyond duty and that a virtuous girl whose has only done one good deed in her life is well above an Académie prize-winner.

I saw an adolescent with an interesting physiognomy and I asked him: "What do you learn in that big house where I see railings, porters and long black robes?"

"I learn Latin," he told me.

"And after that?"

"More Latin."

"What! Nothing else?"

"Sometimes a few Greek words."

"And it's for that, my young friend, that you've quit the paternal house and salutary exercise in the country?"

I addressed myself to the black robes and I said to them: "What are you teaching these children who are at the age of growing and learning?"

"Latin," they told me, "and a little Greek, when they have the memory."

My eyes sparkled with anger. "Pedant!" I cried.

"We're only paid for that," they replied, trembling.

"What! I said. "Latin? Is there no longer any art, no métier, no exact science, nor limbs to develop among that youth? What will all those children do with that almost-useless language? What about exercises of the body, equitation, swimming, living languages, and the knowledge of useful plants? Where will they learn all that?"

The pedants remained mute.

"What! That is public education, then? Latin! Public education has remained the same for centuries, and regents are paid who teach their classes as canons recite their offices, and who limit to insignificant Latin phrases everything that might be taught in the eighteenth century. What! A national establishment is limited to these petty pedantic ideas, and the speech of Rome is taught to children born in Paris! What does Rome matter to them? What is there in common between the duties of civil life and that ancient city? What can the son of a bourgeois divine regarding that ancient mistress of the world, and what benefit will he obtain from the frequentation of those Latin authors? He will lose his health in these sterile studies sand he will emerge from school with the stupid presumptuousness that he has received from his masters."

Suddenly, I made a gesture, and I summoned grooms with horses, joiners, carpenters, blacksmiths and a few designers. The children leapt for joy at quitting their pen for the hammer and compass. They leapt on to the horses and their sad faces were animated by vivid colors. Fencing and boxing were not forgotten.[24] I gave a trade to each of those poor chil-

---

[24] Author's note: "The words virtue and virile drive from *vis*, strength or courage; it is the prerogative of the virile sex to

dren, and they no longer heard any mention of that base flatterer and tippler Horace, whom the regents do not understand themselves and explain to one another in between their exercises. A little natural history amused the young folk and disposed their minds to see the marvels of creation.

Their tastes were studied, and as soon as they showed a decided penchant for a science or an art, they were delivered to specialist masters; they were obliged, at the age of twenty-two, to travel until the age of twenty-six, to leave the capital, and once a week they had to write down what they had seen, and it was on those reports that they were judged in order to obtain positions in civil life.

The regents stood around me, stupefied, and as I had smashed their lecterns they expected compensation from me. The instruction mattered little to them, but the income did.

"And what history do you teach these poor children?"

"Greek and Roman history, in which it is said on every page that it is necessary to detest all kings as so many tyrants; that it was a good thing to expel Tarquin and kill Caesar; that all conspirators are great men, that Cato and Brutus, who killed themselves, performed fine actions in doing so."

---

brave perils and vanquish all obstacles. In the most ordinary tasks it is necessary to combine strength and dexterity; for example, in copperplate engraving and tailoring. The master and merchant tailors I have seen in Lyon willingly employ more boys than girls, although the latter cost them a good third less. *Vir magis patiens laboris quam femina.*

"There is no virtue without the strength of the body and the soul. Demi-talents are only such for want of courage and strength Charles XII was all sinew. Peter the Great had a robust body, a mind more inflexible than any other, a firmer, more confident heart, a stronger will, and an intelligence more active than all of Russia put together. As people only obey force, let us give it to the body and the soul. Courage can be taught, I believe, like equitation."

"And it's the King of France who pays you to teach all these children the fanaticism of an imaginary liberty? To preach the ancient republics twice a day? To render royalty odious to the young inhabitants of the good city of Paris? To imprint in their brains ideas absolutely contrary to the government under which they have to live? Oh, if you hadn't been boring and dull masters, what would have become of your disciples, with principles so opposed to monarchy? But fortunately, they haven't understood the authors you translate."[25]

I armed my arm, and all the colleges were destroyed, to give way to gymnasia in which nothing curtailed the liberty of childhood, the development of physical strength, much less avid and curious young reason.

Three armies in a vast plain were about to fight and slaughter one another. As that appeared to me to be the worst of all human extravagances, and I call that pretended courage dementia and frenzy; as the military mind appears to me to be the infernal breath of the abysm of sin and crime, soling and withering the inhabitants of the earth; as I execrate that abominable fury, I blew swiftly on the ensigns and the flags, and they all became a uniform color.

---

[25] Author's note: "One reads in the history of Florence a fact that merits being known. A regent of the college in 1476, having as sovereign Galeas, Duke of Milan, was prejudiced to the point of fanaticism in favor of republican government. His head excited by reading Greek and Latin authors, he praised to his pupils the advantages of being born in a republic and deplored the misfortunes of a subject submissive to a sovereign. His ideas inflamed three of his disciples so much that they swore an oath between his hands, in a church, to deliver their fatherland from the Duke, their sovereign, as soon as they were old enough. Two perished on the battlefield; the third, who was only twenty-two years old, was condemned to death, and he repeated during his torture, which was long, the Latin passages that the regent had taught him."

Then, those insensates, wanting to fight, could no longer do so; for it was the color of the flags and the ensigns they carried that bore them to massacres and carnage, and it was for the color in question that they went to offer their bare breasts to canons loaded with grapeshot.

What! To see murders and assassinations in a mild climate, in the corner of woods dressed in eternal verdure, alongside flowers born in the midst of a perfumed air? When everything respires life and sensuality, to see men seeking to put one another to death, to slaughter one another over the flowers of spring? What a contrast! How can men reject simultaneously the benefits of earth and those of heaven to abandon themselves to cruel vengeance?

My arm of bronze was not strong enough to choke the monster of war, and its strength is so opposed to that which edifies laws and makes them respected, that I could only curse it and devote it to the execration of sages and celestial justice.[26]

A host of dancers, jugglers and subaltern musicians populated the towns of the provinces; a host of unnecessary workers—hairdressers, wig-makers, etc.—pullulated even in the smaller towns, and yet the rural areas had no surgeons, or,

---

[26] Author's note: "I would like at least to recall those combats, frequent in Italy, in which only one man was killed, although the fighting went on for seven or eight hours; it was still thus in the war of 1460. Good defensive weapons covered the soldiers; it was not easy to kill a man, the supreme danger was falling off a horse. Those unsanguinary battles were no less decisive. They hasted half a day; combats were expelled reciprocally from the battlefield by lance-thrusts. Many contusions, little or no blood soiled. Well, those philosophical battles, which one ought to regret, which I do regret, operated in politics all that is achieved now by cannons, bombs, rifles and the massacre of twenty or thirty thousand men lying in bloody mud."

what is worse, only had bad ones. What! All the help for the capital? The men of the art gathered, crowded at a single point, there was no longer any aid for the unfortunate peasant, and the curative art did not exist for him. Rural surgeons made widows and orphans at their ease; midwives crippled mothers; it was necessary in some cantons to go eight leagues to find a barbaric Aesculapius, who, with six dusty volumes, four bottles of poison, a saw, a lancet and a few grains of emetic formed the forefront of medicine and surgery. The slightest epidemic became disastrous, gangrene accompanied the slightest accidents, and humanity succumbed, sometimes under the scalpel placed in the hands of ignorance, sometimes under the indefatigable lancet and sometimes under a banal and violent purgative.

That dearth of men of the art was a veritable desolation in the countryside; there were only cures for opulent cities. A café idler in a big city, a useless burden to the earth, escaped a malady that would not have caused any void in the state by killing him, while a robust cultivator was stolen from agriculture and his family for want of the most necessary aid. The maladies of country folk were delivered to hazard, or to surgeons devoid of books and medicaments. Shameful mendicity became the recourse of several orphans, who, at the age of passions, soon became brigands. Small towns were devastated; there were no physicians except in the capital and a few populous cities. When they arrived in the wake of a scourge whose renown had spread, mortality had consummated its ravages.

That inconceivable neglect struck me with indignation, and caused tears of dolor to rise to my eyes. What, academies and no pupils? What, so many physicians and no saviors for the countryside? I summoned all those that these abuses ought to strike, and cried to them: "The men, the useful men are in the countryside, they are dying! Run to them; beneficent lights repose in the cities, homicidal darkness envelops the towns and villages; spread out learned men. Is the art of healing only made for the rich, then?"

People ran to my voice; my dolor was so profound that it passed into all souls. A surgeon of recognized capability was placed every four leagues; he was assigned a hundred écus, which were taken from the coffers of actors, strolling players, mountebanks, conjurors, acrobats and puppeteers throughout the realm; and when anyone wanted to open a dance-hall in a city, they began by contributing to the salary of country surgeons and physicians. That title became an honor. Country physicians and surgeons even wore a particular coat, in order that they could be recognized and their help demanded. The physicians of the capital made short tours every year in different cantons to supervise the operations most important to humanity and most inseparable from the salvation of the state.

I encountered the brother of a man who had gone to the scaffold the day before; the brother was a good man. Overwhelmed by that blow, he was walking with his head bowed, not daring to raise his eyes.

"I'm debased," he said.

"What is debasing about a fault that is not yours?" I exclaimed. "What! When opinion has extended its arm over unfortunate humans, they bend their necks in a servile manner and think themselves degraded? They misunderstand their dignity, their liberty, their independence; they think themselves vile because the unjust opinion of others has soiled them? Human soul, image of your God, faults are personal; do not say 'I am vile,' for you are not vile because of someone else's crime."

"People have criticized me."

"People! Get up, get up! People no longer have any power over you. Stand up to the opinion that that defies eternal justice and reason. No one shares the shame of his brother any more than he shares his virtues. It is a servility to obey such a prejudice; it is blind, it is harmful; whoever wants to annihilate it will annihilate it. Do not say 'I am debased,' and you will not be debased."

"If you had been able to appropriate all the salubrious air that flatters the delightful hills of the Seine and the Loire, you would have done it. And if you had been able to enclose the beautiful and vivifying sunlight in your park and your palace for your usage alone, you would have enclosed it, and you would only have left the people, whose blood you believe to differ from your own, the twilight, and then you would have wanted to boast about your noble clemency.

"Fortunately, you have not been able to steal either the air or the light, nor the silvery rays of the moon, nor the brilliant stars of the firmament; and fortunately, your long and avid hands have been too short to embrace the globe of the earth, for it would have required the earth entire to satisfy the imperious demands of a single mad and superb man....

"But what does it matter? The earth is invaded; everything is taken. Aristocrats, you possess it and share it exclusively. Only shreds remain to preserve the greater portion of the human race from starvation.[27]

"Noble and powerful thieves, stubborn leeches, harsh, inexorable proprietors, by what fatality is it necessary that you have everything and other men have nothing? You are now applauded, you posses abundance without remorse, on seeing misery and indigence through the transparent windows of your voluptuous dwellings, you cause the pale and thin crowd to

---

[27] Author's note: "In my opinion, there is a contradiction between birth and lack of property. The man born on the land who has no place to rest his head is necessarily the enemy of those who possess. A Laplander by birth at least has a reindeer for his prerogative; he is assigned a second reindeer when his teeth come through; but in Europe there are millions of men who come into the world without being able to say that they have a tree for their portion. There would be a terrible book to write on the word 'property.' The poorest people are also charged with nourishing and raising the men who, for a modest salary, will one day serve the opulent party. Society is a prodigy."

open before the hooves of your rapid chargers, fearful of being trampled; you continually threaten the lives of your fellow citizens in order to marry more promptly the hours of your delightful enjoyments. But this time will be of short duration; death avenges the human species; soon, your unworthy friends will fly away, naked, and hideous with the crimes of your insensibility; they will fly away to answer for all those public and private tyrannies, the infamous fabric of a personal life; your hard, cold souls will retrogress, far from the gaze of the high and adorable power who counts the actions of every human creature, and who withdraws his divine breath from the wicked, who have scorned and oppressed their fellows. The master who is alone great and alone adorable, will precipitate you into the circle of animality, because you have forgotten the destination of human being, whose life ought to be amour, tenderness and charity."

I addressed those words to the egotists of the century, and I also said to them: "You have not wanted everyone to live, and everyone to live happily; well, your souls will be withered by languor and ennui in the very bosom of opulence; then they will shudder one day at the base actions into which they have plunged. Time flies; tomorrow your pride will be confounded; tomorrow you will no longer be human beings, cast down among the least beings in creation....

"I have read your sentence in the book of eternal justice, of which I am only the shadow down here.... Shudder at the sentence that will reject you from sentimental life...."

There were some who came to me to complain about some imposture or some vexation. The elasticity of my muscles of bronze was in perpetual action, either to protect the weak or to stop or to punish prevaricators, while the host of the culpable increased, and they formed a conspiracy against my justice-administrating person.

It was invulnerable; nothing weakened its mainspring or slowed its march. But what did the multitude of the wicked do? They banded together, formed a mob, joined forces. They finally invented an ingenious and perfidious device that they threw in concert at my arms, thighs and legs. My arms were screwed, thy unscrewed them; then, with a dull file, they sawed through my legs, and, once tipped over, I soon found myself devoid of hands and arms, for that was what they feared the most in me.

Lying on the ground, I no longer had the strength to punish the wicked. They were out of my reach, and I no longer had had anything but the movement of my tongue and head; I was, in sum, no longer anything but a simulacrum, which reduced my power to negligibility.

When people saw me in that state they jeered at me; then I was reduced to proffering a few vain sentences to which they did not listen, or which they made a semblance of admiring in order better to infringe them. I had previously had a coercive strength that maintained or reestablished order; that strength had vanished. Condemned to cast a few wasted words into the air, the chagrin that I had in seeing evil triumphant and being unable to repress it, and the insolence of the wicked, who laughed at my impotent ager when they went past, irritated the generous fibers of my brain so much that the illusion dissipated; I woke up and I said to myself then, uttering a long sigh:

"Alas, what is the use of being an invulnerable iron man and calling oneself Justice? The wicked, always cleverer than the good, are skillful at escaping the power of the law, and hardly ever fail to achieve that end. They would doubtless have much less difficulty in becoming good men again than working day and night on the odious, complicated schemes that remove the arms and legs of Justice, but so profound is the malice of their hearts that they fear self-amelioration more than making war on everything on earth that is most holy.

"Poor Justice! The insidious plots and abominable ruses of scoundrels have made a mutilated body of you, a trunk similar to those that one sees in the studios of sculptors. One can still see the muscles that your generous heart contains, which were once your suppleness and strength, but it is necessary for a guilty party to be very close to you for your terrible voice to

229

frighten him, or that you can punish him by means of a prompt and energetic movement of your semi-mutilated limbs. The torso that Michelangelo still touched respectfully with his failing hands has, alas, become your emblem.

"You once went toward the culpable; today it is necessary for him to be brought to you and dragged before our debris. Who will restore your limbs, your active strength, your proud and rapid stride, as they were in your heyday? The sovereign who will know you, and who will be virtuous enough to become your foremost subject."

THE LAST DAY

I dreamed that I was enchained in a motionless stupor, that an eternal and profound silence surrounded me, and I was beginning to be alarmed by that condition when I heard the faint sound of a trumpet that seemed to be resounding in the distance. The sound was augmented by degrees, became formidable, and I suddenly recognized, fearfully, the sound of the universal trumpet.

That terrible sound broke the stone of tombs and woke up the members of the human race buried since the origin of the world. I got up from the depths of my sepulcher and I heard a voice that cried: "Humans, you may choose to fall back into nothingness, or you may rise with confidence toward the God who will judge you."

Immediately, I saw great figures who were rising before the others, and who were covering their faces with their black and fleshless hands, striving to shout: "Nothingness! Nothingness!" There was Nero, Caligula, Domitian, Tiberius, Philippe II, all the evil kings and their even more culpable ministers, all the tormenters of peoples, all the monsters intoxicated by blood, and all those, finally, who had woven conspiracies against liberty, against human wellbeing; they were afraid of their own existence, imploring the darkness of annihilation, as if to rob themselves of themselves.

The good and the just cried: "We fear God, but we trust in his clemency; let him chastise us, but let him not annihilate us."

An angel with outspread wings, whose span embraced the vault of the firmament, repeated the words for the second time, and the host of murderers, calumniators, ingrates, egotists, unnatural parents, perfidious friends, cried for their part: "Nothingness! Nothingness!" and were afraid that it might not be granted.

The just, raising their timid gazes toward the eternal splendor, said: "Life, the life to come."

The difference of these acclamations served to separate the human flock. I saw on one side the poisoners, the parricides, the thieves, the impostors, and those who had received gold for their iniquitous sentences. On the other I saw the philosophers, the equitable ministers, the generous writers, and all those whom charity had animated. That separation was an irrevocable judgment, which every person had, so to speak, dictated; the cry of conscience had formed the eternal verdict.

I saw a balance that touched the vault of the heavens and which leaned over the abysms of space. Those who had requested life rose up toward the radiant vaults, where I lost sight of them; the others plunged into the tenebrous gulfs, from which I heard groans emerging that resembled the prolonged tones of despair.

THE TOWERS

When the world, still soaked with the waters of the deluge, emerged from its ruins, the new inhabitants of that desolate earth found themselves naked on a sterile beach; but their distress was combined with fear when they heard a distant thunder that threatened to strike them for a second time. They raised their hands to the heavens and said to one another that there was a terrible and hidden power above them, an absolute master of their paltry existence.

I went to sleep on those ideas, and I saw nothing but scattered and consternated people fleeing the bellowing waves, and scaling the summits, where the furious waters still pursued them.

Those unfortunates were naked; they measured the abyss of the waters with the gaze of despair; the slightest rumble of thunder, even if it was expiring, seemed to be returning overhead in order to strike those whom the waters had spared. They withdrew slowly; that vast and lugubrious inundation had something more frightful about it than if waves of fire had rolled over the earth; that liquid abyss in which everything was dormant and motionless, those black and stagnant waters, which uprooted the slightest vegetation, the ornament of the earth, which swallowed its branches and its fruits, offered a spectacle of desolation, and that vast overflow struck the eyes with terror.

It was a comet that had suddenly poured down its waters with a terrible din; the birds of the sky could no longer find anywhere to alight; the vegetal earth, sadly dissolved, was swirling in a great quantity of mud. I saw again the tower that fearful men had built in order to protect themselves from such a disaster; that monument to their weakness and their extravagance had remained imperfect; the colossal tower only announced vain projects and a futile enterprise; the hasty work-

233

ers were interrupted in the midst of their audacious hopes when God mingled, with nuances so fine and do different, the organs of speech in such a way that it was impossible henceforth for them to do anything in perfect accord.

The voice of God had said to them, in a rather striking manner: "Go, live in peace, each in your place, without fatiguing yourselves in such vain endeavors."

Mortals had not understood the divine wisdom; then the most ridiculous spectacle was seen; each of them tried to build a tower on his own part, and wanted to build it all the way to the heavens; only a few had constructed a few cubits, which they imagined to be very high, because the mountains, in the distance, seemed to be beneath their gaze.

All those builders who cried discordantly that they were building the most reliable stairway to rise to the heavens, sheltered from all danger, had given one another the lie reciprocally; every one, perched on the summit of his tower, had cried: "Come to me, it's me who is the nearest to heaven."

One sustained that the God they sought was surely the sun, that the moon was his wife and the stars his children; others, more materialistic, had prostrated themselves before a calf, a sheep, or a dove; in sum, they all made grotesque gods; but what proved most fatal was that each pontiff substituted himself for the idol hoisted to the summit of his tower, wanting to be adored with it, and cried out: "Strike, kill the refractory, they are as many impious individuals." To the voices of those pontiffs, victims were dragged who requested in vain to be allowed to build a tower in accordance with their own architecture.

All the follies that they committed in order to honor their idols were innumerable; the height of the tower had turned their weak heads; there was no bizarre figure that did not appear in pomp as an object of adoration; the pontiff of the idol had a particular language and behavior different from his neighbor: one danced, another held his arms in a cross; one remained immobile, another abstained from drinking and eating, finding a singular virtue in only having skin stuck to his bones; there were some who cut off certain body parts, and those enthusiasts wanted others to follow their example.

In sum, I saw the follies of the nations, from Pharaoh's magicians to the saint of the Saint-Médard cemetery, as well as the jugglers, the shakers, the thaumaturges, the exorcists, the sorcerers and the chiromancers, shouting loudly from their particular tower. What confusion! What disorder!

Further away, I saw a sage who was saying tranquilly to the people around him: "The universe is the temple of the Divinity; the serenity of the heavens corresponds to his soul." And, comparing all those towers with the immense expanse of the firmament, it was soon converted in my mind into a true temple, in which the Divinity presented himself to us in the most sensible manner; the heavens are the limit of the religious edifice, and that imposing grandeur is not too vast for nature and the presence of God that it contains.

Erect again the vaults and domes of Saint Paul's in London and Saint Peter's in Rome, add by thought to the boldness of the construction; how small all that becomes before the vault of the temple that is open everywhere at every hour, and where every man can, by raising his eyes, worship and prostrate himself.

Sometimes a temple is illuminated by candles, but they pale and are consumed; but they need to be renewed; here is a torch, an abysm of inexhaustible light; when it visits another hemisphere it is suddenly replaced by an innumerable quantity of other torches that open to our eyes the limitless field of a radiant magnificence; the soul is seized by admiration; it falls into silence or prayer.

Are not those variously colored clouds that border the horizon, the transparency and glow of which the painter's brush only imitates imperfectly, worth as much as the drapes that art hastens to deploy?

In that high-ceilinged temple, where is the altar? Where is the priest? They are united in the human heart when the conscience is pure, simple and innocent; from that altar humans can cause the perfumes and incense of their adoration and praise to rise all the way of God; they can present to their beneficent Creator the sacrifice of their actions of grace, for the faculties with which their soul is enriched, for the divine flame that illuminates them, for the inestimable privilege of knowing and loving the source of those graces; the priest devotes his existence to him, and consecrates it to praise and adoration; he is the former poet who teaches us to praise the grandeurs of God; it is only necessary to repeat to him:

"Eternal, my God, you are marvelously great; you are clad in majesty and magnificence; all your works are made with wisdom; you have put your majesty above all the skies."

At those words, I saw all the towers metamorphose into columns, pavements, vaults, supports and ornaments; the Alps were enclosed beneath that magnificent vault; a brilliant sun illuminated that immense expanse; the eye lost itself there, but it was still a temple, and the beautiful words of Solomon resounded in my ear;

"Behold the heavens; but the heavens of the heavens cannot contain you; how much less is the house that I have built you!"

The voice that was speaking became so loud, so great and so majestic that my organs could not suffice, and I woke up.

NEWS FROM THE MOON

The account I am writing is perfectly true, although the reader might deem me a madman. Believe me if you will; I shall offer no proofs to the incredulous. Let us begin.

I had a friend: a good man whom everyone called inestimable, but with whom very few people were closely acquainted. Friendship is a tree that cannot put down roots in bad ground; it requires everyday virtues to put forth good fruit, and moral defects usually cause it to wither. Two men who do not respect one another rarely come to like one another; in order to be friends they must be able to confide in one another, and they must earn the right to speak frankly to one another by repeatedly proving themselves worthy of trust. Let us return to my friend.

We had become acquainted in middle age; we helped one another through awkward crises more than once. Our characters were not perfectly in tune, but amity and tolerance bridged the gap. Resolved to run a similar course for the rest of our days, we took up residence in the same house. I passed my happiest years in his pleasant company. His death left me alone, prey to regrets which still endure, but I have continued to live under the same roof.

Ordinarily, one does not like one's thoughts to dwell on those whose loss afflicts us, but for me that was my sole consolation. Always alone, revisiting in my thoughts through the places I had discovered with my friend, I recalled our most interesting conversations incessantly. The memories returned so vividly to mind that I was sometimes able to enjoy his imaginary company.

All those who have the habit of reflection know from experience how conducive a fine evening's moonlight is to meditation. Late one night, when the heavenly body in question was full, I was lingering in the garden, thinking continually of the one I had lost, when my sight was suddenly struck by a bright and vivid point of light. It seemed to stay in front of me no matter which way I turned. Eventually I stopped, looked directly at it, and examined it more closely. I perceived that the shining point was the tip of a luminous arrow, inscribed on the ground—and that the arrow was an immensely extended ray proceeding directly from the moon.

Astonished by this phenomenon, I became more attentive. When I approached it, the point of light withdrew, as if to guide me. When I followed it, it stopped on a newly-whitewashed wall, where I saw it trace visible letters, and I read:

It is me! Have no fear! It is your friend. I am living on the star that lights your way. I can see you. I have long sought a means of writing to you, and I have found one. Prepare a set of planks of wood, so that I can more easily trace thereon all that I have to tell you. Come back to the same place tomorrow; it is too late tonight—the star is turning, my line is no longer direct, and it is....

The fiery point abruptly disappeared.

This marvelous apparition threw me into utter confusion. I remained immobile for a long time, my eyes staring by turns at the moon and the wall. My mind was so agitated that I passed the rest of the night without being able to sleep a wink. The following day I made ready a large number of planks, which I arranged myself in the place where I impatiently awaited the return of night.

Never had the sun seemed to set so slowly. The moon displayed its shining disc at last, but so many clouds gathered around it that it was masked by an impenetrable veil. Fatigued by waiting in vain, and not having slept at all the previous night, I could not help falling asleep, much to my regret.

When I woke up I saw a clear and serene sky, in which the moon was already close to the horizon. My eyes immediately went to my planks, and I found the following inscribed upon them:

You are asleep, my friend. That is an imposition to which the beings of your world are subject; when you awake you will see this evidence that I am thinking about you. I want to reveal secrets to you that no other living man has ever penetrated before. Do you remember the moment when I died in your arms? Well, it has not been nearly as painful for me as you have presumed.

No, death is not what one imagines; the living have an idea of it that is false and frightful. Its convulsions, so frightening for the spectator, are a gentle passage into sleep for the dying man. The somber ceremonies with which a corpse is surrounded perpetuate dread and terror, but death is not what is represented by the fearful imagination.

When I felt the beating of my heart stop, I found myself endowed with the faculty of entering into more durable bodies, whose density could not prevent my elevation. All matter appeared to me as porous as a sieve, and my will took control of my ascension. I could transport myself to any place I wished, traversing immense distances without difficulty or dread.

The more I projected myself the more I felt the flame of life empower and activate me. My understanding, memory and imagination brightened with a new clarity. When I had lifted myself up I could descend just as rapidly towards any object that I wanted to reach; the wings of a bird are an inadequate analogy for the free movement of which every part of my being was now eminently capable.

What delighted me more than anything else was that a host of ideas that I had never previously entertained became familiar to me. A ready intelligence immediately allowed me to conceive all the marvels of creation--but the one which imported the sweetest rapture into my being was that of rediscovering all those I had loved. Our souls were instantaneously drawn together, and a delicious sentiment bound us together inextricably.

239

Our bliss comprises an inexhaustible and incessantly-satisfied curiosity. Every day we apprehend more, and never tire of apprehension. Science, uncertain on the Earth, is supported here by the clearest evidence. There is no object that our eyes cannot easily penetrate; we see so profoundly at a distance that I can even read, at this moment, the words that I am writing. I can bend rays of light to my will, making pencils of them that I sharpen according to my taste, and in this manner I can engrave my thoughts in the deepest regions of the sky and touch the boundaries of the universe.

By this means the Creator has given the eye the privilege of reaching the most distant globe, has deigned to afford to thought the power of manifesting itself in every system populated by sentient reasoning beings. I converse with those whose writings I have admired; distance is no obstacle to the rapid flight of ideas, and print is only the gross simulation of that privileged art by which the inhabitants of the celestial spheres communicate their thought.

I have descended to the moon in order to select its gentlest ray, for the benefit of your feeble eyelids; your eyes would be dazzled and blinded by a brighter one. I will return tomorrow, if there are no clouds to get in our way, and if I still have permission to reveal to you the strange truths of the sublunary world.

Seeing these last words. I took a piece of chalk in my trembling hand, and I wrote on the plank: My friend, is it possible that you are on the moon, and that your sight can penetrate as far as this? Can you read these words?

Yes, perfectly. There is no need to write such large letters. Write quickly and easily, in your own hand.

Oh, how many questions I have to put to you! So, it really is in the radiant spheres I observe in the sky that all the races of humankind who have lived on Earth will be reunited. Tell me, will the wicked and the good be mingled together without distinction? That is the first and most important thing I want to know.

The most secret actions of a past life will be revealed to every gaze; the entire history of our lives is painted on our faces in a manner that is universally intelligible. The wicked are forced to discover their own wickedness; it is by seeing one another, and what they are, that they are themselves horrified. This perpetual display inspires in them a profound repentance, which is their torture, and they try to erase those iniquitous characters that torment them. By performing good deeds they can remove the black imprint that disfigures them; it is necessary that they are without the stain of dishonor in order to communicate with beings who are strangers to all deformity.

If those who are blackened by numerous vices ask questions of those resplendent with light they obtain no reply; they are punished by disdain, and they feel the distance that separates them from children of divinity. Consternated by their debasement, they seek to escape it, for the record of their sins passes from mouth to mouth and they hear again all the maledictions heaped upon them on the Earth, where their memory excites horror. Whenever they hope to enjoy a few moments of tranquility, the feeble voice that accuses them becomes thunderous, reclaiming their attention, and that accusation is spread throughout the worlds of the cosmos. Crushed beneath the weight of their shame, conscience becomes a dagger that pricks them incessantly: they flee, but they are naked to every gaze; they hide themselves behind uninhabited worlds, in solitude, but the angels of light cry out to them as they pass by: "I see you, and your every iniquity."

As the sentiment of justice ranks above all others among us, our pity must be set aside. We sense in ourselves the necessity of the order that governs us. Everyone expiates his sins by a proportionate shame; no one complains of its magnitude, because it is equitable to endure a just chastisement.

Given the manner in which you speak, and according to what I know about you, it seems to me that you ought not to be too discontented by your lot.

That is true; I have the good fortune not to be among those who suffer the most, even though I have not yet attained the rank of the happiest.

What, then, constitutes your pleasure and your pain?

It is hardly possible for me to make you understand all that. Your joyful emotions are so feeble, and of such short duration, that they cannot be compared to the transports that are excited here by the memory of the good one has done. We also enjoy friendship and love, to a degree which can only increase further and further. Beings of merit are very nearly equal in resemblance, and form a delectable society. Those who are not made to figure in it are excluded.

Must they remain forever in that miserable state, without hope of release?

Nothing in the second world is eternal; everything is temporary, as it is in yours. Those who progress to an advanced age feel a strong desire to elevate themselves towards another sphere; it is a great pleasure to nurture such ideas. Friends and parents understand the sensuality involved in advancing the study of creation, in ascending further, as far as their Author.

Death to you is fearful; here one looks forward to it and celebrates it with glad cries. We are conscious of the glorious destination and future of humanity, the contemplation of all beings who pass and events which occur; for us it is a spectacle, which adds to the sum of our knowledge. In sum, the better one has lived on the Earth, the less one suffers here, and the more pleasure one has in passing further on. Those who retain various hideous stains upon their wings appear to us to lose themselves on a different path, and thus disappear from our view. I cannot tell where these and others like them go.

But you make me envious of the dead—I would like to die now, in order to have the unique pleasure of being with you. Is it permissible to cut short one's term of exile?

No, refrain from suicide; it is an infamous stain that you would be unable to efface for a very long time. One who has lived but little counts for less than one who has borne the burden of life for a long time; those who have sacrificed themselves for a genuinely good cause are the only ones granted a dispensation in the number of their years.

What becomes of infants then, who often die soon after birth and pass away without every knowing anything of good and evil?

They have the opportunity here to make use of their intelligence. They attach themselves to their parents, and the mother rediscovers the son she believed to be lost forever. The bonds of blood and affection are not broken; souls made for life draw closely together. In sum, love reigns supreme here, and reigns without jealousy

.

Is that because what we have down here is naught but instinct, whereas love in your world is a sentiment?

I have said all that needs to be said in revealing to you that love has dominion here, in all its strength and all its purity. It is not necessary to add to these words: all that is loving is virtuous.

I AM DEAD

I dreamed that I was dead, and I considered the body from which my soul had just emerged, lying on my bed. How much pity I felt! But I was very glad no longer to be linked to that carnal vestment that nailed me to the earth, and to be flying through the air with the rapidity of thought.

No overheated tragedian, weary of his role, ever cast of his dramatic costume with the same pleasure that I felt in shaking off my terrestrial envelope. I made two or three sudden voyages through the planets in order to take an initial glance, as I throw myself into a new city the first time I visit it, going astray deliberately and taking pleasure in asking the way back to me hotel when, very weary, I find myself lost.

After that little excursion I returned to my defunct body, which was being wrapped up in the worst of my sheets; it was the most hideous maidservant in the quarter who was rendering me that service; then a kind of carpenter came in, who, singing a popular song, nailed me between four ill-fitted planks, and an unknown voice in a corner said: "There won't be any candles or bells, and as for what you're giving him, it'll be put in the big ditch in the cemetery."

A priest came, drank his bottle right beside me, and went to sleep; he only woke up to grab the twenty écus that my burial cost, for in every country in the world the fields of the dead have been farmed by priests.

While a few indifferent faces entered the room and some said: "He's dead?" and others "Where are his friends?" one, joking about my defunct profession, said; "A printer ought to make him a funeral notice," and I approached my writing desk. Obedient to force of habit I tried to pick up my pen in order to write, but my soul, alas, in the title of spirit, was incapable of lifting a pen. That was a great pity, for I sensed a host of ideas that would have astonished the living. I ran my eyes over my bookshelves, and I saw that I had just learned more in an instant than all those books would have been able to teach me.

I recognized the nullity of human sciences, and the universe appeared to me to have a perspective very different from what they had imagined. I read in the great book, of which the planets and the sun were the letters or punctuations marks; my delight was immeasurable, and I ridiculed my writings utterly, in which I had, however, divined a small portion of the marvels that surrounded me.

My heirs came in, but they were not joyful, because I had left nothing but papers; there as mention nevertheless about putting them under seal, but as someone made the reflection that it would cost money and that I probably had none, they dispensed with summoning the commissaire.

They had soon made an inventory of my clothes, for I never shone in that regard; my self-respect forbids me to repeat what was said over my ashes, but at least I had not imposed on faces a deceit of relationship; they went to bury me with all possible tranquility.

I expected to emerge from the house after a few hours to arrive at my last refuge; a stone-carver and a second-hand dealer were waiting for me to be their neighbor, and that seemed perfectly all right to me, for the vicinity of Turenne and Louis XIV would no longer have been flattering to me at the moment when everyone is leveled again; I still had no bier, however, and I saw that the delay was caused by the fact that one of my heirs wanted all my qualities printed on the funeral notice. He read it aloud in my presence and that of the neighbors of both sexes who had arrived seemed seized by respect during the list; but, reflecting subsequently that it had not made me very rich, they resumed their former familiarity.

I heard a noise outside the threshold, and I was thinking: *Here come the officers of the parish to take me away*, when a black-clad man came in and said: "I've come to look at the papers."

I tremor seized me as if I were still a vile mortal; but I soon saw that I was a soul, and I placed myself on top of the examiner's head.

He ran his eye over a multitude of loose sheets, in which he could not decipher anything, everything being Greek, Hebrew or Latin to him. The papers, covered with deletions, were hieroglyphs so far as he was concerned

Everything was carefully searched: no notes in the account-book, no notes to the porter; nevertheless, in all that mess they discovered a small wad of oblong sheets. "Those are bills of exchange!" cried one of the witnesses, and leapt forward to open them.

They were, in fact, bills, but bills from booksellers, all settled, which dated back twenty years. Then a voice moved by compassion said, in a low voice: "Perhaps we should envy his repose. Journalists won't attack him anymore, and he won't have to pay for judgments against printers anymore."

All my papers were put in a box, saying that they would let an academician see them, and then a grocer. My spirit emerged from the house before my body was outside. I followed the route of my papers for a while, and I saw the academician shrug his shoulders disdainfully. He treated me very severely, alas.

I finally went out, carried by four men, two of whom were lame and the other two as thin as my skeleton. I was going rather slowly when I was stopped in my progress by an illustrious and rich corpse whose superb procession, candles and the curé's embroidered stole contrasted so sharply with my poor black and spoiled shroud that the rabble, who were admiring the beautiful burial, did not want to stand aside to make way for mine.

To the sound of bells, the illumination of candles and the funeral chant of a hundred priests in elegant surplices, the rich man plunged into the regal church where a private resting-place awaited him a few toises from the main altar, and I went to see myself lowered, with the aid of a rope, into my grave.

The coffin missed its mark and I fell on to that of a seamstress who had died in childbirth two days before.

I thought that I was as well there as anywhere else, but what cheered me up was that at two o'clock in the morning I saw the illustrious dead man buried with so much pomp disinterred and deposited alongside me; I could not help smiling, recognizing that every pendant of life is merely a simulacrum

Absolutely dead and having read the brief eulogies in the newspapers, I abandoned this globe and everything it carried and launched myself toward the etheric region. To begin with, I looked for Socrates, Seneca and Fénelon, and finally, all the worshippers of the divinity. I asked them to initiate me into the language of adoration. Music is the language in which intelligences talk to God; it is the language of sentiment, the one that we employ in a profound, religious and filial prostration.

I renewed acquaintance with all the great individuals of antiquity, and it was then that I was plunged into science, that ineffable radiation of bright light. It enlightened my soul and set it ablaze The vain phantoms of error no longer surrounded me, and I discovered in all their absurdity the theses of obscure scholasticism, arrogant sophistry and he chimeras on which bigots nourish their extravagant zeal. My eye discovered the origin of those thoughts that launch into space and incessantly seek the measure of eternity. I saw the mystical ladder that, by the gradation of beings, raises reason toward the creator God; but profound respect stopped me, and although I had other eyes and another intelligence, I feared advancing, and I did not sound that bottomless abyss of glory and light.

But there was no happiness without the contemplation of the Supreme Being.

My soul could not exist without the influence of that divine sun; there was no felicity far from its radiance. I forgot the earth and preceding centuries to such an extent, my sensations were so vivid and so profound, that I imagined having always lived in that state of harmony, sentiment and liberty; I was floating in that delightful intoxication, while my miserable body, which I believed to be interred, I know not by what imperceptible thread, pulled my soul from its holy ecstasy and I saw, dolorously, that I was not dead.

Here I am again, submissive to material operations; where is the dream in which I marched without feet, where I gave form to objects without hands, where I saw without eyes, where my head commanded and all the rest of nature obeyed?

SF & FANTASY

Adolphe Alhaiza. *Cybele*
Alphonse Allais. *The Adventures of Captain Cap*
Henri Allorge. *The Great Cataclysm*
Guy d'Armen. *Doc Ardan: The City of Gold and Lepers; The Troglodytes of Mount Everest/The Giants of Black Lake; The Abominable Snowman*
G.-J. Arnaud. *The Ice Company*
André Arnyvelde. *The Ark; The Mutilated Bacchus*
Charles Asselineau. *The Double Life*
Henri Austruy. *The Eupantophone; The Olotelepan; The Petitpaon Era*
Barillet-Lagargousse. *The Final War*
Barbot de Villeneuve.*The Naiads/Beauty & The Beast*
Cyprien Bérard. *The Vampire Lord Ruthwen*
S. Henry Berthoud. *Martyrs of Science; The Angel Asrael*
Aloysius Bertrand. *Gaspard de la Nuit*
Richard Bessière. *The Gardens of the Apocalypse; The Masters of Silence*
Chevalier de Béthune. *The World of Mercury*
Albert Bleunard. *Ever Smaller*
Félix Bodin. *The Novel of the Future*
Pierre Boitard. *Journey to the Sun*
Louis Boussenard. *Monsieur Synthesis*
Alphonse Brown. *City of Glass; The Conquest of the Air*
Émile Calvet. *In a Thousand Years*
André Caroff. *The Terror of Madame Atomos; Miss Atomos; The Return of Madame Atomos; The Mistake of Madame Atomos; The Monsters of Madame Atomos; The Revenge of Madame Atomos; The Resurrection of Madame Atomos; The Mark of Madame Atomos; The Spheres of Madame Atomos; The Wrath of Madame Atomos* (w/M. & Sylvie Stéphan); *The Sins of Madame Atomos* (w/M. & Sylvie Stéphan)
Jean Carrère. *The End of Atlantis*

Félicien Champsaur. *Homo-Deus; The Human Arrow; Nora, The Ape-Woman; Ouha, King of the Apes; Pharaoh's Wife*
Didier de Chousy. *Ignis*
Jules Clarétie. *Obsession*
Jacques Collin de Plancy. *Voyage to the Center of the Earth*
Michel Corday. *The Eternal Flame; The Lynx* (w/André Couvreur)
André Couvreur. *Caresco, Superman; The Exploits of Professor Tornada* (3 vols.); *The Necessary Evil*
Gaston Danville. *The Perfume of Lust*
Camille Debans. *The Misfortunes of John Bull*
Captain Danrit. *Undersea Odyssey*
C. I. Defontenay. *Star (Psi Cassiopeia)*
Charles Derennes. *The People of the Pole*
Georges Dodds (anthologist). *The Missing Link*
Charles Dodeman. *The Silent Bomb*
Harry Dickson. *The Heir of Dracula; Harry Dickson vs. The Spider*
Jules Dornay. *Lord Ruthven Begins*
Alfred Driou. *The Adventures of a Parisian Aeronaut*
Odette Dulac. *The War of the Sexes*
Alexandre Dumas. *The Return of Lord Ruthven; The Man who Married a Mermaid* (w/P. Lacroix)
Renée Dunan. *Baal; The Ultimate Pleasure*
J.-C. Dunyach. *The Night Orchid; The Thieves of Silence*
Henri Duvernois. *The Man Who Found Himself*
Achille Eyraud. *Voyage to Venus*
Henri Falk. *The Age of Lead*
Paul Féval. *Anne of the Isles; Knightshade; Revenants; Vampire City; The Vampire Countess; The Wandering Jew's Daughter*
Paul Féval, *fils. Felifax, the Tiger-Man*
Charles de Fieux. *Lamékis*
Fernand Fleuret. *Jim Click*
Charles-Marie Flor O'Squarr. *Phantoms*
Louis Forest. *Someone is Stealing Children in Paris*

Alain le Drimeur. *The Future City*

Georges Le Faure & Henri de Graffigny. *The Extraordinary Adventures of a Russian Scientist Across the Solar System* (2 vols.)

Gustave Le Rouge. *The Dominion of the World* (w/G. Guitton) (4 vols.); *The Mysterious Doctor Cornelius* (3 vols.); *The Vampires of Mars*

Jules Lermina. *The Battle of Strasbourg; Mysteryville; Panic in Paris; The Secret of Zippelius; To-Ho and the Gold Destroyers*

Maurice Level. *The Gates of Hell*

M.-J. L'Héritier de Villandon. *The Robe of Sincerity*

André Lichtenberger. *The Centaurs; The Children of the Crab*

Maurice Limat. *Mephista*

Listonai. *The Philosophical Voyager*

Jean-Marc & Randy Lofficier. *Edgar Allan Poe on Mars; The Katrina Protocol; Pacifica 1, 2; Robonocchio; Return of the Nyctalope;* (anthologists) *Tales of the Shadowmen 1-14; The Vampire Almanac* (2 vols.)

Ch. Lomon & P.-B. Gheuzi. *The Last Days of Atlantis*

Charles Malato. *Lost!*

Maurice Magre. *The Marvelous Story of Claire d'Amour; The Call of the Beast; Priscilla of Alexandria; The Angel of Lust; The Mystery of the Tiger; The Poison of Goa; Lucifer; The Blood of Toulouse; The Albigensian Treasure; Jean de Fodoas; Melusine; The Brothers of the Virgin Gold*

Victor Margueritte. *The Bacheloress; The Companion; The Couple*

Camille Mauclair. *The Virgin Orient*

Xavier Mauméjean. *The League of Heroes*

Joseph Méry. *The Tower of Destiny*

Hippolyte Mettais. *Paris Before the Deluge; The Year 5865*

Louise Michel. *The Human Microbes; The New World*

Miral-Viger. *The Ring of Light*

Tony Moilin. *Paris in the Year 2000*

Michael Moorcock's *Legends of the Multiverse*

José Moselli. *Illa's End*

John-Antoine Nau. *Enemy Force*
Marie Nizet. *Captain Vampire*
Charles Nodier. *Trilby and The Crumb Fairy*
C. Nodier, A. Beraud & Toussaint-Merle. *Frankenstein*
Oksana & Gil Prou. *Outre-Blanc*
Henri de Parville. *An Inhabitant of the Planet Mars*
Gaston de Pawlowski. *Journey to the Land of the 4th Dimension*
Georges Pellerin. *The World in 2000 Years*
Ernest Pérochon. *The Frenetic People*
Pierre Pelot. *The Child Who Walked on the Sky*
Jean Petithuguenin. *An International Mission to the Moon*
J. Polidori, C. Nodier, E. Scribe. *Lord Ruthven the Vampire*
P.-A. Ponson du Terrail. *The Immortal Woman; The Vampire and the Devil's Son; The Police Agent*
Georges Price. *The Missing Men of the* Sirius
René Pujol. *The Chimerical Quest*
Edgar Quinet. *Ahasuerus; The Enchanter Merlin*
Jean Rameau. *Arrival; in the Stars*
Henri de Régnier. *A Surfeit of Mirrors*
Maurice Renard. *The Blue Peril; Doctor Lerne; The Doctored Man; A Man Among the Microbes; The Master of Light*
Restif de la Bretonne. *The Discovery of the Austral Continent by a Flying Man; Posthumous Correspondence* (3 vols.); *The Fay Ouroucoucou* (2 vols.)
Jean Richepin. *The Crazy Corner; The Wing*
Albert Robida. *The Adventures of Saturnin Farandoul; Chalet in the Sky; The Clock of the Centuries; The Electric Life; The Engineer Von Satanas; In 1965*
J.-H. Rosny Aîné. *Helgvor of the Blue River; The Givreuse Enigma; The Mysterious Force; The Navigators of Space; Pan's Flute; Vamireh; The World of the Variants; The Young Vampire*
Marcel Rouff. *Journey to the Inverted World*
Marie-Anne de Roumier-Robert. *The Voyage of Lord Seaton to the Seven Planets*
Léonie Rouzade. *The World Turned Upside Down*

Han Ryner. *The Human Ant; The Superhumans*
Henri de Saint-Georges. *The Green Eyes*
Louis-Claude de Saint-Martin. *The Crocodile*
X.B. Saintine. *Jonathan the Visionary; The Second Life*
Frank Schildiner. *The Quest of Frankenstein; The Triumph of Frankenstein; Napoleon's Vampire Hunters; The Devil-Plague of Naples*
Nicolas Ségur. *The Human Paradise; Penelope's Secret*
Pierre de Selenes: *An Unknown World*
Norbert Sevestre. *Sâr Dubnotal: Vs. Jack the Ripper; The Astral Trail*
Angelo de Sorr. *The Vampires of London*
Brian Stableford. *The Empire of the Necromancers (1. The Shadow of Frankenstein; 2. Frankenstein and the Vampire Countess; 3. Frankenstein in London); The Wayward Muse; Eurydice's Lament; The Mirror of Dionysius; The Pool of Mnemosyne; The New Faust at the Tragicomique; Sherlock Holmes and The Vampires of Eternity; The Stones of Camelot* (anthologist) *News from the Moon; The Germans on Venus; The Supreme Progress; The World Above the World; Nemoville; Investigations of the Future; The Conqueror of Death; The Revolt of the Machines; The Man With the Blue Face; The Aerial Valley; The New Moon; The Nickel Man; On the Brink of the World's End; The Mirror of Present Events; The Humanisphere*
Jacques Spitz. *The Eye of Purgatory*
Kurt Steiner. *Ortog*
Michel & Sylvie Stéphan. *The Wrath of Madame Atomos* (w/André Caroff); *The Sins of Madame Atomos* (w/André Caroff)
Eugène Thébault. *Radio-Terror*
Edmond Thiaudière. *Singular amours*
C.-F. Tiphaigne de La Roche. *Amilec*
Simon Tyssot de Patot. *The Strange Voyages of Jacques Massé and Pierre de Mésange*
Louis Ulbach. *Prince Bonifacio*

Théo Varlet. *The Castaways of Eros; The Golden Rock.; The Martian Epic* (w/Octave Joncquel); *Timeslip Troopers* (w/André Blandin); *The Xenobiotic Invasion*
Pierre Véron. *The Merchants of Health*
Paul Vibert. *The Mysterious Fluid*
Villiers de l'Isle-Adam. *The Scaffold; The Vampire Soul*
Gaston de Wailly. *The Murderer of the World*
Philippe Ward. *Artahe; Manhattan Ghost* (w/Mickael Laguerre); *The Song of Montségur* (w/Sylvie Miller)

www.ingramcontent.com/pod-product-compliance
Lightning Source LLC
Chambersburg PA
CBHW060348030726
47497CB00003B/646